# Advance Praise for *GTO*

"In this delightful novel Roger blends the passion of automobile enthusiasts with his ability to turn an intriguing tale of suspense and adventure. This is a great read for car guys, those holding a special place in their heart for Ferraris, as well as anyone who enjoys a good adventure. Easy to read and hard to put down, you will enjoy this latest work of a talented writer and knowledgeable car collector."

**Jim Weddle**
Managing Partner, Edward Jones Investments

"While I loved the multimillion dollar Ferrari GTO in this novel, I was much more inspired by the thrilling story of a man attempting to overcome a terrible injustice and at the same time trying to discover his own lineage and identity. It is definitely one of the most inspiring novels I have ever read and I strongly recommend to anyone who would like to lose themselves in an exciting adventure."

**Marie Fisher**
High School English Teacher

"*GTO: Race to Oblivion* is not just for car aficionados—it is a true page-turning thriller. To the last page, *GTO* brings intrigue, suspense, and a great plot with surprising and unbelievable twists and turns. The author brings together unrelated but true historical events and then asks, 'what if?' I couldn't put it down. Enjoy!"

**Bob Harden**
*Bob Harden Show*, Naples, Florida

"The author spins a tale of intrigue that encompasses the GTO, the *Andrea Doria*, and royalty (the Grimaldi family) that is both entertaining and full of suspense and surprises."

**Bill Warner**
Chairman and Founder Amelia Island Concours d'Elegance

"Life doesn't always turn out the way we planned, but we make the most of our circumstances. Whether a car person or not, you will truly enjoy this captivating novel that taps into our core values and all that is special about relationships in life."

**Marc Corea**
President and Founder MotorCarTrader.com, LLC

"We were very much intrigued by the thrilling story about difficult choices and how those choices affected four generations of a family. We also loved the suspense surrounding the Ferrari GTO. It is truly an amazing story!"

**Howard and Doug Sharp**
The Sharp Team, Winners 2011 and 2015 Great Race

"*GTO: Race to Oblivion* surprised me by its depth of intrigue, mystery, and thrills. I read it through in one sitting. I could not put it down. The many plot twists, historical flashbacks, and dramatic final ending made for a very enjoyable read. I was fascinated by how well the characters were developed, and the fast-paced thrills were woven together to fully engage my attention, imagination, and left me anxious for the each new chapter."

**Ben C. Smith**
Former Executive Vice President at Wells Fargo,
Vice Chairman of GMAC Real Estate and Relocation Services

"To fully appreciate Roger's most recent novel, you don't have to be a 'car person.' The car is only the frosting on the cake, not the cake itself. The cake is the need of the leading character, Tommy Grimaldi, and his friend Rebecca Ricci, to make right an injustice that has been in place for many years. If you are among the portion of humanity that screams for justice when an injustice is perpetrated, your time spent reading this novel will be well rewarded."

**Bob Tobin**
Classic Car Enthusiast


"Set against the backdrop of the classic automobile industry, Roger Corea takes us on a page-turning romp across oceans and generations, exploring the value of treasures that are sought, as well as those that are found along the way. Corea continues to make his mark as a wonderful storyteller."

**Peter J. Pullano, Esq.**
Top-Rated Criminal Defense Attorney

# By the Same Author

*The Duesenberg Caper*
*(2015)*

*Scarback:*
*There is So Much More to Fishing Than Catching a Fish*
*(2014)*

# GTO

## Race to Oblivion

*A Thriller*

ROGER COREA

SelectBooks, Inc.
*New York*

This edition published by SelectBooks, Inc.
For information address SelectBooks, Inc., New York, New York.

First Edition

ISBN 978-1-59079-397-8

Library of Congress Cataloging-in-Publication Data

Names: Corea, Roger, author.
Title: GTO : race to oblivion / Roger  Corea.
Description: First edition. | New York : SelectBooks, [2017]
Identifiers: LCCN 2016028850 | ISBN 9781590793978 (softcover)
Subjects: LCSH: Antique and classic cars--Fiction. | Ferrari
  automobile--Fiction. | Family secrets--Fiction. | BISAC: FICTION /
  Thrillers. | GSAFD: Suspense fiction. | Mystery fiction.
Classification: LCC PS3603.O73428 G86 2017 | DDC 813/.6--dc23 LC record
available at https://lccn.loc.gov/2016028850

Manufactured in the United States of America
10 9 8 7 6 5 4 3 2 1

*This novel is dedicated to Donald Quinn,
my high school football coach,
who taught me how to win on the field of life.*

# Contents

## A Bag of Tools

Isn't it strange that princes and kings
And clowns that caper in sawdust rings
And common folk like you and me
Are the builders of eternity.

To each is given a bag of tools,
A shapeless mass and a book of rules;
And each must make, ere time is flown,
A stumbling-block or a stepping-stone.

—R. L. SHARPE
*(1872–1951)*

# Foreword

## by Bill Warner

WHENEVER A GROUP OF CAR PEOPLE get together and the subject of the "favorite car" comes up, very infrequently, if ever, do they all agree on one particular car. To some, the 1938 Alfa Romeo 8C 2900 is their favorite. To others it could be a Ferrari 250 GT SWB Berlinetta. But nearly all would have the Ferrari 250 GTO somewhere in their top two or three cars.

Roger Corea has utilized the GTO for the basis of this book, and I think most would agree that it is the postwar car to aspire to owning. With only thirty-nine of this model built, they generally change hands privately and are not subject to public scrutiny at an auction. However, one did pass through the Bonhams Auction in Monterey several years ago at an astounding $38.5 million, a number that could represent the GNP of some Third World nations. And this was for a GTO that had been seriously crashed at one period, taking the life of its driver. Rumors of a GTO changing hands in a private transaction at slightly over $50 million have been circulated, but have not been confirmed.

The aura that surrounds this motoring icon allows Corea to build a case for the passion driving his characters to recover the "lost GTO" from its perceived watery grave. Writing a fictional novel based on such an important and historic vehicle requires some latitude in times, places, and people. The author spins a tale of intrigue that encompasses the GTO, the *Andrea Doria*, and royalty (the Grimaldi family) that is both entertaining and full of suspense and surprises. As any good novel of this ilk, the story wraps everything up and ties it with a bow in the very last pages, leaving the reader with an "aha" moment as all the facets of the story fall together. Could a prototype GTO have been lost in the sinking of the *Andrea Doria*? Not likely, in that there is a six year spread between the sinking and the unveiling of the first GTO. However, fiction allows the compression of time that makes for an entertaining read.

Is the novel strictly about the car? Not really, as the car sets the theme for the story. It is more about people and the family that were involved in the manufacture of the "lost GTO." And the convoluted relationship of the Grimaldi family to Commendatore Enzo Ferrari makes for an entertaining tale. Enjoy the story woven by Roger Corea, and bear in mind that the Chrysler Norseman is, in fact, still available in the hold of the *Andrea Doria*, but that's another story for another time.

Bill Warner
Chairman and Founder
Amelia Island Concours d'Elegance

# Acknowledgments

ENCOURAGEMENT FROM MY FAMILY AND FRIENDS has been a significant catalyst for the completion of this novel. I am grateful for their genuine interest, shared opinions, and ongoing enthusiasm for my literary travails.

I immensely appreciate the efforts of my good friends Dick Rice and Bob Tobin for spending countless hours reading an early manuscript and providing valuable feedback.

My words of gratitude extend to Kenzi Sugihara, publisher and founder of SelectBooks, Inc., for his eagerness to publish *GTO: A Race to Oblivion*, Kenichi Sugihara for his marketing expertise, and Nancy Sugihara and Molly Stern for their insightful final edits and outstanding teamwork.

Thank you to Bill Warner, Chairman and Founder of the Amelia Island Concours d'Elegance, for his excellent foreword. Bill has developed this event into the premier classic car show in the country with the proceeds assisting more than six thousand patients annually at the Community Hospice of Northeast Florida.

And last, but certainly not least, thank you to my son, Marc Corea, who owns MotorCarTrader.com, a successful classic car business in Charlotte, NC. His wonderful introduction captures the heart of the magnificent Ferrari GTO. It brings to mind the numerous car events and auctions we have attended together over the last forty years. His knowledge of the classic car business has grown exponentially, and I am proud of the many outstanding testimonials he has received for his sound business ethics.

# Introduction

## By Marc Corea

As a child, my father gifted me a coveted model of a 1962 Ferrari 250 GTO. The car was gorgeous and had sensuous lines and a look like no other. It was one not to be destroyed, or mixed with other ordinary model cars.

The first time I saw a real 250 GTO in person I was totally awestruck. The rosso corsa paint was captivating. From every angle it was simply sensational, with its high shoulders, covered headlamps, and swooping muscular rear spoiler. No other car could match its style, grace, and allure.

In 2012, when we attended the Amelia Island Concours d'Elegance, there was not one, but over a dozen of these legendary sports cars on the field. As we drove through a tunnel of Spanish moss, twenty police cars passed us with sirens blaring, stopping traffic on each side of the road. For a moment, I thought the president was in town. Cars on each side of the road pulled over and stopped. We had no idea what going on. Then, we noticed the first one in line, a 1962 Ferrari 250 GTO, with about twelve others following in a straight line behind it. Now, I love my classic rock music, but the exhilarating sound of this car trumps anything I have ever heard at a concert. These GTOs were the ultimate rock-and-roll stars, producing a symphony of noises that could never be recreated by any instrument.

Today, the Ferrari GTO is one of the most collectible cars in the world. It sells for more than $40 million. Yes, $40 million for a car, but not just a car, a significant piece of automotive history. Discounting prototypes, only thirty-nine GTOs were made, including three of the "330 GTO." This car is the quintessential Ferrari of all time.

All of us car guys and gals yearn for the "the hunt," or to find that special car which is hidden away, and hasn't seen the light of day for decades. A one of a kind car that people know about, but only you know its current status and location. We search for that truly special automobile with the heritage and provenance that cannot be replicated by restoration or rebuilding. Through my professional career of buying and selling vintage sports cars at my company, MotorCarTrader.com, I have always enjoyed the hunt or the chase. This is where all the excitement of classic car collecting begins, because predictability and routine are not the norm for us.

Some questions: What could be behind those garage doors? Where the hell am I going? Am I at the right house? Does anyone live here? What is under that car cover? The hunt can take you on several twists and turns, slippery slopes, and sometimes to the middle of nowhere. No matter what, it is all about the hunt for good, bad, wow, or ugly, all the while hoping for that once in a lifetime find.

*GTO: Race to Oblivion* is an exciting story which features the unicorn of all unicorns—a Ferrari GTO Prototype. This is a pivotal story about doing the right thing while simultaneously facing an incredible injustice. The story alludes to integrity, grit, and pushing forward to see beyond what is immediately obvious. As we all know, life doesn't always turn out the way we planned, but we make the most of our circumstances. Whether you are a car person or not, you will truly enjoy this captivating novel that taps into our core values and all that is special about relationships in life.

Marc Corea
President and Founder
MotorCarTrader.com, LLC

# Quail Lodge Auction

### Quail Lodge, Carmel, California

*August 14, 2014*

The audience is witnessing automotive history, and they know it. The 1962 Ferrari 250 GTO Berlinetta "3851GT," the nineteenth GTO out of thirty-nine made, is being sold at the Bonhams' Quail Lodge Auction in Carmel, California. Never before has a classic automobile garnered so much attention.

The atmosphere is electric. The auction pavilion is overflowing on to the lawns with the crowd watching proceedings live on the numerous flat-screen TVs. Spectators stand five deep at the rear of the pavilion. Aisles are jammed. Reserved seats for wealthy collectors are full. Against the sidewall, auction representatives settle behind rectangular tables as they prepare to accept telephone and Internet bids from all over the world.

The auctioneer speaks in a slow, rhythmical cadence with only a slight inflection as bidders set their own pace. Before long, a passionate bidding war erupts that at times resembles a tennis match, complete with moments of silence interrupted by cheers.

"Going once," the auctioneer says as he surveys the crowd. He pauses and the anticipation builds. "Going twice," he says louder. He raises the gavel toward the sky and holds it there for one final solicitation. His eyes methodically scan the inside of the pavilion searching for a hand in the air or even a discrete nod. The crowd waits in dead silence. Finally he shouts, "Sold! Sold! Sold! You have the car, sir!" and pummels the gavel to the top of the podium as if he is driving an iron spike into a railroad tie. The audience breaks into a thunderous applause as the fall of the gavel confirms the staggering final price of $38.1 million. It was all over in less than five minutes.

☆　☆　☆

The 1962 Ferrari 250 GTO Berlinetta "3851GT" set an auction record at the Quail Lodge in Carmel, becoming the most valuable car in history. But what about the *first* GTO made, the 250GT 56Comp 001 Prototype? *What if this car went to auction?* Prominent vintage car aficionados have projected its value in excess of $100 million. *But where is this car? Who owns it? Why has it been kept under wraps? Does it even exist?*

## Italy

### *July 1956*

Captain Piero Calamai of the ill-fated *Andrea Doria*, Italy's most luxurious ocean liner, makes the following entry in his logbook for the ship's manifest:

> Departure Naples. Thursday, 19 July 1956. A total of 1,134 passengers (190 First Class, 267 Cabin Class, 677 Tourist Class), 401 tons of freight, 522 pieces of baggage, 1,754 bags of mail, nine automobiles parked in the general garage area, and two sealed in watertight auto containers. Cargo hold #1 has the container with the 1956 Prototype #9999CN Chrysler Norseman. Cargo hold #2 has the container with the 1956 Prototype 250GT 56Comp 001 Ferrari 250 GTO Berlinetta.[1]

---

1   *Collision Course: The Andrea Doria and the Stockholm* by Alvin Moscow. The information given in the captain's logbook entry about the contents of the ship is factual with the exception of the listing of the GTO.

Seven days later, on July 26, 1956, the world watches as the *Andrea Doria* capsizes and sinks in the foggy North Atlantic Ocean fifty miles south of Nantucket Island. The damage done after being broadsided by the Swedish liner *Stockholm* is fatal. Fifty-one passengers lose their lives. It is the first maritime disaster to be televised live, and the only one where two priceless experimental automobiles are included in the ship's manifest: the 1956 Prototype #9999CN Chrysler Norseman and the 1956 Prototype Ferrari GTO Berlinetta.

The Chrysler Norseman, a concept car built by Ghia in Torino, Italy, was truly a monument of automotive design technology. Chrysler was hoping to integrate the Norseman's advanced and innovated design features into future production models.

The Ferrari 250 GTO Berlinetta Prototype, considered by many to be the most beautiful sports car ever made, was the first example of the thirty-nine eventually produced. Its aerodynamic design was a major technical achievement and a tribute to the genius of Italian design engineering. The Colombo all-alloy 3.0-liter V12 engine developed 300 horsepower and was the most admired engine in the world.

News of the cars being on board the *Andrea Doria* spreads quickly throughout the world of wealthy car collectors. Dive boats on Long Island and New Jersey begin to advertise dive expeditions to the *Andrea Doria*. Incentives to salvage the cars, fueled by rumors of actual sightings, escalate, prompting affluent collectors from all over the world to finance costly dive operations to locate and raise the cars.

But gaining access to the cars is very dangerous; they are down 240 feet inside the ship on forward Deck C. Drawn by the lure of fame and riches, divers take unnecessary risks inside the ship. Several get their lines tangled in the twisted metal of the wreckage and die of nitrogen narcosis. Some cannot find their way out of Deck C and drown. Several are still missing.

Collectors eventually abandon their quest to find the GTO. Not until fifty-two years later, when the bow of the *Andrea Doria* collapses, is interest in raising the GTO rekindled.

# 1

# Enzo's Ultimatum

## Italy

### *July 17, 1956, Tuesday at 2:00 a.m.*

High on a ridge in the western Alps near Torino, Italy, a 1956 Fiat Bartoletti auto transporter owned by Ferrari S.p.A. meanders south toward Genoa. Its oversized coach tires crunch the wet gravel of the Strada dell'Assietta, the treacherous thirty-five-mile road known for its soft terrain, steep hills, and sharp curves. While the rain has stopped, visibility is nearly impossible as muddy grime sticks to the windshield like mortar. The howling wind makes the transporter unstable and difficult to control.

Despite the turbulent weather, Antonio Grimaldi and Giancarlo Bandini are determined to complete their mission. One year ago, the longtime members of Enzo Ferrari's inner circle were assigned a secret project to build the most beautiful and competitive sports racing car in the world. Built by hand for his personal approval, the car was designed for the racetrack as well as the highway.

However, the prototype never saw the production line. Il Commendatore, or Knight Commander, the official title and venerable sobriquet of the man who led the Ferrari autocracy, flatly and angrily rejected it. So now, under the cover of darkness, Antonio and Giancarlo are secretly transporting the car to the Port of Genoa for shipment to the United States aboard Italy's most luxurious ocean liner, the SS *Andrea Doria*. Once it arrives in New York City, it will be placed in secret storage away from the public eye.

But navigating the Assietta is pushing Antonio's driving skills to their limits. Moreover, the transporter's 92-horsepower six-cylinder diesel engine provides only a small amount of torque, making it difficult to navigate the steep mountain grades of the road.

"You should slow down on the curves and hills, Antonio. When you touch the brake pedal, I can feel the tires slip!" Giancarlo says in a disturbed voice. His gangly outstretched legs push down hard against the floorboard as his bony fingers squeeze the armrests with a deathlike grip.

"Is this your first roller-coaster ride?" Antonio asks with a playful smile.

"This is no time to make a joke. We could get killed on this road!"

"Giancarlo, my friend, if I go any slower I'll be in reverse. Just relax. We'll be okay."

Riding anyplace in any kind of weather with Giancarlo is enough to give Antonio a throbbing migraine. Even his good-natured taunts cannot calm Giancarlo's uneasiness. They're good friends, and most of the time good friends tolerate each other's idiosyncrasies, if not their imperfections. But today, Antonio has his hands full keeping the transporter on the road. Today, he wishes Giancarlo would just shut up.

"This is not a smart thing that we do—to be on the Assietta in this kind of weather—it's *stupido*!" Giancarlo's wire-framed Ben Franklin glasses with foggy, oval shaped lenses keep sliding down his nose. "I'm not in a laughing mood," he says, as he pushes his glasses back up where they belong. Sweat beads form on the wide bald patch on his head, saturating what little hair he has on the sides. "We should have waited for better weather!"

"When the boss says 'go' I go," Antonio says without hesitation. "You have to trust him."

Giancarlo cringes as small rocks bouncing under the front and rear wheel wells remind him of flak he encountered while flying a dive-bomber for Regia Aeronautica Italiana during World War II. One of the few Italian pilots who survived the war, Giancarlo still suffers from the trauma of air combat. It isn't uncommon for him to become catatonic in stressful situations. His doctor calls it combat stress reaction. Antonio just calls it combat fatigue.

"I hear strange noises from the Berlinetta in the back. The straps seem too loose," Giancarlo says. "If they come off, the car will be ruined, and so will we! And what if the *sospensione* breaks? We won't be able to drive it off! Then what are we gonna do?"

"Stop worrying," says Antonio. "The car is insured for one million. I placed the straps over the tires instead of the axles. That way, the suspension does all the work."

"I don't know, I still don't trust it."

"If we keep stopping to check it every time you hear something, by the time we arrive at Genoa the *Andrea Doria* will be halfway to New York. Then you know what happens to us?"

"What?" Giancarlo asks.

"You and me, we'll both be working for Fiat!"

"I'll never work for that company! I design beautiful racers, not tomato cans!"

Antonio smiles affectionately at his friend, then struggles to keep his eyes on the road. He is a tall, handsome man of thirty-four years with broad shoulders and a muscular build. His dark brown eyes are bloodshot from lack of sleep, and his long black hair, streaked with silver, is soaked with rain, since he has manually wiped the mud off of the windshield several times. His normally clean-shaven, angular face is starting to show signs of stubble from having spent the last two nights in the transporter.

"I can't believe Enzo—to just shut down our project like that!" Giancarlo bursts out with chagrin. "Zero to sixty in 4.5 seconds, the quarter mile in 11.5 seconds, the best design and best engine ever made, and Enzo—he no longer wants to make the car!"

"I was there the first time he saw it," Antonio says. "He slammed his fist on the hood and left the building." Antonio hesitates, weighing his words, feeling an immense loyalty to Il Commendatore. "I told him I thought it was the most magnificent sports car ever made. He ignored me and said it would be the last time those bastards screwed him."

"Ah . . . once you get on the wrong side of the International Automobile Federation, you pay a big price. Not even Il Commendatore can change the certification rules for racing, the *omologazione*."

"But Giancarlo, the rules were changed after the car was built. Originally, he only needed to produce twenty-five cars to sell to the public. Now the rules say he must produce one hundred. That's unfair! He intended to play by the rules until the IAF blindsided him."

"He makes a big mistake! I don't care what you say, Antonio!"

"Ah, but Il Commendatore—we should never question him. Remember how much he has done for us?"

"More for you than for me," Giancarlo says somewhat defiantly.

Antonio thinks to himself how Enzo Ferrari graciously hired him after his release from serving five years' prison time at Regina Coeli in Rome and Gorgona Island Penal Colony north of Elba. He was accused of stealing a new Ferrari Tipo 166 back in 1948 from the factory showroom in Modena.

"It still makes me very sad for you," Giancarlo says.

"I've been out for two years now. Life goes on, my friend."

"But you didn't do it!"

"No, I didn't."

"Life is unfair."

"Yes, sometimes it is."

Giancarlo is finally quiet. Antonio's unjust treatment upsets him. He finds it difficult to understand how Antonio can be so nonchalant about spending five years of his young life in prison for a crime he didn't commit. *Life really is unfair.*

"You know, Antonio, I think I'm going to retire to Le Marche when we get back," he says wistfully. "I'll sit by the Adriatic, soak up the rays of the sun, and stay out of trouble. After all the work I did on the Berlinetta, no one cares. It's very discouraging. And to lock it up in storage at Chinetti Motors—oh my God, I'm very disappointed!"

"It's true, the world will never be able to appreciate the best Ferrari ever made!" Antonio remarks. "And Luigi Chinetti, even though he could make a fortune if he decides to sell it, I don't think he will. I wouldn't be surprised if someday Il Commendatore will want the car back. Maybe he'll build a museum for it someday."

"You make me cry, Antonio!"

"Just remember," Antonio says, "no matter what happens there will always be just one 1956 Ferrari Prototype GTO Berlinetta—the one that *we* built together from scratch!"

A harsh thump suddenly reverberates in the front section of the transporter and the steering wheel jerks violently downward, nearly breaking Antonio's wrists.

"Let it go!" Giancarlo yells. "Let it go!"

Antonio leans back and quickly surrenders his arms to the forceful gyrations of the steering wheel, then plunges both feet on the brake pedal. The transporter rocks side to side as it planes across the loose, slippery gravel for thirty feet, coming to rest on a small shelf overlooking a deep gorge.

Removing his hands from the safety bar on the dashboard and folding them in a prayerful position, Giancarlo squirms desperately in his seat. "Thank you, Lord! Thank you!" he says. Then making the sign of the cross he looks at Antonio with relief. "Another ten feet and we'd be *finito!*"

"Get the flashlights!" Antonio shouts.

They open their doors and leap the short distance to the ground, their feet sinking into the muddy terrain. The transporter lies crooked in the road, covered with mud due to its sudden stop.

"Check the front steering and suspension," Antonio shouts as he walks to the front of the transporter.

They study the steering apparatus under the front bumper, stand up, and look at each other. One wheel is turned to the right and the other to the left. Neither one has to explain the problem to the other.

"*Morto!*" Giancarlo clamors. "We are *morto!* Now what are we going to do? You are the best mechanic I know. You must fix that damn thing right now!"

"Sure, I can fix it! But tell me, where do I find tie rod parts out here?"

"Antonio! We have to be at the Port of Genoa before daylight! Do something! The *Andrea Doria*—she'll board in six hours! Enzo doesn't want anyone to see the Berlinetta, remember?"

"I know, I know!" Antonio says. He hesitates, then points to the back of the transporter. "It's the only way!"

They run to the tailgate, disengage the chain holding the ramp, and tug on the ramp handles until they become fully extended. Antonio detaches the front tie-down straps; Giancarlo detaches the rear straps, then jumps into the bare aluminum cockpit with seats like paper napkins. Antonio lifts the hood with one hand and holds a fire extinguisher in the other, just in case. He shakes his head in disbelief as he admires the six dual downdraft Weber carburetors. *They look like a dozen silver trumpets,* he says to himself as he shakes his head in awe. The 3-liter V12 all-alloy engine explodes to life. Pure bedlam erupts. Oil and gasoline fumes smother the inside of the trailer. Giancarlo backs the GTO down the ramp. After he locks the doors and rear gate of the transporter, Antonio places the keys in his pocket. Then they head south to Genoa.

# 2

# Little Deuce Coupe

**Fairchester, New York**

*October 17, 2008, Friday*

Tommy Grimaldi is sitting on the edge of his bed in his small one-bedroom apartment. His broad shoulders and well-built physique fill his new gray pinstripe business suit.

*It will be another stressful day of watching market gyrations,* he says to himself. *It's getter harder and harder to make a living in this business.* He places his onyx and gold rosary beads on the nightstand, then gets up and re-combs his neatly parted sandy brown hair. It's become messy. He's been nervously finger combing it all morning.

Usually, the combination of his fresh morning mind and the solitude of his bedroom allow him to formulate a clear strategy for his day. After his early morning prayers, sometimes he'll sit on the edge of his bed for hours thinking through financial alternatives for his clients, including methods to maximize their percentage return. He analyzes their temperament and risk tolerance level, making sure his advice does not create inordinate discomfort for them. Tommy has great empathy for the stress his clients feel, especially in down markets like the one they are currently experiencing.

The early morning edition of NPR News only magnifies his uncertainties. The Dow Jones Industrial Average is falling like a large stone in a deep pond. And it's been dropping for several weeks now. The day before yesterday, on October 15, the Dow dropped 733 points. On September 29 it dropped 778 points, the worst point drop in history. On October 9, it dropped another 678 points. Not since the Great Depression had the market suffered such a free fall. He keeps asking himself, *With the apparent collapse of our monetary system, exactly what advice should I give my clients? Should I tell them to sell, get their money out and run for cover, or should they hang on, ride it out, and wait for the market to bounce back? Then again, given the extent of the losses, is it reasonable to assume the market will ever bounce back?*

Tommy feels a grave responsibility. While he has always preached the merits of long-term financial planning, he fears his clients might do something rash, something from which they can never recover. His own personal investment account, meager as it is, has also plunged into the abyss. But Tommy is a young man; he can always start over. Most of his clients are seniors taking payouts from their investments. They need sound advice. They need reassurance. They are counting on him.

When Tommy brings himself back to real time, he hears his best friend, Mike Bender, fumbling around the kitchen. He wonders if it really was a good idea to give Mike the key to the side door entrance to his apartment. It doesn't matter the time of day, Mike has shown up as late as midnight with female companions and a six-pack.

Despite the annoyance Mike sometimes causes him, they've been like brothers for most of their lives. Their friendship goes way back: grammar school, high school, college, and Afghanistan. They were US Army Rangers together under the Buddy Program, and enlisted right after college when President Bush launched Operation Enduring Freedom on October 7, 2001.

After military duty, Mike and Tommy decided to pursue careers in the field of education. Tommy taught English while Mike still coaches and teaches physical education at Fairchester Academy, a small upstate New York high school. Two years in the classroom was enough for Tommy. He entered the financial services industry with renewed incentive and enthusiasm. His shingle reads: Tomasso A. Grimaldi, CFP, Independent Financial Advisor.

"Let's go, Grimaldi," Mike hollers from the staircase. "I haven't got all day!"

Lately, Tommy's social life is suffering from monotony. Hitting the bars for a few drinks, watching TV, and going to bed early has become a boring weekly routine. At twenty-eight, he feels too young to have fallen into such a rut.

Nevertheless, Tommy can't deny how much fun he and Mike have when they're together. When Mike does his John Wayne imitation, it's like the Duke is right there in the room, and Tommy looks like a younger version of Brad Pitt. A few years ago, they attended a Halloween masquerade party. Neither one had to wear a mask.

Tommy finally saunters down the stairs, opens the fridge, and plunges into a cold, two-day-old Egg McMuffin. "Tastes like shit," he says. "At least you could have made breakfast while you waited, Bender."

"No time, Grimaldi, gotta pick up Jessica. She's buying me breakfast."

"Well at least you're taking care of yourself."

"She wants me to buy her a new car later," Mike says. "Do you believe that?"

"Are you?"

"Of course! She's hot, I want to keep her around for a while."

"No classes today?" Tommy asks with a mouthful.

"Teachers' convention," Mike replies. "Just another excuse for a day off."

"I should never have left teaching," Tommy says. "Just kidding. I *love* my job." Mike gives him a curious look.

"The F40 is fired up in the driveway. Let's check it out!" Mike says eagerly. "I'll shoot you to the office. That'll clear your brain and you'll be like a brand-new man!"

A striking red Ferrari couldn't have been more conspicuous parked in the middle of the short driveway on the side of the apartment building. Of course, it would present a striking picture suitable for framing no matter where it was parked. The car, built to commemorate Ferrari's fortieth anniversary, was the last new car Ferrari produced prior to Enzo Ferrari's death in August of 1988. It is a masterpiece. The seductive body, designed by Pininfarina, is radical, low, and mean looking with an array of cooling slots and intake ducts from the front hood to its triple tailpipes. A panoramic rear window covers the mid-mounted V8 with twin turbochargers that produce a power output of 478 horsepower. Tommy stands frozen in the driveway gaping at the F40 as if he is admiring a curvaceous, tempestuous model from Victoria's Secret.

This isn't the first time Tommy has ridden in the F40. Nevertheless, as he enters the passenger seat, the Spartan-like interior strikes him along with the felt-covered dashboard, the absence of power windows, and the lack of interior trim. The door release catch is a pull wire in the bare door pockets. Indeed, this F40 is strictly a racer for the road, and Ferrari purists will have it no other way. Attached right above the ashtray is a small brass plate that says: *Built exclusively for Michael Bender.* Every time Tommy sees that plate, he is amused. The plate was originally inscribed: *Built exclusively for Rick Bender.* Rick was Mike's father.

Mike sits behind the satin-finished, three-spoke, leather-rimmed steering wheel and positions his feet near the drilled aluminum foot pedals. They buckle their four-point nylon racing harnesses and seatbelts. When Mike turns the key, a throaty roar blasts through the Tubi exhausts making pops, bangs, crackles, and even a backfire.

"Sounds like a sick chicken," Tommy says with a degree of testiness.

"It's like an Italian woman," Mike responds. "It takes her time to warm up, but then hold on to your drawers!"

"For what this thing costs," Tommy asserts, "she should be warmed up before you stick the key in!"

"Yeah, $500,000 new!" Mike gloats. He stares at the instrument panel with a certain smugness. Mike wants people to know he has something special.

"Well then, why not buy a couple dozen of them? We both know you can afford it." While Tommy enjoys teasing Mike, at the moment, he's trying to conceal his growing aggravation.

"They're selling for $1.5 million now," says Mike.

"Aw, damn, just buy a dozen then!" Tommy says with a grim voice. "Seriously, Bender, take me to the office, will you? The market crapped the bed yesterday and I have some urgent postmortems to deal with."

Mike chuckles with an uneasy overconfidence as he shifts into fifth gear and slams the red Ferrari F40 toward the horizon with lightning speed. The twin turbocharger screams like it's begging for mercy and the engine growls like an angry bear.

"Hey Grimaldi, did you know this thing spits flames out of the tailpipes?" Mike says with a wide-eyed, childlike grin.

"Bender, I don't care if the damn thing spits chewing tobacco out the tailpipes! Just get me to my office, will you please?"

Then Tommy starts to laugh. He's thinking how absurd Mike looks driving a million dollar car with his whistle hanging around his neck. The whistle is a permanent part of Mike's attire. On the football field, it is his badge of authority. Whether he's on a date, in the grocery store, or hanging out in his twenty-five-room mansion, he always wears it. The brown t-shirt he wears that says *Property of Fairchester Eagles Football* in bold white letters on the front, complements the rest of his wardrobe.

In recent months, Tommy has been very concerned about Mike. His string of county championships used to be all he needed to feed his voracious ego. However, due to his recent acquisition of amazing wealth, that has been changing. And, as far as Tommy is concerned, the change is not for the better.

"You know, Mike, the coach driving a million dollar Ferrari is a complete violation of teaching protocols. Teachers are supposed to drive Chevys like me!"

"And kids should be seen and not heard, right Grimaldi? I'm getting sick of those silly expectations they have for teachers. *I* live my life the way *I* want to live it!"

"I'm just saying you're going to get yourself in hot water with the principal if any parents see you," Tommy remarks.

"Listen, I'll drive whatever the hell I want to drive," Mike snarls as he puts the accelerator to the floor. "Relax!"

"Mike, please learn how to shift this thing, will you? You keep looking down at the shifter instead of the road. That's pretty dangerous, don't you think?"

"It's the damn gated shifter; it takes some practice," Mike explains.

"You're doing seventy, the speed limit here is fifty-five!"

"How many times I gotta tell you, Grimaldi? You don't drive a Ferrari like it's an old lady. Especially not an F40. That's like drinking a fine wine out of a beer can!"

Mike tightens his grip on the steering wheel. As he hogs the center lane on the three-lane highway leading to farmland outside

Fairchester, the F40 is pushing eighty and Mike is still having trouble with the gated shifter.

Then it happens. An intimidating image suddenly fills Tommy's side-view mirror. A street rod coupe with a yellow body and red flames painted on the sides is rudely tailgating them. The large chrome supercharger protruding high above the front windshield makes it impossible to see the driver.

"Mike, just in case you're interested, some sort of prehistoric beast is behind us. Looks like a '32 deuce coupe with an attitude."

"My God, that's a big block Chevy with a Roots blower and nitrous!"

"That sounds scary as hell to me! Just ignore him."

"I have to find out who owns that monster," Mike says, somewhat offended that he doesn't know the driver. "That thing can't be from around here, I know all the guys with street rods! Hurry up, turn on the CD player. I have *The Beach Boys Greatest Hits* in the glove box. Find 'Little Deuce Coupe.' It'll be fun to listen to as I leave this pork chop son of a bitch in the dust!"

Mike floors the F40. The g-forces from Mike's acceleration fling Tommy's body deep into the red cloth sport bucket seat. All he sees is blue sky, and as hard as he tries, he cannot bring his head back down to a level position.

"I'm going a hundred and he's still right on my ass!" Mike exclaims.

The roar of the F40 and the high-pitched whine of the deuce's blower suffocate Mike's words. The catchy lyrics of one of the Beach Boys' most famous songs about a little deuce coupe are barely audible . . . until Mike cranks up the volume.

"Hey!" Tommy shouts. "Enough! Let them pass you!"

"Pass *me*? Are you crazy? Admit defeat? Never! You know me better than that!"

Just when Tommy thinks there are no more gears, Mike finds another, and the F40 takes off like a nitro-gulping dragster lurching toward the finish line.

"The little bastard is still hugging my tail and if I stop, he'll smash right into our ass!" Mike shakes his head in disgust and cranks the volume up even higher.

Tommy looks in his side-view mirror again. "Damn thing's gone. Thank the Lord!" he exhales in relief. "Okay, slow down now! There's nothing more to prove."

"The hell he's gone! The son of a bitch is passing me on my left! Do you believe it—a freakin' deuce coupe bastard passing an F40. Nothing passes an F40!"

Tommy stretches to see the driver. The dark tinted windows of the deuce coupe obscure its cockpit.

"Shit, I missed the gear!" Mike curses. A horrible grinding noise comes from the gearbox. The deuce coupe accelerates. In a matter of seconds it disappears over the hill, leaving Mike behind to lick his wounds—but he just might need a blood transfusion.

"You need to depress the clutch when you shift! That's in Drivers Ed 101!" Tommy yells.

"That damn gated shifter! It's a nightmare! I need to get back on the track and refine my driving skills."

Tommy starts to laugh. "'Refine your driving skills,' huh? Maybe you should just leave the damn thing in the garage."

"Shut up, Grimaldi."

"Bender, do you realize what just happened?"

Mike is too busy trying to mentally repair his damaged self-respect to answer at first. "I'm not that bad of a driver. Son of a bitch!" he finally hollers as he slams his open hand on the steering wheel. Then he angrily depresses the brake pedal so hard he forces the front suspension of F40 downward. A loud thud accompanies a long scrapping sound from the front of the car. As Mike panics, he slams on the brakes a second time, losing control as the car goes into a violent counter skid. As he overcorrects, the car skids in the opposite direction.

Tommy feels like he's on a toboggan sliding sideways down a steep slope. *We're dead men!* he says to himself. Then the car becomes airborne, leaving the pavement and careening across a field of recently harvested beans. Fortunately, clods of old manure slow them down. Grateful they aren't upside down, the terribly pungent odor is somehow painfully tolerable. They sit quietly for a few minutes trying to collect themselves.

Tommy is the first to speak. "I can just see the headlines now. *Local schoolteacher and financial planner die of manure suffocation.*" Mike remains rigid, still languishing over his embarrassing debacle and in no mood for Tommy's humor.

"It can't be! No freakin' way a deuce is going to overtake a Ferrari," Mike exclaims. "It can't happen. No way!"

"Well, Bender, my good friend, not only did he overtake you, he gallantly disappeared into the horizon like the Lone Ranger and left us buried here in yesterday's gardenias! That's about as humiliating as it gets, don't you think?" By now the next song on the Beach Boys album, "All Dressed Up for School," is playing loudly.

"You can turn that damn thing off now!" Mike shouts vehemently.

Meanwhile, cars gather along the side of the road to take pictures of a million dollar Ferrari in the middle of a bean plantation with all the trimmings. Amid the fifty or so onlookers, a tow truck arrives and winches the Ferrari out of the manure. Mike immediately drives the car to the nearby Boomerang Carwash for a serious bath, and does his best to conceal the shattered portion of carbon fiber on the front spoiler with the license plate.

Feeling humiliated, Mike is completely silent on the ride to Tommy's office. When they arrive, he says sarcastically, "Now go make me some freakin' money!"

Tommy realizes Mike's ego has been savagely brutalized and he is smoldering over his embarrassing defeat, not to mention his dubious driving skills. He sees the situation as an opportunity to rankle Mike even more.

"It's okay, Mike, I still love you even though you just allowed a 1932 Ford to clean your clock. You know what?"

"What?" Mike replies as he nervously taps his fingers on the steering wheel.

"I'll bet the driver was a girl!" Mike lunges for Tommy from the driver's seat. Tommy quickly pulls the wire to open the door and escapes before Mike can choke him to death. Then he convulses with laughter.

"Hey, Mike, make sure you avoid the boys' lavatory this afternoon. The way you smell, you'll get flushed and I may never see you again!"

"Shut up, Grimaldi!"

Tommy laughs to himself as he walks up the stairs to his office. *Of all people! Bender will never get over this one!* Tommy will definitely file the event for future reference and take full advantage of the opportunity to bring it up whenever the need arises.

When he reaches the top of the staircase Margie, his secretary, is outside the door waiting for him. "Tommy," she says, "ten of your clients are waiting in the reception area. I've been making excuses."

As a conscientious financial advisor and a dedicated student of the financial markets, Tommy's practice has grown exponentially over the past few years. People trust him. He, in turn, treats his clients like they are members of his family.

"I thought I only had five appointments this afternoon."

"Yes, five that were *scheduled*. The others showed up unannounced. You need to speak with Lilly first," Margie adds. "She's getting quite agitated." Suddenly she squints and looks sideways at him. "Oh, Tommy! What's that horrible smell?"

"Just give me about five minutes." Tommy walks into the lavatory in his office, opens the medicine cabinet, and sprays his suit coat and pants with a can of Right Guard deodorant. Then he washes his hands and face with soap and water. He slides quietly into his office and sits behind his desk, looking as officious as possible considering his recent bout with a manure patch.

Lillian Brandt is one of Tommy's high net worth clients and a close personal friend. Her mother was an art teacher and her father was the minister at the local Presbyterian Church in Fairchester where she grew up. Everyone in Fairchester knows Lilly. A vice principal in charge of discipline at Fairchester Academy for nearly thirty years, she retired five years ago only to find herself busy volunteering for just about anything and everything. She is still a legend at the academy, and some of the students she disciplined the most as children have become her closest friends as adults.

Two such examples are Tommy and Mike, although she is more of a maternal figure to them. Crossing her was unthinkable. More importantly, students trusted and respected her. She would say, "My job is giving students what they need, when they need it, and in a manner in which they can use it." Of course "need" and "manner" had a myriad of interpretations—all of which were subjectively construed and applied by Ms. Brandt.

Just about the only religion Tommy and Mike ever received in high school was when they were sent to Lilly's office. She had a padded piano bench against the wall across from her desk that not only served as a place for visitors to sit down, but also a place for misbehaving teenagers to kneel and atone for their "sins." Tommy and Mike remember it well, especially since Mike's mother once called the principal to complain about Lilly imposing her religious values on the students. But that didn't stop her.

She is just about the smartest person Tommy knows. But she has other noteworthy traits as well. A remarkable specimen of physical fitness, no one will ever mistake her diminutive size for fragility. At sixty years young, Tommy marvels at her stamina. Her dark blue eyes turn steel blue when she is angry. Her short, knotty white hair is rarely brushed, and almost always looks like a patch of wild dandelions. On Valentine's Day, Tommy inserted a small comb inside her card as a joke, which she promptly tossed into a wastepaper basket saying, "Next time give me a blowtorch. That's what I really need!"

One day, Tommy asked her, "What's your secret, Lilly? How do you stay in such great shape?"

"I kick ass and take names! Who wants to know?" she laughed.

"I do, Lilly. Seriously. How do you do it?"

"Seriously? I try to experience everything life has to offer and I have no fears because I rely on the good Lord to take care of me," she said. "That's my solution for a positive attitude. To keep my gorgeous body in shape, I run and swim every day, and recently started lifting weights. Nothing real heavy though, fifty to sixty pounds for about thirty minutes three times per week. Then I do yoga to keep my balance, flexibility, and mental health. I pray a lot, too. You ought to try it sometime, Tommy. It works wonders!"

"You'll have to coach me."

"You're a big boy, coach yourself! I haven't got time." Lilly liked to pretend to be angry. Before Tommy knew her well, he felt guilty, like he had done something wrong and needed to apologize. Now all he does is laugh.

Lilly loves conversing with Tommy in his office. One day he asked her why she never married. "I intimidate men," she said, without batting an eye. "I've never met a man that could keep up with me. Not only that, I don't trust them. All they want is my money." When Tommy offered to marry her on the spot, she said, "No thanks. You won't be able to handle me either." She was probably right.

Lilly's considerable assets have been derived from years of assiduous investing. Managed portfolios in ultraconservative high-grade commons are her mainstay. She's very comfortable with Tommy as her financial advisor. She has a special fondness for Tommy and Mike and, to a large extent, has been a surrogate parent for both of them ever since grammar school. There is no one in either one of their lives they respect more.

"Now, Tommy, I told you," she says, as she waves her index finger at him. "We're going to have another crash. Only this time, it's going to be worse than '29!"

Tommy doesn't react even though she's been saying the same thing for the past three years.

"Not only that," she continues, "exactly one hundred years ago today, John Kenneth Galbraith was born, you know, the famous economist and author of the book *American Capitalism*. You know what he said?" She waits for Tommy to react, then sits down in the armchair in front of his desk, clasping her knees together and leaning forward.

"No Lilly, I can't remember. Tell me," he says, with a gleam in his eyes. He loves to spar with Lilly on the economy.

"He said that all markets, left to their own devices, provide optimal solutions. Today, there is far too much government interference in the markets. The banks? Wait until you see how many of them fail over the next few days. And it's all because of the Federal Reserve. Greenspan! He's the culprit! He turned on the spigots and hosed us all! The Fed held the money rate at 1 percent for too damn long. That's why we have a housing bubble. Mark my words, Tommy. The government will try and bail out the banks. You wait and see. The die has been cast!"

"I was listening to NPR this morning and several analysts say the collapse of our global financial system is imminent," Tommy replies.

"Well, when the markets decline, the world is full of naysayers. This time, they might be right. Anyway, it makes us all feel good to jump on the bandwagon of despair."

Doom and gloom was her initial mantra. Now she is talking about all the *other* naysayers. Tommy is confused. "Okay, so what do you really think?" he asks.

"You have to ask? I always have a positive outlook!" says Lilly.

"I wasn't sure. How come your outlook is positive with all the negative news?'

"Hard assets. That's where money should be. Hard assets. Gold, silver, art, and . . . oh yes . . . llamas."

"Llamas?"

"Tommy, have you read about the tax deductions? Lord! All the trucks and barns can be depreciated. Do you know that one llama fetched $190,000 at an auction?"

"Where are you getting this information from?" Tommy asks.

"I get a magazine called *Llama Life*. It comes from Durango, Colorado, where llamas are raised by the thousands." Tommy can feel a small smile part his lips. "They say you can make a 50 percent return or more!"

"I hear what you're saying, Lilly. That's not true anymore, though. It's just another bubble that has already burst, and now there are thousands of llamas running around the country that no one wants." He hesitates a moment as he thinks how stupid that really sounds. "It's true," he says. Then he starts to laugh.

"Good time to buy 'em up," she says. "Buy 'em low, sell 'em high!"

"But what if they haven't bottomed out?" *How the hell does a llama bottom out?* Tommy asks himself and starts to laugh all over again.

"Well then let's buy 'em high, Tommy! Buy high, sell low, and make up the difference on the volume!" That did it. They both laugh hysterically.

"Are you sure you didn't come here on a rescue mission?" Tommy asks. "I feel a hundred times better than I did before you graced me with your presence."

"Listen, Tommy. I want you to pray to St. Matthew. Did you know he is the patron saint of sound money management?"

"I didn't know that."

"Yes," says Lilly, "but last I knew, he doesn't work at the SEC and he's not licensed to sell."

Tommy smiles. "Maybe we can call upon St. Matthew to calm things down a bit."

The rest of his day isn't nearly as entertaining, but thanks to Lilly he gets through it. After she leaves, Tommy sits back in his chair, closes his eyes, and prays to St. Matthew for guidance. *Hey, I got nothing to lose,* he says to himself. He prays that St. Matthew will advise his clients with wisdom and resourcefulness, and help him get through the rough days ahead.

By the end of the day, Tommy counsels all his clients to keep their investments intact. Their portfolios are mostly conservative with principal preservation as the main objective. If total financial collapse *is* imminent, their money wouldn't be of value anyplace else either, so why not hang on and hope and pray for the government to resolve the crisis. The way Tommy sees it, there are no other palatable investment alternatives—not even llamas.

At six foot four inches and 230 pounds of rock-hard muscle, Mike Bender is an imposing figure, though his innocent, childlike facial expressions belie his Herculean build. The symmetry between his very blue eyes and his broad smile is magnetic. While demanding and sometimes brusque, he loves the kids and is easily the most approachable teacher at Fairchester Academy. Students ascribing to his high expectations, uncompromising physical fitness regimen, and refusal to accept defeat, have high respect for him. He teaches them how to win at all costs.

Mike came very close to NFL stardom. Viewed as a potential All-Pro linebacker during his short stint with the Buffalo Bills, his career ended prematurely. Had it not been for the hip injury he suffered tackling a 364-pound defensive end turned running back, who knows; Mike might even have made the Hall of Fame. He was that good.

Mike's father, Rick, was killed in a horrendous airplane accident about the time Mike won his third county championship with the Fairchester Eagles. Rick was only fifty-four years old when he and a woman friend flew to Lake Placid for a skiing trip in his private Learjet. On the return trip, his plane crashed into the side of Mount Marcy, the highest peak in New York State. Stormy weather, thick clouds, and mountainous terrain were blamed for the accident. For some reason, his traveling companion didn't accompany him on the trip home and was spared a similar fate. Mike has been strangely passive about the tragedy, not wanting to discuss the subject with Tommy or anyone else.

Nevertheless, Mike is no stranger to grief. His mother died of lung cancer during his freshman year of high school. After that, Lilly became Mike's rock. She asked Tommy to watch over him when they went away to college. Initially, Tommy wasn't at all excited about joining the Buddy Program with the Rangers. Lilly just didn't want Mike going to Afghanistan without Tommy by his side. Also, Mike was very persistent about Tommy going with him.

That's another thing about Mike. He's more stubborn than a block of granite. Once he's made up his mind, no one, with the possible exception of Lilly, can change it. Winning three consecutive county football championships does not come from an ordinary resolve. His headstrong nature filters down to his players, too, and they learn to overcome almost any obstacle. He once informed Tommy, "I'm not stubborn. My way is just better. Get used to it."

Mike's net worth markedly increased upon his father's death. As an only child, Mike inherited a $50 million estate that included an impressive stock portfolio, a valuable car collection, a luxurious mansion, and a highly successful business.

In the early 1980s his father began a company called Safety Guard. Over the last twenty-five years Safety Guard has been the leading manufacturer of seatbelt pretensioners. This made Rick a very wealthy man. Fortunately, Rick was smart enough to have a buy and sell agreement in place with one of his partners. It was funded by a large life insurance policy and Mike was the beneficiary. In the event of Rick's death, the agreement forced Mike to sell the business to his father's partner. This was a good thing. Mike knows nothing about pretensioners or the intricacies of running a global business enterprise. He was grateful he could continue teaching and coaching and not be dragged into a business he knew nothing about.

A few weeks ago, just after his father's estate was settled, Mike sat down with Tommy to implement the long-term financial plan

Tommy had designed specifically for him. Tommy was very much relieved since he knew Mike's dad considered estate preservation the most important financial objective for his son. Tommy strongly believes it is *his* responsibility to advise Mike with that objective in mind. Accordingly, Mike invested $35 million in ultraconservative investment instruments. The non-liquid $15 million balance of his assets includes a first class car collection and a palatial mansion on the outskirts of Fairchester.

Still, Tommy worries about Mike, especially when it comes to financial matters. Something seems to be gnawing at Mike in a bad sort of way. When they are out together, Mike exhibits unpredictable and sometimes impulsive behavior. Tommy wonders if Mike is having a tough time coping psychologically with his sudden wealth. As his best friend, Tommy is very concerned, although he is unable to clearly identify exactly what is going through Mike's head lately.

☆   ☆   ☆

At 6:00 p.m. Mike charges into Tommy's office like a blitzing linebacker attacking the quarterback, his typical entrance routine on Friday nights.

"Hello," Tommy says, unsurprised by his friend's sudden appearance in front of his desk. "Did Ferris Bueller put the wimpy Ferrari with the gated shifter to bed yet?" Tommy knows how to push Mike's buttons. "Wimpy" is Mike's least favorite word.

"Shut up, Grimaldi. Do you like your knuckle sandwich naked or with fingernails?"

"Wait a minute," Tommy says. "Wasn't that you I was with when you missed the gear and we ended up in the cow chips? The way you were driving today, I thought maybe you'd be paws up at the morgue by now."

"You're never getting rid of me, Grimaldi," Mike replies. "You and me—we're joined at the hip, even though mine is sore as hell. Listen, I have to pick up the Daytona in Toronto tomorrow. It just had its 15,000-mile service."

"I'll bet that's gonna cost some coin."

"Fifteen grand—*only* one dollar per mile."

"Glad I drive a Chevy Cruze," Tommy says proudly.

"Buy American, Grimaldi, what's wrong with you?"

"It's a Chevy!"

"C'mon, it's a Chevy wannabe! It's made in China! Buy a new Corvette. It has great lines and really is a big bang for the buck."

"That's BS," says Tommy. "I'm not a Corvette kind of guy. Anyway, my 15,000-mile service cost me $57. And look who's talking about buying American. How many foreign cars do *you* have in your garage? Jags, Mercedes, Ferraris . . . give me a break!"

"You forgot to mention my Ford GT. That's American," Mike complains.

"Sure. One American car out of how many immigrants?"

"Maybe thirty or so. I'm gonna pare down at the RM Auction next March. You wanna ride along with me tomorrow, Grimaldi?"

"What—no football tomorrow?" Tommy asks.

"Have a bye," says Mike.

"When the hell *do* you work?"

"Next Saturday is our final game. We play Northport for all the marbles."

"I know. Hope you give 'em hell, too!"

"So do you want to come with me, or not?" Mike persists.

"Do you think you can learn how to shift before we leave?"

"Do you want to come or not? Just say yes or no."

"Sure, I'll come along," Tommy says. "Someone's gotta watch over the big guy."

"Hey, tell me. What the hell's my account worth, anyway?"

"You want me to check?"

"Yeah, just for the hell of it."

Tommy isn't sure whether Mike has paid much attention to the recent market downturn. Just about the only time Mike mentions the stock market is when he wants to tease Tommy or make a large withdrawal.

Mike hurls himself down on the sofa, stretching his legs over the armrests. "By the way, Tommy, why the hell are you making the market tank so badly?"

*At least he's smiling,* Tommy notes. *That'll change when he sees the value of his account.*

"Let's take a look." Tommy scrolls down to Mike's account on his computer monitor and clicks the heading entitled "current value." His heart sinks. *Can't be,* he says to himself.

"You look like someone just kicked you in the groin!" says Mike. "Did someone die? I knew it. You just ain't cut out for the business world, are you?" He rolls over on the sofa laughing like a lunatic. Tommy doesn't understand what's so funny, but Mike is Mike and he can't stop laughing.

"Shut up, Bender!" Tommy exclaims, as he scrolls further down the page until he comes to a minus $350,000. "Hey! You liquidated $350,000 without telling me! Am I your financial advisor or not?" Tommy is genuinely peeved.

"Well, if you're my financial advisor, why the hell did you put me into that damn AutoNation stock? Now no one can get a loan to buy a car and the stock is in the toilet! I got out with $50,000 less than I invested! It could have been much worse had I waited for you to get up off your ass and tell me what to do."

"C'mon, Bender, that was your idea! How many times have I told you to get rid of that dog?"

"Well, I did just that. I got rid of one dog and you ain't gettin' any of the money back, either!" says Mike, wagging his finger from side to side.

Tommy feels more and more agitated. "So what are you going to do with it?" Tommy asks, unsure if he really wants to know. *Mike is up to something. Making a prudent investment decision is not his style.*

"Just bought a new Bentley Azure. What an amazing car! I may as well have some fun with my money instead of getting screwed over in the market." Mike sits up on the sofa, bends forward, and says, "Well, Mr. Buffet, now what do you think of *that* investment strategy?"

"You've completely lost it," Tommy says patiently. He's becoming accustomed to Mike's newly acquired pomposity, even though he finds it repugnant.

"You're the one who's lost it—to the tune of $50,000—fartin' around in that AutoNation trash," Mike counters.

"Listen, Bender. Just be honest with me. If you wanted to buy a Bentley, all you had to do was tell me."

"That stock's been colder than your last girlfriend! Just admit you screwed up, I've had enough!"

"I think we've both had enough," Tommy says, as he stands up. "It's seven o'clock and just to prove I harbor no hard feelings, I'll buy you dinner."

"Can you still afford it? With your tiny portfolio, *you* probably got wiped out!" Mike says with an unusual smugness.

Tommy is a little surprised at Mike unkind words. "Fish n' chips tonight!" he says, ignoring the slight from his best friend.

Mike laughs. "I'm the one with the hard feelings, and you buying dinner won't do squat to get rid of them!"

"Okay, then you buy."

They both laugh, but Tommy is quietly perturbed over Mike's display of arrogance. He wonders why Mike didn't call him before he purchased the Bentley and ask him to liquidate enough shares to buy it. It's so inconsistent with Mike's usual conduct that Tommy worries about his state of mind. Ever since his father died, Tommy has noticed a gradual but reckless change in his temperament. Mike was never the most deliberate thinker in the world, but in the past when he needed to make an important decision, he would seek the advice of Lilly or himself. This afternoon he was caustic and rude. As his best friend, he needs to talk to Mike. Maybe he'll have a chance on the way to Toronto tomorrow.

A mutual friend, Billy Amato, owns an Italian place in downtown Fairchester. He has a large dimple on his right cheek that Billy says is some kind of birthmark. Given some of the characters that frequent his restaurant, Tommy wouldn't be a bit surprised if it's from a gunshot wound. Other than that, Billy is a rather ordinary looking person. He is a pudgy man with a large midsection and a wide bald spot. Somewhat top-heavy when he walks, he leans forward as if he is constantly dodging punches in a boxing match. He sits on his stool behind the bar most of the time and allows the help to do most of the running around.

Mike and Tommy go to Billy's every Friday night for a fish fry and, when in season, strawberry rhubarb pie. On weekends, especially after Saturday football games, Billy's is the most popular gathering location in Fairchester.

Jessica, a high school Spanish teacher and Mike's friend, usually meets them later, bringing a different female friend with her each time, hoping one of them might spark Tommy's interest. Tommy tries telling her he's gay and that Mike is his secret lover, but she just laughs and brings the girls anyway. Tommy has even gone on dates with a few of them, but somehow never finds himself wanting to go on a second one.

Mike and Tommy usually hang at Billy's place until after midnight, then head to Denny's for a late-night breakfast and sleep until noon, unless it's football season. That's when Mike is all about X's and O's and adheres to a strict curfew.

Billy Amato is a big classic car buff, and Tommy suspects he is responsible for brainwashing Mike into selling his stock and buying the Bentley. After dinner they sit at the bar and drink a couple of Michelob Ultra Lights.

"Billy, tell me," Tommy says, "how come you corrupted my good friend Mike?"

"Ha! You gotta be kidding me. You mean Shula?" Billy smiles, then lights up a cigarette. Billy wrote the book on barroom give-and-take. "Your good friend was corrupt long before I met him. How do you think he wins so many championships? The big one is next Saturday. I've already hired extra help for the big victory party."

"What do you think, Coach?" Tommy asks. "Are you going to guarantee a win for our friend?"

"It's in the bag. Place your bets now, folks! Anyway," Mike says, "how can any of you even think of questioning me?"

Tommy struggles to smile.

"Well, then, I'd better order the food and booze right away!" Billy laughs loudly.

"Just make those calamari and smoked salmon antipastos like you did last year," Mike says. "Only make enough! Last year you ran out and some people got pissed."

"You got it, Coach. Hey, I can't wait to see the new Bentley! Listen . . ." Billy says as lowers his voice, "I bought a 1954 Corvette at a Kruse auction in 1988 for $50,000. Last month, one sold for $102,000 at a Mecum auction in Florida. That's a lot better than Kodak stock now, ain't it?" Billy beams with pride, as if he's discovered the mother lode.

"Even AutoNation is better than Kodak stock," Tommy asserts. He tries to avoid debates on the stock market when he socializes. Most people who are enamored with a get rich quick mentality reject his long-term investment philosophies. Tommy tells them, "Buy intelligently, not emotionally." He considers any other strategy as speculation, a refined word for gambling, and always advises against it.

"So what's your latest stock tip, Tommy?" Billy asks. Tommy doesn't respond right away. "Well? Spit it out, good buddy!" says Billy.

Tommy motions for him to come closer so he can whisper in his ear. "That's not close enough," he says. Billy stretches his neck and as Tommy places his hand sideways over his mouth, he whispers in Billy's ear, "Buy low and sell high!"

"That's a hot tip? Ha! Everybody knows that!"

"I just wanted to give you a heads-up, that's all," Tommy grins.

Mike laughs and shakes his head. "Some people don't practice what they preach," he says.

"The '54 Vette turned out to be a great investment," Billy says proudly. "Don't you think so, Mr. Investment Advisor?"

"Well, sure," Tommy says, "but in my opinion, classic cars are for recreational purposes. You take them to car shows, impress your girlfriend, and take them on Sunday drives. They're not for investment purposes."

Mike is unusually quiet, scratching the back of his head. He finally chimes in. "What about my Ferrari F40, Grimaldi? It went from $400,000 to a $1.5 million in 20 years!"

"Okay. Let's put things into perspective," Tommy says. "Have you guys ever heard of the Rule of 72?" He pulls his cell phone from the inside pocket of his suit coat and goes right to his time value of money app. "If you have an investment growing at 10 percent per year, it will double in 7.2 years. So let's calculate the return on the '54 Corvette." He punches in the numbers. "Accordingly, if you double your money in twenty years, that means you are earning 3.6 percent per year on your money." Then he plugs in the CPI or inflation index from 1988 to 2008, the same twenty-year timeframe. "That $50,000 you invested into the Corvette in 1988, due to inflation, is the same as $91,000 is today. So it will cost you almost twice as much to buy in 2008 what you could buy in 1988 for the same dollars. Do you guys understand this?"

"Yeah, so it's almost a breakeven deal," Mike says.

"Not quite, but my point is that the return on the Corvette is certainly not the slam-dunk return most people think it might be."

"Well how did the stock market do during that same period of time?" Billy asks.

"I'm so glad you asked!" Tommy searches the Dow Jones Industrial Averages. "In 1988 the Dow ended the year at 2,753. At the end of 2007, the Dow was at 13,264. Do I really need to calculate the rate of return or do you guys get the picture?"

"Okay, but now it's going to hell in a handbasket," Billy points out.

"It's shittin' the bed all right," Mike can't help but add his two cents.

"It did the same thing in 1987. It always bounces back. You guys need to be long-term investors and think about your retirement rather than putting so much of your money into hot cars. Anyway, just think how many cars you can buy when you retire wealthy by investing with me." Tommy waits for some return flak. For a brief second, he thinks maybe they understand what he is telling them.

"Well," Mike concedes, "I hate to admit it, buddy, but you *are* pretty persuasive. I'd still rather have my car collection than a damn stock portfolio, though."

"What time do we hit the road tomorrow?" Tommy asks as he looks at his watch.

"I'll pick you up at six so we can beat the traffic over the Lewiston Bridge."

"In that case, I'm out of here." Tommy starts to get off the barstool to leave.

"Hey Grimaldi! Where do you think you're going?" It's Jessica Smallridge, Mike's friend and, not surprisingly, she has brought along another woman who just happens to be very attractive.

"Tommy Grimaldi—say hello to my friend Rebecca Ricci." Tommy is trapped. It's okay, though, Rebecca looks interesting, like someone Tommy might like to know better.

"It's a pleasure." Tommy brings another barstool over for her, and then sits down next to her. She seems just as uncomfortable as he is when it comes to meeting strangers in a bar. Clearly, she is unlike the other Jessica girls.

"Not a good day for stocks, huh?" she says. Tommy feels her sincerity. "Jessica says you're a stockbroker," she adds. "I don't know how you cope with all the ups and downs."

"The ups and downs are easy," Mike quickly answers. "It's the jerks that drive you crazy!" Tommy smiles tactfully while everyone laughs at Mike's one-liner.

"Yes, I'm a financial advisor, not really a stockbroker. My job is to assist people with their financial planning by helping them identify their needs and goals, then I make recommendations, almost all of which are long-term in nature."

"I need a good financial advisor. Got any good stock tips?" Rebecca asks with a pretty smile.

"Yeah, buy high, sell low," Billy interjects. "That's what he'll tell you!"

"I think you have it reversed," Tommy laughs, nearly spilling his drink.

"Oh, sorry. I mean sell low and buy high. Wait a minute. Oh, I don't know what the hell I mean. See how confused you get me, Tommy?"

"Rebecca loves cars," Jessica notes. "I told her you own a nice Chevy."

"Mike calls it a wimp wagon. Of course, *he's* been driving an F40 today."

"A Ferrari F40?" Rebecca is grinning from ear to ear.

"It's the only one around here," Mike quickly answers.

"Are they very fast?" Rebecca asks.

"Not when up against a hot '32 deuce coupe," Tommy replies, seizing the opportunity to hassle Mike. He can't wait see his reaction.

Mike nervously clears his throat, then looks at Tommy with daggers in his eyes.

"It was that damn gated shifter, that's all," he responds. "There's no way any freakin' deuce coupe, no matter how souped-up it is, can take an F40."

Given his response, Mike is clearly in a state of profound denial. Tommy has to turn his head away so he won't laugh in his face.

"Excuse me? I'd like to order a honey deuce cocktail, if I may?" Rebecca says as she nods in Billy's direction.

"Did you say honey deuce, sweetie?" Billy asks.

"Yes, that's right. Honey deuce. Do you know how to make them?"

"Oh, yes. I know how to make them all right," Billy assures her.

"Deuce? She did say deuce, right?" Mike asks.

Tommy wishes he could take a picture of Mike's helpless and forlorn expression. Then Mike looks right at Tommy as if to say, *You're my friend. You're not going to let this happen to me, are you?*

"Tell 'em, Rebecca, tell 'em!" Jessica urges. "He needs to be humbled."

"Jessie," she says self-consciously, "show some mercy."

"Oh, I know Mike can handle just about anything!" she laughs. "At least he *thinks* he can!"

Picking up on Rebecca's clever little word game, Tommy starts to laugh uncontrollably. "Mike," he says, between spasms, "I think Rebecca has something she wants to tell you, ole buddy. Better brace yourself."

Mike maintains his totally baffled expression. Rebecca folds her arms, hesitates a little, and then looks at Tommy and winks.

"Well . . . *my* deuce . . . I think it beat *your* F40 today," she trills as Billy hands her the honey deuce she ordered. She raises it into the air in a triumphant salute and says, "Here's to my little deuce coupe! *You don't know what I got!*"

Tommy raises his drink and they all laugh and salute with Rebecca. Everyone except Mike, that is. He's somber as a stone and suffering from a serious affliction called disillusionment, or maybe something even worse, like shell shock.

"C'mon Bender, loosen up. It's just a car," Jessica says sharply. "It doesn't hurt that much to lose once in a while. You're a big boy, right?"

"That's right," Tommy says, on the brink of hysteria. "It's just a car and Mike is definitely a big boy! There's no doubt about that!"

# 3

# Andrea's Secret Treasure

**Fairchester, New York**

*October 18, 2008, Saturday*

Mike picks Tommy up early Saturday morning in his new Bentley Azure convertible. It is an exquisite shade of cerulean blue with a gorgeous creamy leather interior. The car has every conceivable accessory known to modern man, not to mention that it's zero to sixty times are under five seconds. With 450 horsepower and weighing over 6,000 pounds, their trip to the Ferrari dealer in Toronto promises to be exciting. At around $350,000 per copy, Bentley has sold only a few of them. Now with the global financial crisis, as incredible as the car is, Tommy can't help but wonder about their future sales.

Tommy is anticipating calls from his clients today, so his cell phone is charged and at hand. The Lehman Brothers bankruptcy, the biggest in history, is front-page news. Things are ugly, and fear of total economic collapse permeates the minds of serious investors all over the world. The previous night at Billy's place was wonderful comic relief, but Tommy fears the dark financial clouds might cause an end to his career. While that possibility has him tense and uneasy, he tries to conceal it from Mike.

"Well Bender, you have a nice button-down shirt on today. I like it," Tommy says.

"Thanks," says Mike. "I need to look the part. I have my new Ferrari watch on, too. Thought it might look a little weird with the whistle and the t-shirt. Anyway, those things are becoming part of my boring past."

"Never forget your roots, big fella."

"I don't know, Grimaldi, I think teaching is becoming too monotonous for me. There's got to be more to life than babysitting adolescents every day. If it weren't for football, I'd resign and play with my cars all day."

"What are you talking about?" Tommy replies. "You're the best thing that's ever happened to Fairchester Academy. Look how many young lives you've influenced."

"It's getting old," Mike says. "Really it is. Maybe you should consider changing professions, too. I know the market has been pretty rough on you the last month. I can tell you're stressed out most of the time."

"No way!" Tommy doesn't mean to be so abrupt, he just hates it when people question his resilience.

"You know what?" Mike glances at Tommy and says, "I'm gonna beat that damn deuce if it's the last thing that I do."

"It just might be," Tommy says. "Next time I'll stay in the dugout."

"Oh, and don't tell anyone either. Someone will blame it on my driving, not the car!"

"You'd better prepare yourself," warns Tommy. "Your friend Jessica will probably announce it on the public address system Monday at school. She seems to be on your case lately."

"You know, Jessie is starting to get on my nerves," says Mike. "Maybe I should find someone who doesn't require so much attention. She hates to be alone and is always calling me."

"How about that Rebecca, she's some girl, huh?" Tommy says.

"That girl has some serious hang-ups."

"She sure does, and I like them a lot!"

"You're kidding me, she's not your type," Mike scoffs.

"Okay, tell me. What's my type?" Tommy asks.

"More straightlaced. You know what I mean—someone low-key and quiet, the peaceful agreeable type." Mike is having difficulty restraining his smile.

"I think you're describing the ideal woman for you, not me."

"No, no, no," says Mike. "I'm not just going after any old woman. She has to be a highly successful professional woman. She needs to make the big bucks or be independently wealthy like me. Unlike you, I have to be careful. Most chicks are after my money."

"Unlike me?" Tommy asks.

"Yeah! Chicks are drawn to me because of my good looks. When they find out how much money I have, they get a little crazy."

"That's not Jessica, is it?"

"It isn't?" asks Mike. "Two things about Jessie: she's too much of a drama queen and she doesn't make enough money as a teacher to feel comfortable with me. She's got a great body, though, so she'll do for now."

"Do you think Rebecca's hot?" Tommy asks.

"As hot as a frozen potato!"

"You know what I think, Bender?" say Tommy. "You should get your ego serviced after we pick up the Daytona. Your spark plugs are misfiring! Not only did Rebecca trounce you on the highway, she did quite a number on you at the bar last night. Imagine that! And a woman, no less. How do you live with yourself?"

"Good thing I have broad shoulders, huh?" quips Mike.

Tommy laughs. "Yeah, good thing. By the way, she told me she needs a financial advisor. I'm calling her Monday to make an appointment."

"That's a likely excuse."

"It's a pretty good entrée, though, don't you think?"

"Find out where she got that deuce coupe," Mike says. "It's probably her old man's street rod. I really would like to know what's in that thing. And tell her I want a rematch too!"

"You're a real glutton for punishment, aren't you?"

"It ain't over till it's over!"

"Okay, Yogi, suit yourself. She'll probably accept the challenge, too. By the way, what route are we taking to Toronto?" Tommy adds.

"Hamlin Beach Parkway. The New York State Thruway is quicker, but no cars are on the Parkway so we can open up the Azure. It's like driving on the Bonneville Salt Flats. No speed restrictions! Cool, huh?"

"Yeah, cool," Tommy says impassively, as he looks out on the Lake Ontario shoreline.

As they approach the Hamlin Beach Parkway, Mike immediately floors the Bentley. It feels like the Azure is being shot out of an iron slingshot. Just then Tommy's cell phone rings. As he answers it, he glances at the dash instruments. Amazingly, at 130 mph, he feels the comfort of a first-class seat on a jumbo jet. No noise, no shaking, no bumps; the ride is perfect.

"Hello Tommy," comes a soft voice over the phone. "It's Rebecca, remember . . . from last night?"

Mike reaches toward the posh instrument cluster, pushes the Bluetooth button, and like magic surround sound fills the car.

"Who says you could listen in?" Tommy whispers, as Mike projects a sardonic smile.

"Oh, hello, Rebecca! We have you on speaker," Tommy says matter-of-factly. "Mike and I are on our way to Toronto to pick up his Daytona. How are you doing?"

"I'm well," she says. "Just wanted to apologize for last night. I didn't mean to embarrass either of you."

"I don't know, Rebecca," Tommy replies, "I think some irreversible damage has been done to my dear friend's enormous ego." Out of the corner of his eye, he can see Mike's head bobbing up and down. "He may have to see a shrink on Monday."

"I'll never get over it!" Mike exclaims. "And I want a damn rematch too!" Mike attempts a feeble laugh, but Tommy knows, for him, this is no laughing matter.

"Rebecca," Mike asks, "where did your old man get that deuce, anyway? That thing's a rocket ship!"

"Oh, my dad lives near New York City and doesn't even own a car."

They wait for her to say more. Mike looks at Tommy and shrugs his shoulders as if to say, *it's your move buddy.*

"Well then, it must be your brother's car, huh?" Mike continues to probe.

"No brothers," she replies. Again she delays—waiting for Mike to hang himself high.

"Who did you borrow it from?" Mike asks. "I thought I knew every fast car in Fairchester."

"Bender, you idiot, it's *her* car! Ignore him, Rebecca! Thanks for calling. I'll call you Monday. Maybe we can have lunch?"

"Love to!" she says.

"Great!"

## Toronto, Ontario

They arrive at Ferrari Maranello of Ontario early in the afternoon. As they enter the showroom, they are immediately mesmerized by the bright red Ferraris strategically arranged on the showroom floor.

"These cars are such a beautiful shade of red," Tommy observes.

"The official color name is rosso corsa," Mike quickly informs him. "That's the color most often seen on cars driven by the international Ferrari racing teams. French cars are blue and British cars are green. Germany uses mostly silver and white. The United States uses white and blue, and Japan uses white with reddish orange sun colors."

Tommy wonders why Mike thinks he needs instruction on racing colors from around the world all of a sudden. "Is this a geography lesson?" he asks.

"If you're going to hang with me, I just want you to be *informed*," says Mike. "See this car here? Did you ever hear of Leonardo Fioravanti? He's the design genius who used to work for Pininfarina where he designed the Dino, Boxer, 308, my F40, and the Daytona, too."

"This car looks very different," Tommy remarks. "What is it?"

"It's on loan," comes a distant voice. "Hi, I'm Jaclyn Le Harve."

An attractive woman walks over to them and extends her hand. Mike immediately extends his right hand exposing his Ferrari Hublot wristwatch. Tommy always wondered why he wore his watch on his right arm instead of his left. Now he knows.

"Your watch . . . it's the MP-05 LaFerrari by Hublot. Isn't it the most expensive Ferrari watch in world?" she asks.

"With 637 individual components, $318,000 might be considered a bargain," Mike replies with unflinching bluster. Mike's strategy, at least in his mind, has just paid off.

"The watch resembles the LaFerrari hybrid engine that's coming out next year," Jaclyn explains enthusiastically. "Only this hybrid has 963 'prancing horses' with zero to sixty times under three seconds! Would you like to order one today?"

"I hate hybrids," Mike answers curtly. "Any kind whatsoever. If you can afford a Ferrari, you can afford the gas, even if you only get nine miles per gallon!"

"Well, I suppose that's true, especially for a diehard Ferrari guy like yourself."

Jaclyn is able to read Mike quite well. She is stunning, and the more Tommy looks at her, the more he realizes she is the literal embodiment of a Ferrari mainliner. Her gold prancing horse earrings are only slightly visible under her long black hair, which drapes over her narrow shoulders. Tommy can tell that her charcoal eyes are making Mike want to write her a check on the spot and select the car later. Bright red lipstick matches her bright red blazer, and an open collar black silk blouse matches her knee-high black skirt. Her Louboutin stilettos with "sammy red-bottoms" accentuate her beautiful long legs. Tommy doesn't mean to stare, but he can't help but notice an elegant double chain gold ankle bracelet with a heart shaped pendant just above one of the stilettos.

While Tommy sees her as an interesting dinner date, Mike pictures her in one of those red-hot bikinis from the recent *Sports Illustrated Swimsuit Issue*, the kind he just bought for Jessica, only hers is white. *White would work for Jaclyn, too*, he thinks.

"I'm Mike Bender. This is my friend, Tommy Grimaldi."

"Your last name is Grimaldi?" Jaclyn asks with an unusual curiosity. "Any relation to Antonio Grimaldi?"

"Antonio Grimaldi? Never heard of the guy," Tommy answers. "I've never been into the family ancestry thing."

Jaclyn smiles graciously as she explains, "Antonio was one of Enzo's best Formula One techs during the 1950s. I hope he isn't related to you. He had such a tragic life."

"Tragic life?" Tommy repeats.

"Hmm." Jaclyn squints thoughtfully. "Don't worry. If you haven't heard of him, you're probably not related to him, although in Ferrari circles he's becoming sort of an icon. He and only a handful of others were responsible for the design of the first Ferrari 250 GTO Berlinetta, my all-time favorite car."

"What's that?" Tommy inquires with a quizzical look. "I've never—"

Mike interrupts, "You've never heard of the Ferrari GTO? Only a few were made, and each one of them is worth millions today. The prototype—the one Jaclyn mentioned—that thing has to be worth gazillions, right Jaclyn?"

Jaclyn smiles tactfully. "Maybe, one day, someone will find it. I sure would like to be the one who does!"

"What part of Italy is Antonio from, any idea?" Tommy asks.

"Well, there's a rumor that he was part of the Grimaldi family that rules Monaco," she responds. "I believe there's a large Grimaldi family spread throughout Genoa, too."

"That's interesting. My aunt and uncle were Genovese."

"Someday we should go there, Grimaldi, and find your compatriots," Mike suggests.

"Your friend Mike seems wise and resourceful," Jaclyn smiles.

While Jaclyn seems a bit calculating to Tommy, he is sure Mike is becoming quite enamored with her. Mike's body language does the communicating: his quick, accommodating reaction when she speaks, his penetrating eye contact. And after the coming-out party for the Hublot watch, she is probably just as enamored with him.

"Yes, he is," Tommy agrees. "He's one of the most resourceful people I know."

"Speaking of me, how do I find out more about the GTO Berlinetta?" Mike asks.

"Some of the information is most likely rumor or part of Ferrari folklore," Jaclyn surmises. "That being said, it's true that GTOs are fetching millions at auctions. Antonio Grimaldi and Giancarlo Bandini have become popular characters in Ferrari pop culture lately. They were the two main architects of the prototype. Enzo, for some reason, was very unhappy with the prototype. He had them secretly haul it off to the Port of Genoa for transport to America. It was supposed to go to a storage facility in New York City. Too bad it never made it. It's not just the monetary value, it's the historical significance, too. If the car existed today, it would be an Italian national monument."

"God, I'd give my eyeteeth to own that car!" Mike says spontaneously.

Jaclyn ponders for a moment, as if she isn't sure what to do next. "For what it's worth," she finally says, "there's a long article about Antonio Grimaldi in the latest issue of the *Prancing Horse*, the Ferrari Club magazine."

"How can I get my hands on a copy?" Tommy asks.

"I have several copies in my office. Hang on. I'll run and get one for each of you."

Within a minute, Jaclyn returns. "Take these home. You'll like the pictures of the GTO being hoisted onto the *Andrea Doria*. There are pictures of Antonio, too."

"The *Andrea Doria*? So this car is at the bottom of the ocean?" Tommy says as he folds the magazine under his right arm.

"That's where it is," Jaclyn answers. "I heard the front part of the bow on the *Andrea Doria* has recently fallen and cargo holds are much more accessible now."

"No kidding!" Mike exclaims. Tommy notices his wheels turning. His eyes telegraph something more than mere enthusiasm.

"No kidding," Jaclyn confirms, detecting Mike's growing fascination.

"Thank you for the magazine, Jaclyn," Tommy says.

"Let me know your thoughts after you read it," Jaclyn replies with a certain probing curiosity. "People in the know think Antonio was involved with some unscrupulous characters. I heard that a group of Ferrari enthusiasts are attempting to clear his name."

"Why?" Tommy asks. "What happened to him?"

"You have to read the article. I couldn't begin to describe what happened to him."

Tommy's distant relatives are of little concern to Mike. The lost GTO, however, excites him almost as much as Jaclyn.

"I'm surprised the GTO hasn't been salvaged from the *Andrea Doria* before now," Mike says. "Restoration costs would be nothing compared to what it would sell for at a high-end classic car auction like Gooding or RM Sotheby's."

"I can't answer that," Jaclyn replies, "but did you know another famous car was in the number one cargo hold on the *Andrea Doria*? Rumor has it that the GTO is in the number two cargo hold. Both were placed in watertight containers."

"The Chrysler Norseman," Mike answers. "That was a big loss for Chrysler, too."

"Right again, Mike," Jaclyn winks. "It was built by Ghia in Torino at the same time as the GTO prototype. It had a dramatic effect on American car design, even though it never made it to America."

"It looks like a Plymouth Barracuda on steroids," Mike observes.

"That's sad," Tommy says. "I've always liked Plymouths."

"Plymouths, Grimaldi? You've always liked Plymouths?"

"It's very sad we lost *both* great cars," Jaclyn says, coming to Tommy's rescue.

"Didn't I read somewhere that a guy died recently trying to salvage it?" Mike asks.

"That's probably true," Jaclyn acknowledges. "The *Andrea Doria* went down near Nantucket after it was broadsided by the Swedish liner *Stockholm*, ripping open a seventy-foot gash in her starboard side. Fifty-one passengers died. A lot of people have tried to recover the Norseman and the GTO, and several of them got their lines tangled in the twisted metal of the wreckage and died. Some couldn't find their way out and drowned and several are still missing. They call it the 'Mount Everest of wreck diving.' It's 240 feet down!"

"Jaclyn," Mike says, "you seem to know quite a bit about the *Andrea Doria* and diving in general. Have you ever been scuba diving?"

"I used to dive the Main Duck Islands on Lake Ontario with my former boyfriend. Now, he does more diving trips to the *Andrea Doria* than anyone. If you're ever interested, I'll give you his number."

"A trip like that might be a possibility," Mike concurs.

"He's a good diver, he has the experience, and he has all the latest diving gear."

"He's your *former* boyfriend, right?" Mike asks.

"Yes. It's a boring story. Anyway, the first thing he'll tell you about, if you call him, is something called the 'whiskey factor.' It's when you—"

"I've heard of that!" Mike jumps in the middle of Jaclyn's explanation.

She continues, "At every fifty feet of depth, it's like taking a shot of whiskey. Listen guys, I don't mind getting smashed on terra firma, but getting blitzed in several hundred feet of dark, freezing water? No way! That's why today, at those depths, divers need the latest technology, especially the correct mixtures of helium and oxygen. I've done some deep dives with Al, and he has all the right stuff. He knows what he is doing."

Tommy begins to wonder why all of a sudden Jaclyn seems to be selling a dive trip.

"Yeah!" Mike agrees. Not to be outdone, he adds, "I know all about diving, too. I used to dive the Bermuda Triangle with my father when I was in college. I'll bet I've seen at least half of the three hundred wrecks scattered on the bottom of the triangle. It really took my breath away when I saw the *L'Herminie*. It was a French warship that sank in 1838. Seeing her cannons and masts—what a sight! Really breathtaking."

"Yes, I've heard about that," Jaclyn says. "It hit a shallow reef, right?"

"Yup. It's only in thirty-five feet of water, so it's pretty accessible."

"Well, thirty-five feet is a helluva lot different than 240 feet," Tommy notes. "Why would anyone be crazy enough to go that deep?"

"Treasure seekers," Jaclyn replies. "There's supposed to be millions still on the *Doria*. They raised one safe back in the nineties. It only had some silver certificates and some other worthless foreign currency in it. Locating and salvaging the GTO prototype would be the greatest automotive discovery ever. That would take a lot of money, though, certainly more than I have, that's for sure!"

"I'm putting it on my bucket list," Mike says. "Hey, Tommy, what do you say? Want to join me? Maybe we can find the GTO and that other safe. Between the two, we'll make millions! Listen. I'll pay for the whole deal, the charter, the dive equipment, and all the accommodations. The whole gig is on me! What do you say, buddy?"

"Forget it, I want to live long enough to collect my Social Security checks."

"C'mon, Grimaldi, you got to live a little. Life's too short!"

"Count *me* out," Tommy says emphatically. "Completely and totally out. Forget it!"

"What do you think, Jaclyn? I'll bet you're the adventurous type."

Jaclyn smiles at Mike, then turns her head away. It seems hard for her not to say "yes." "Look . . . fifty feet . . . that's my new max. I'm afraid I'd be very boring company. Thanks for asking, anyway."

Tommy is skeptical. For some reason, he doesn't believe Jaclyn is being candid.

"Can I call and try to convince you?" Mike asks with a hopeful smile.

"Of course," Jaclyn says. "I wouldn't mind at all."

Mike extends his arm with the Hublot. "Let's shake on it."

"Sure!" she agrees, as she looks at his watch again. "Can we talk business now?"

"Absolutely," Mike says. "But that information about the GTO prototype—it's got me all psyched up!"

Jaclyn nods. "Maybe we can discuss it again sometime."

"I'd like that a lot," Mike replies. "Sometime soon, I hope."

Jaclyn walks near the front window of the showroom. "This is another one of my favorites," she says, pointing to the car they are standing beside. "It's a Ferrari SP1, also designed by Leonardo Fioravanti. Sorry, I can't sell it to you. It's the first one-off custom as part of the Ferrari Special Portfolio Program. The president of the Ferrari club in Japan owns this one. It cost him about seven million to have it built to his specs. It's based on the F430 platform and the lightest Ferrari ever made. It's almost all carbon fiber!"

"I love the eye shadow they added around the headlights," Mike remarks. "The greenhouse appearance seems much more pro-nounced. Where can I get more details about this project, Jaclyn?"

"Come with me," she says quickly, realizing the hook has been effectively set and it's time to reel in the catch.

Mike places his arm around Jaclyn's shoulder as he walks with her to her office, leaving Tommy alone in the showroom.

*Will Mike spend seven million? He's crazy but not insane,* Tommy muses. *But then again, he's about as malleable as a clay monkey lately, especially when he's at the mercy of a seductive woman and an ostenta-tious red Italian sports car.*

"Hey," Tommy says, "don't you two be gone for long, I need to be back by midnight!" They both ignore him.

Jaclyn leads Mike into her office. It's ornate and the deep pile navy blue carpeting and red suede wallpaper remind Mike of his father's executive office when he was alive.

"You must be the CEO of this place. I'm very impressed!" he says, as he sits on the plush red leather sofa.

Jaclyn laughs. "Not quite, but I sell a lot of Ferraris. That's why I get the big corner office."

Mike points to an oil painting of the GTO Prototype in the middle of the wall across from her desk. The bright red car presents a striking contrast to the frosty gray clouds above it, yet there is just enough sunlight to amplify its curvaceous lines.

"That picture is absolutely incredible!" Mike exclaims. "That's the *Andrea Doria* in the background, isn't it?"

"Yes. The ship is docked at the Port of Genoa. The GTO looks gorgeous, doesn't she? The painting has been replicated from a picture taken by Antonio Grimaldi. You'll see it when you read the magazine article."

The pure elegance of the painting captivates Mike, but the immense symbolism it represents affects him deeply. Here is a gorgeous image of the most significant Ferrari ever built, just before its terrible demise.

"Imagine," he says, "this beautiful icon rotting away at the bottom of the ocean."

Jaclyn ignores Mike's nostalgic moment and begins her sales routine. "Let's talk *new* Ferraris, okay? I want to show you something I know you'll love!"

As Tommy peruses the plethora of beautiful cars on the showroom floor, he starts to recap in his mind what has just transpired.

*I wonder which portfolio Mike is more interested in—Ferrari's or Jaclyn's. Knowing him, he'll score with both. Jaclyn's different than most sales people in the business. She's very astute about Ferraris and their history. That story about the GTO and the Norseman is quite intriguing, and perhaps I should learn more about Antonio.* Then he starts to get nervous. *I should have never let Mike go into Jaclyn's office without me. He'll probably do something stupid like throw another chunk of money at a car he doesn't need just to impress her.*

After checking out the showroom cars, Tommy walks into the service area and discovers the most immaculate, antiseptic garage area he has ever seen. It is hospital clean. The technicians are dressed in spotless white uniforms with open collared shirts. They look like brain surgeons getting ready to operate. Sophisticated diagnostic machines, many with Wi-Fi, Bluetooth, USB connectivity, and LCD touch screens are at every workstation, and designed to measure every conceivable function on a Ferrari. *No wonder the 15,000-mile service cost $15,000!*

Mike emerges from Jaclyn's office with a huge smile on his face. "I ordered one," he says to Tommy. "It'll take at least a year to manufacture. I'll show you the build specs later. Listen, Grimaldi. I want you to sell $10 million worth of my stock. I don't care what you sell—just sell enough and place it in my cash account. I'm going to need it next week."

"Bender! Can we talk about it first?" Tommy's shock and frustration are clearly apparent. Ten million dollars is a large percentage of Mike's portfolio. Selling shares now, especially in a down market, will mean substantial losses.

"What's there to talk about? The decision is made."

"Hold off for a few weeks and allow the market to rebound," Tommy asserts. "It could mean a couple million, even more. After this kind of dramatic decline, the market always bounces back. Don't be so damn impulsive!"

"Piss on the market! Just dump enough shares for ten mil and put the cash in my money fund, okay? I'll be writing a check from that account next week."

"Bender, think through what you are asking me to do."

"I told you what to do. Now do it or I'll call and have it done myself."

Tommy has never seen Mike this headstrong. His eyes have a mean, unwavering look, as though he might physically attack Tommy if he continues to challenge him.

"Listen Bender, we have a serious disagreement here. Please, we have to discuss this more," Tommy insists.

"Maranello manufactures only one Ferrari portfolio car a year. Jaclyn was telling me the CEO of a large supermarket chain ordered one, then changed his mind and now wants his money back. She said I could take his place on the list if I get the money in next week."

"I thought a custom-made Ferrari cost seven million. Why ten?" Tommy queries.

"I ordered one with the F12 Berlinetta platform. It's the fastest Ferrari ever made! It has 740 horsepower with zero to sixty times at three seconds, and eleven seconds in the quarter mile. And that's before all my modifications. It has active brake cooling, carbon-ceramic brakes, and a suspension feature I can hardly pronounce. It's called the magnerhetorical . . . no, wait it is the magneorbital suspension control system. Jaclyn explained that it has no small moving parts that can break. It has a smart fluid that is filled with magnetic particles to increase the fluid's viscosity. When it's turned on, it's charged and reacts to a magnetic field. Sensors monitor road conditions while a controller modifies the damping characteristics up to one thousand times per second. Pretty neat, huh?"

"I have no idea what the hell you just said. I don't think you do either."

"Never mind. Just sell, don't argue with me!"

"You're crazy, Michael," Tommy says angrily. "Fine, I'll sell first thing Monday morning."

"Good, let me know when the money is in the account."

"Do you want me to email the trade confirmations with the sell prices or do you want to wait for your monthly statement?"

"I don't really give a damn what the prices are. I'll check the monthly statement."

Mike's answer conveys to Tommy just how profoundly indifferent he is about his money. Indiscriminately liquidating stocks, losing millions, and not seeming to care is inconceivable to Tommy. He is raging mad at Mike and it is making him sick to his stomach. *Here I am losing sleep over my clients' losses, exerting every possible effort to communicate with them in order to put their minds at ease, implementing detailed strategies to minimize their losses, and Mike drops millions with one stubborn request—millions he doesn't need to lose.* And what really incenses Tommy is that Mike doesn't give a damn.

# 4

# Bull and Bear

**Fairchester, New York**

*October 19, 2008, Sunday Morning*

As they do every Sunday at 10:00 a.m., Tommy, Mike, and Lilly attend mass at the St. Ignatius Chapel on the campus of St. Ignatius College near Fairchester. While Tommy and Mike are willing participants, Lilly has been a staunch catalyst for their church attendance ever since they were kids. In the absence of parental guidance, she sees it as her obligation to make sure the Lord is a meaningful part of their lives. The Lord will take care of them, she believes, as long as they remain faithful and practice their religion.

Yet Mike and Tommy are preoccupied this Sunday morning. Mike can't stop thinking of the oil painting of the GTO Prototype in Jaclyn's office. He is unable to clear his mind of the *Andrea Doria* resting on its side in 240 feet of water. Could the GTO be salvaged? Could he restore it and bring it back to its former majesty? He had to find out.

Tommy is also distracted. He resurrects thoughts of his ancestry, thoughts he has sequestered for years. For the first time in his life, he wonders why he has shied away from them. Was he afraid of what he might discover? Maybe it's time to find out more.

Sitting between them like a mother trying to separate two unruly little boys, Lilly notices their minds drifting off. Like she has always done during Mass, she pokes them with her elbows to bring them back to real time. But this morning, Lilly's pokes are to no avail.

"Say your prayers!" she whispers firmly. "This *is* the Lord's Day and he knows you are ignoring him!"

After Mass, they go to Billy Amato's place for breakfast. It's crowded, as it always is after Sunday Mass. When Billy arrives at their table, Lilly demands, "It's my turn to buy. Don't take their money!"

"You two guys freeloading again?" Billy teases. His white apron is stained with egg yolk and grease.

"Billy," Mike says, "wait till you see the ride I just purchased in Toronto."

Billy grins with stubborn pride. "Can't possibly be nicer than my Vette, right?" he says.

"Not even close," Tommy replies as he flashes an engaging smile in Billy's direction.

"Now what did you go and do?" Lilly asks. "Do I have to watch you every minute?"

"Tell her!" Tommy says. "Maybe she can drill some sense into that thick skull of yours." Tommy is still fuming over the $10 million Mike had him liquidate from his investment account.

"Well, I just purchased a new Ferrari, that's all," he says. "No big deal."

"No big deal, huh?" Billy asks. "How much did you pay for it?"

Mike lifts his coffee cup, takes a sip, and remains tight-lipped.

"Tell them, Bender!" Tommy insists. "See if I'm the only one who thinks you're insane."

"Almost $10 million," Mike replies. "So what?"

"Ten million dollars for a car?" Lilly asks. "Do me a favor next time, *don't* tell me!"

"You're kidding me," Billy is startled. "The coach driving around a $10 million dollar Ferrari? That sends the wrong message, Mike! You're supposed to be a role model for these kids. You should focus more on coaching and less on your damn cars."

"And you should mind your own business," Mike retorts. "I don't need some hash-slinger telling me how to spend *my* money."

"You mean your father's money, don't you, chump?" says Billy.

Mike kicks back the chair and stands up to confront Billy.

"What are going to do, tough guy, hit me? Go ahead! You know, Mike, you've become a real jackass lately."

Tommy quickly rises to separate them. "Calm down, Bender. You're twice his size!"

"Mike! Sit down!" Lilly hollers in a loud, penetrating voice. All eyes in the restaurant are on them. Billy throws a towel over his shoulder and walks away, angrily shaking his head.

"No way am I putting up with his insults!" Mike protests angrily. His face is blood-red.

"Bender, like it or not, small town values don't include $10 million cars!" Tommy says assertively. "And school teachers are supposed to drive Pintos! That's the mindset here. Accept it and adapt or be miserable."

"Then I'm selling the house and moving the hell out. I don't need this crap!"

"What the hell's wrong with you, Mike," Lilly snaps. "You've become totally incorrigible!" She throws her cloth napkin on the table and storms out of the restaurant in a huff.

Mike and Tommy look at each other in silence, startled by Lilly's harsh reaction.

"Grimaldi, don't forget to sell the stock!" Mike finally exclaims.

"After all that, all you can say is 'don't forget to sell the stock'? Relax, Michael, I've already placed the damn sell order!"

"Good. Make sure you let me know when I can write the check to Jaclyn."

Tommy doesn't respond, rubbing his hand across his forehead to relieve the stress.

"So why are you pissed at me?" Mike asks. "What the hell did I do?"

"I *am* really pissed at you right now, just leave it at that!"

"You'll get over it," Mike says with apparent indifference.

"Don't be so sure!"

For a minute or so, there is total silence between them. Making eye contact is difficult. Mike is the first one to break the ice.

"Listen, Tommy. I should be able to drive whatever car I want to drive. It's a free county, isn't it?"

"Yes, that *is* up to you," Tommy replies. "Someone once said to me, 'Few people can stand success, especially when it's someone else's.' That's just human nature. Couple that reality with the culture of this town and all you are going to do is antagonize everyone."

Mike shakes his head and leans back in his chair. Then he changes the subject as if Tommy has been talking to the wall behind him.

"Hey, listen to me," Mike says, "last night I signed us up for a diving expedition to the *Andrea Doria* wreck on the *Ocean Diver* out of Montauk. You know, Jaclyn's former boyfriend's boat. It has all the latest technical diving equipment."

"Why didn't you *ask* me first? You're really pushing our friendship lately."

"I saved you the trouble of thinking it over; you're so damn indecisive."

"Oh yeah? You need to understand something right now. There's absolutely no 'us' in that arrangement. Just get that straight before we go on, okay? How's that for decisiveness?"

"I'm not going without you Grimaldi, so don't bother objecting," says Mike.

"Then just cancel the damn trip, okay?"

"Can't, already sent in the ten grand deposit."

"Then get your money back!"

"No way, I never ask for refunds."

"Look, Bender. Schedule a diving trip to Bermuda in July and I'll go with you."

Mike gives Tommy one of his aloof smiles. "This is not like diving in Bermuda and going down thirty-five feet. This is big boy diving. We're going down 240 feet to find the GTO. After we find it, I'm going to salvage it and then restore it. When I'm finished, I'll have the most valuable car in the world!"

"That's if you don't end up in a pine box first," Tommy interjects. "Then who's gonna need restoration?"

"What are you worried about? Hundreds of people dive to the wreck every summer."

"Then don't you think if the GTO were easy to find, someone would have found it by now? You've not been thinking right lately. I'm getting very concerned about you."

"I spent all night on the Internet researching this stuff," says Mike. "The front bow of the *Andrea Doria* collapsed to the ocean floor. Now you can get inside the cargo holds from the upper deck near the chapel on Deck C. That's right where the GTO is supposed to be!"

"You're going to need a chapel all right!" Tommy warns. "Say a few prayers for yourself, you're going to need them!"

"The reason people have never found the GTO is they don't have the balls to go deep inside the ship. They do it for bragging rights! They dive down to the wreck with a tether attached to the mother ship, spend about twenty minutes or so, reach out and touch the wreck, and then come right back up again. Trained monkeys can do that!"

"And, of course, macho Mike Bender has balls big enough to perform a thorough inspection of the ship, right?" Tommy scoffs. "Don't you remember what Jaclyn said about divers getting their lines tangled in the twisted metal of the wreckage and drowning? Some got lost inside the wreck and couldn't find their way out. Many are still missing. C'mon, Bender, like you tell your kids, get your head screwed on right. This is insanity."

"Well, you think about it," says Mike. "I'll pick you up after work and we can talk more."

"Don't bother," Tommy replies angrily. "Here, Mr. Fat Cat! You can pay the damn check!" Tommy throws the check in Mike's direction. With his blood pressure soaring, he slams his palm onto the table and storms out of the restaurant.

Tommy drives around town for about an hour to cool off, wondering why Mike is squandering his money—and why he's so damn arrogant about it. Before his father died, Mike was never like this. The Hublot watch, a Bentley, and the millions of unnecessary losses in the stock market baffle Tommy beyond belief. *And the cost for the custom Ferrari? It represents 20 percent of his total assets!* Then there's his obsession with salvaging the GTO. While Tommy realizes the diving expedition will be expensive, the recovery operation to raise the GTO would be unconscionable, not to mention its astronomical restoration costs.

In Tommy's mind, Mike received a sacred bequest from his father. He wants him to spend it wisely so it will last through his retirement years. If Mike continues his compulsive spending binge, he'll be broke before he's thirty-five.

Yet as Tommy's anger dissipates, his feelings turn to sadness. Mike is his best friend and they are drifting apart. Tommy has seen it before in his financial planning practice, how money changes people's priorities and they suddenly become selfish and insensitive to others. If Mike's destructive behavior continues, Tommy and Lilly need to do something. Exactly what, however, is the million-dollar question.

# 5

# House of Grimaldi

**Fairchester, New York**

*October 20, 2008, Monday*

Although Tommy finds himself plowing through a myriad of phone calls on Monday morning, he hopes the luncheon appointment he intends to schedule with Rebecca will be the high point of his day. Tommy hasn't dated much. After struggling through his childhood and later assuming a large college debt, he's shied away from serious relationships. He could barely afford the rent for his apartment, let alone a wife and family.

When he calls, he is surprised by her immediate enthusiasm. "Yes, of course I'm free for lunch today."

"That's great! Meet you at Kristi's Shoreline at noon?"

"Sure, can't wait!"

In the meantime, there's work to do in the office. Today, for a change, the stock market is surging forward. Tommy feels some relief. At 10:00 a.m., the Dow is up 300 points. While an encouraging sign, Tommy realizes there are still critical economic problems remaining. He has to be careful when speaking to his clients, not to give them false hope. Volatility is still a daily reality so he needs to be a calming force, managing their expectations and reinforcing their long-term investment strategies.

When Tommy and Rebecca arrive at the restaurant, the hostess leads them to a small table set for two on the outside patio deck overlooking the Lake Ontario shoreline. Rebecca isn't overly tall, but her hourglass figure turns heads as she walks through the restaurant. Her dark blue pantsuit is exquisite, a calm self-assurance lights her turquoise eyes, and her wavy blonde hair is as smooth and silky as a velvet chemise. Tommy cannot picture her under a street rod with a wrench in her hand.

*Wow!* Tommy thinks to himself. *She looks stunning! Better than I even remember.*

"I like quiet restaurants," he says, as they sit down. "This may be the perfect opportunity for us to really get to know each other," Tommy smiles.

Rebecca blushes as she smiles and says, "That sounds inviting, especially when two people want to learn more about one another."

Most women might be hesitant to be so direct on a first date. Not Rebecca. She radiates excitement. Even when she isn't smiling, she looks happy, confident, and intelligent. An inner beauty glows in her eyes and softens her features. Tommy can't wait to learn more about her. He immediately feels connected in a way he cannot explain.

"It feels great to be out of my office. Sometimes the incessant phone calls have my head spinning," Tommy says.

"I know," Rebecca replies. "The speed shop is full of people complaining about their cars not being ready. I'll be glad to get out of there this fall. Working sixty hours each week takes a toll on my social life, and it's become impossible for me to have a serious relationship."

"I've never really even thought about being in a serious relationship," Tommy replies.

"I haven't either," Rebecca says, smiling warmly. "Between school and work, who has the time?"

"I have a really, really important question for you, Rebecca."

"Are you going to propose?" she quips.

Tommy laughs. "Not just yet. But I haven't ruled out the possibility."

"Good. So what's the big question?"

"Why did you annihilate my friend, Mike, like that? He still hasn't recovered, I don't think he ever will."

Rebecca bursts out laughing. "He's just a big old jock with an even bigger ego. I grew up with guys like that."

"You called that one right," Tommy laughs. "Mike's still shell-shocked. He simply cannot believe a street rod pummeled his Ferrari F40."

"Yeah, but I could tell he was getting his shifting mixed up. Sometimes those gated shifters are stubborn. With someone who knows how to shift them, there's no way my street rod would take an F40."

"That's still quite an awesome machine you have!"

"That was my first opportunity to crank the monster up since I installed the new nitrous system," says Rebecca. "It felt really, really good! Right now, I'm working on a Cadillac V16 engine, the Cadillac 452. That's one of the biggest engines ever made."

"Amazing! A 1932 Ford Coupe with nitrous. Mike thinks that's pretty astounding."

"Well, obviously, street rods aren't *his* thing. I've been around them all my life. Remember John Milner's yellow deuce coupe in *American Graffiti*? I fell in love with that car. I built my street rod on a '32 chassis I've owned since I was a kid. Ray's Speed Shop hired me for the summer to help build street rods while I work on my doctorate degree. I have two years left to get my degree. In the meantime,

I'll be teaching European history here at St. Ignatius College this coming January. I can't wait. I like the speed shop, but my first love has always been European history."

"I love history, too," says Tommy. "In college I majored in English, but I have a minor in history. How did you get into street rods?"

"My dad aroused my interested in them as a kid. He was an excellent auto technician who adapted very well to what I call the automotive electronics revolution. He went back to the classroom to learn about microprocessors and advanced diagnostics. When we moved to the Greenwich, Connecticut, area he was hired at Millers."

"Millers? The beer company?"

"Tommy!" Rebecca laughs. "Miller Motorcars. You've heard of them, right?"

"Sure. I think they sell Plymouths, don't they?"

Rebecca smiles. "They sell Ferraris and Maseratis. They used to be called Chinetti Motors and were originally located in Manhattan. They were the first Ferrari dealership in America. Luigi Chinetti used to be a champion race car driver in Italy and was a very good friend of Enzo Ferrari's. He imported the first Ferrari and brokered Ferraris to wealthy people in Westchester, Long Island, and Greenwich. My dad knows all the guys managing the dealership now. He travelled with NART for several years—you know, the old North American Racing Team that Luigi Chinetti started back in the sixties. My dad got to know some of the best drivers in America. Phil Hill and my dad were good buddies. Now my dad's in a nursing home in Greenwich. Alzheimer's disease ended his career a long time ago. I can't wait to show him pictures of my street rod! That'll definitely put a wide smile on his face. What about *your* family, Tommy?"

"Oh, I was raised by my aunt and uncle here in Fairchester," he says. "It was a pretty austere life. My uncle worked in a shoe store and my aunt was a seamstress. They were private people who avoided *any* kind of social involvement—and I do mean *any*! We lived on Thompson Street, the poorest section of Fairchester. My aunt and uncle both died in 1998, about six months apart. I was only eighteen years old. That's when I went to live with Lilly Brandt, a teacher who became like a mother to Mike and me. Between working full-time in a gas station and some hefty college loans, I somehow managed to get myself through St. Michael's College in Toronto. "

"And what about your parents?"

Tommy shook his head then looked down somberly at the table. "I never knew them. My mother died from AIDS in the early eighties and my father . . . I haven't got a clue. My aunt and uncle forbid me to ask about them. When I persisted, I was punished. Then I just stopped. But my desire to find out about my parents has always been in my heart."

Tommy moves his head backward, like he is attempting to relieve a stiff neck. "It's been distressing and still gnaws at me terribly. Someday, I'll find out more. I have too."

"I'm so sorry," Rebecca says, as she leans toward him.

"I can't believe I'm sharing this with you," says Tommy. "Here we are on a first date and all I can do is monopolize the conversation with my personal issues. I apologize."

"Please, don't be upset. I'm interested in hearing all about your life."

"It's just that there is nothing really exciting about it. I have no extended family. According to my uncle, my grandparents were killed in the war." He pauses and shrugs his shoulders. "That's about it," he says, not really wanting the conversation to end.

"I'm sure there is a much more to your life than that."

"Funny," he continues, "a sales woman we met last Saturday at the Ferrari dealership mentioned a member of the Monaco royal family by the name of Antonio Grimaldi who, as a young man, lived in the

Genoa area back in the fifties. We probably aren't connected, but it got me thinking."

"You know with all the new genealogy software available today on the Internet, you should at least be able to find something about your mom and dad."

"I did check out one of the popular genealogy sites once, but I didn't have the money to spare at the time. And those European databases . . . I had zero faith in them. I did a Google search and found Grimaldis all over the world. So I just dismissed the whole idea."

"You know, I took an advanced genealogy course and I'm a member of the Phi Alpha Theta History Honor Society. I have special access to the Center for Public Dissemination and Discourse at St. Ignatius College—we could check their databases. They're quite extensive."

"Well, sure," he says, "maybe that would be a good place to start."

"I'll make an appointment and let you know, okay?"

"Rebecca, thank you. You're busy and I appreciate it," Tommy says.

"Not a problem. So, Tommy, tell me, what else did the Ferrari salesperson say?"

"She gave me a magazine article from the *Prancing Horse*, the Ferrari Club monthly magazine. I'm reluctant to read it."

"Why?" she asks.

"I don't know," Tommy shrugs.

"So why did she give it to you?"

"Apparently, Antonio Grimaldi drove the Ferrari 250 GTO Prototype to Genoa so it could be loaded onto the *Andrea Doria*. The destination was America. That was back in July of 1956. We both know the outcome of that trip."

"Really?" Rebecca asks. "The first GTO? And it went down with the *Andrea Doria*? I never knew that."

"Apparently not too many other people did either. Did you ever see one?"

"At Millers once," Rebecca recalls. "I remember my father being totally blown away. It's a spectacular car. Still, I have a hard time understanding why they're bringing millions at auction. Then again, why any car is worth that much money is beyond me."

"I think it's all about buyer perception. Like stocks, sometimes desire trumps the true value. Prices run up and then the bottom falls out . . . just a big bubble."

"I guess when you have all the money in the world, you can create your own value."

"No doubt," Tommy says as he reflects on Mike's recent spending escapades.

"What was the saleswoman's name?" Rebecca asks.

"Jaclyn Le . . . Le Harve . . . I think."

"That's a popular name around Normandy," Rebecca notes. "I wonder what *her* ancestry looks like."

"If it's anything close to what she looks like, it's full of beauty queens!" says Tommy.

"A real looker, huh?"

"Mike's got a thing for her," he explains, "just another distraction to cloud his good judgment."

"Have you ever heard of the House of Grimaldi?"

"Sounds like a steakhouse."

"No, no, no," Rebecca laughs. "It's an ancient royal family in Genoa that goes way back to the twelfth century. They were warriors, ship owners, and bankers. They developed quite a commercial empire financing popes, kings, emperors, and even explorers like Christopher Columbus."

"Like the wealthy Medici family from Florence?"

Rebecca smiles politely. "The House of Medici."

"I learned a little bit about the Medici family," Tommy remarks. "They initiated the concept of collateralizing loans and pretty much invented our modern banking practices."

"Yes, that's exactly right," she nods. "These two powerful families of Europe have been major concentrations in my postgraduate study. Speaking of the Medici family, did you know that during the Renaissance they cultivated the art of poisoning their adversaries? They were experts at it."

"I only know them as great bankers," Tommy replies.

"Well, Cosimo de' Medici, back in the 1500s, kept the recipe for a deadly poison in his private papers. Mixing rhubarb leaves with water and soda created a deadly poison called oxalic acid. He noted in his papers that it was 'an excellent toxin that could simply be put in a drinking flask.'"

"Were the Grimaldis that devious?" asks Tommy.

"Compared to Cosimo and his offspring, the Grimaldis were saints!" Rebecca responds.

"They were bankers too, right?"

"The Grimaldi Bank of Genoa had almost as much wealth and influence as the Medici Bank of Florence. They've ruled Monaco since 1297. Prince Albert and Prince Rainier of Monaco are descendants of the House of Grimaldi."

"Funny. I tell my clients if they want tax breaks, move to Monaco. There is no income, capital gains, or inheritance taxes there. It's not that hard to move there either, all you need to do is deposit about a million bucks in one of their banks."

"Let's go!" Rebecca says. "I'm more than ready."

"Okay, you deposit the million," Tommy replies, "and I'll buy the plane tickets!"

Rebecca nods in agreement. "Actually, in my opinion, with all of its beautiful mountains, ski resorts, not to mention the French Riviera, there isn't a more exciting place to visit in all of Europe. I'd really love to go there sometime."

"How about the Monaco Grand Prix? It's in May."

"Okay," Rebecca says with a straight face. "All that glamour and prestige—have you ever seen the race?"

"I watch it every year on TV," Tommy replies, "even though I'm not much of a car buff. The streets of Monte Carlo seem to make the perfect racetrack, despite that Grand Hotel Hairpin. It really turns me off to see powerful cars go that slow in a Formula One race."

After lunch, they leave the outside patio deck to walk along the Lake Ontario shoreline. Their warm conversation blends nicely with the blue sky, soft breeze, and gentle waves on the shore.

Tommy is already looking forward to their next date. Rebecca's fun, fascinating, and even gets a kick out of his trite one-liners. Buoyed by her encouragement, Tommy feels his self-confidence growing.

"Are you going with anyone to the big game Saturday?" he asks so delicately she can hardly hear him.

"The game Saturday? What about it?" Rebecca inquires as she looks out at the water.

"Yeah, the game Saturday," Tommy says. *Time to get shot down.* He braces himself.

"I hope I'm going with *you*!" she says.

"Oh?" he pauses to relish her answer. "That would be great!"

In the early afternoon, when Tommy finally returns to his office, he feels as though his day couldn't possibly get any better.

"Best lunch I ever had!" he remarks to Margie.

"You should get out of the office more during lunchtime," Margie suggests.

"Yes, I'm definitely planning on it."

# 6

# GTO Road Trip

### Italy

### *July 17, 1956, Tuesday*

Despite almost zero visibility and powerful winds, Giancarlo refuses to relinquish control of the GTO to Antonio. His lanky arms are stiff and straight to the wheel, forcing his back to strain against the thin, aluminum bucket seat, making his driving responses sudden and unsure. His left leg presses hard against the narrow, flat-bottomed floor, dislodging the loose floor mat and impeding the interaction between the clutch and gearstick. The transmission responds with a loud admonishing grind that offends Antonio's sense of automotive propriety. *This is not how you treat the greatest Ferrari ever built!*

"Giancarlo, stop! Pull over! You're going to ruin the gearbox." Antonio is livid.

"I'm driving now!" Giancarlo insists. His chin is upright and his lips are tight as he squints uncompromisingly.

It's torturous for Antonio to watch. *He* is the engine and driving guru and Giancarlo—well, *he* is just a design engineer who knows nothing about how to treat the mighty Colombo V12 Ferrari engine, let alone shift the metal gate of the 5-speed dogleg gearbox on the tight slippery curves of the Assietta.

Mud splatters the windshield and creeps through the scanty side curtains, splashing across their faces and on to the circular instrument cluster. The tires spin, losing their grip on the wet gravel.

Antonio recoils. *This is a Grand Prix racer, with its daunting front engine and rear wheel drive, not some converted mud bogger!*

When Giancarlo overcorrects, the GTO fishtails sliding sideways. He recovers soon enough and somehow manages to maintain control. As he heaves on the brakes, the GTO skids to a stop just short of Buco di Satana, Satan's Hole, the steepest cliff on the Assietta.

"Thank God!" Antonio cries in a loud voice that seems to echo across the large canyon. They sit in silence and frustration. Then Antonio shouts, "*Uscire*! Get out!"

Giancarlo's arms tremble, his hands are welded to the steering wheel, eyes dilating like large black agates. He is in an aerial dogfight and has just been outmaneuvered by an American P-51 Mustang. The pilot has honed in on his target and is coming in for the kill. Giancarlo is hovering on the edge of hysteria.

"Giancarlo! Giancarlo! Take it easy!" Antonio has never seen such bizarre behavior from Giancarlo.

Suddenly, Giancarlo bolts. Violently throwing open the door, he sprints as fast as he can in the direction of the transporter. Then he keeps running until he disappears from Antonio's view. Antonio's cries are ignored. He is baffled. Giancarlo's apparent meltdown disturbs him deeply.

But Antonio has little difficulty assessing his priorities. Il Commendatore is counting on him. The GTO's safe delivery to the *Andrea Doria* for its voyage to America is uppermost in Antonio's mind. If, for any reason, Antonio is unable to fulfill that expectation, he knows his prominent role in the Ferrari organization as a respected Formula One technician will be over. After all his hard work and sacrifice, he couldn't risk that outcome. Losing his job means losing his ability to save money to pay the private investigator he hired to locate his wife and son, and he will do anything to bring his family together again.

Antonio is already running late, and the weather isn't getting any better. Giancarlo can wait in the transporter until he returns. He'll be okay. Maybe all he needs is a good night's sleep. Antonio climbs behind the wheel of the GTO and drives off.

Once he passes Moncalieri, it is clear sailing. He drives to Alessandria, then directly south to Genoa until he sees the 249-foot Lanterna, the main lighthouse and landmark in the Port of Genoa. Having spent summers in the Genoa area while in college, Antonio has no difficultly locating the terminal where the *Andrea Doria* is docked in preparation for its voyage to America.

An icon of Italian national pride, the *Andrea Doria* is an incredibly beautiful ship. At seven hundred feet long with a ninety-foot beam, it occupies the most prominent position in the port, yet is small enough to be appreciated for its yacht-like appearance. It is fast, luxurious, and its stance in the water is as graceful as a swan. The ship conforms to all the latest safety standards, and is considered one of the most dependable ships ever built. The colorful signal pennants stretching from stem to stern above the ship whip in the wind, beckoning the *Andrea Doria* to the sea.

As per his instructions from Il Commendatore, Antonio drives behind the port. He navigates downhill on the gritty, narrow, twisting streets and arrives at a small Quonset hut recently put in place to accommodate the GTO Prototype and the Chrysler Norseman. The latter is an experimental fastback coupe Chrysler contracted to Ghia and built in the same building under the same veil of secrecy as the GTO.

Chrysler is hoping to capitalize on the Norseman's advanced and innovative design features. It has a glass window that can be retracted up into the roof, hideaway headlamps, a broad oval grille, a pair of modest fins, and broadly flared wheel openings. Painted in a two-tone metallic green with red accents in the wheel openings, it's long, low, clean, and beautiful. Four power-assisted bucket seats are upholstered in green and gray metallic leather. The engine is a 235-horsepower 331 Hemi, but upon its arrival in Detroit, Chrysler will remove it and install the giant 340-horsepower letter car engine.

The Norseman and GTO are strange bedfellows sitting side by side, the only two cars in the building. They would perhaps be the two most desirable cars in the world, if the world only knew of their existence. The only inhabitants in the building, besides the armed security guards at the entrance, are two men in white uniforms—men who are surely trusted confidants of Enzo Ferrari. With their clipboards, they walk around the cars taking notes. Antonio wonders what they can possibly be writing down. Both cars are perfect.

After they tuck the clipboards inside a metal briefcase, they drive the cars to the Italian Line port quayside next to the *Andrea Doria*. An ominous sensation fills Antonio. In another four hours people and luggage will swarm the area. Right now, other than the two workers, the place is eerily uninhabited, as if time is standing still and the *Andrea Doria* will forever occupy a permanent place in the port.

Antonio loads his Polaroid Land Camera. He wants evidence for Il Commendatore. He has one of the workers take the first picture—one of him standing beside the car with a big smile on his face, as if he is modeling for *Motorama*. Antonio clicks more pictures when the horseshoe frame of a yellow and red gantry crane hovers over the cars like the giant squid straddled Captain Nemo's *Nautilus*. Three-foot wide belts are carefully placed under the cars and attached to the crane boom lines. Then each car is meticulously lifted and placed beside a freight elevator in front of the deck near the foremast. Each car is carefully lowered into watertight metal containers in the lower cargo hold of the ship and securely anchored by ratchet straps to ensure stability during the long trip to America. Antonio keeps clicking the shutter on his Polaroid as the camera spits out picture after picture.

Later, he waits patiently for all the passengers to board. At 11:00 a.m., *"La nave sta partendo,* the ship is departing," blares from the ship's loudspeakers. Passengers migrate from Spumante-soaked bon voyage parties to the Belvedere Deck to wave goodbye to family and friends standing on the wharf. Steam billows from the red, white, and green funnel as whistle blasts echo against the hills of Genoa.

The great ship disembarks slowly, passing a panorama of pink and red buildings and church domes against the backdrop of the majestic Apennine Mountains. Antonio cannot take enough pictures as the Polaroid continues to flawlessly eject them.

Despite the cold, rain-filled atmosphere of the morning, Antonio feels good, and relieved too. The wishes of Il Commendatore have been fulfilled and he has the pictures to prove it. Now he can afford to think about Giancarlo, his erstwhile friend, and the stranded Fiat transporter on the Assietta. He will need to repair it quickly. Another critical assignment awaits his undivided attention.

Antonio rents a small Alfa Romeo Giulietta from a shop nearby. The 1.3 liter 50-horsepower engine is a far cry from the GTO's amazing power plant. He purchases parts for the crippled transporter at a nearby automotive store and borrows some tools at his friend's automotive service garage just outside of town. Then he heads for the Assietta, Giancarlo, and the stranded transporter.

The sun filters through the clouds, signaling the end of the rain. Antonio has all the windows open in the Alfa. He places his elbow out the driver's side window and welcomes the stream of fresh air entering the Alfa from all directions. He feels cleansed by the air. Even if he continues to be alienated by the Grimaldis, as long as he can get his son and wife back, that will be good enough for him. As his star rises in the Ferrari organization, he hopes and prays no one discovers what he is about to do. *Just this one time, I have to appease Charone. Just this once.*

Giancarlo's unpredictable and irrational behavior has added significantly to Antonio's thoughts. Thankfully, his next assignment will be without Giancarlo. When all his assignments are completed, the expensive King of Denmark cigar given to him by Il Commendatore will taste good. Then he can sit back and celebrate—and write another check to the private investigator.

When the transporter comes into view, Antonio hopes to find Giancarlo leaning against the front fender smoking a cigarette or sitting on the running board patiently awaiting his return. He is sorry Giancarlo doesn't have a key, but he ran away so quickly, Antonio didn't have a chance to give him one. The weather is improving and traffic is increasing on the Assietta. Quite possibly Giancarlo found a ride back to Torino. One less inconvenience right now would be gladly accepted.

Antonio drives past the transporter, makes a quick u-turn, and parks the Fiat directly behind it. He wants to check its overall condition before he repairs the front tie-rod assembly, and slowly walks around the large vehicle looking for any additional damage.

After Antonio completes the repairs, he jumps into the driver's seat and fires up the transporter. *What a catastrophe it would be if it failed to start!* he thinks. He has a long trip in front of him, 420 miles to be exact. He also has a deadline to meet.

The transporter slowly moves forward as he lets up on the clutch. Out of the corner of his eye he sees a shadow and then a hand touches his shoulder. He is so startled he nearly falls off of the seat. He hits the brakes hard. The transporter stops on a dime.

"Antonio! Maybe you should let me the hell out first!"

"Giancarlo! How did you get inside? I thought I had the only key."

"I remembered to bring the extra one. I tried to sleep in the back until you returned. Sorry I ran from you. Ever since the war, you know, I have a big problem with stress."

"Don't worry about it. I'm just glad you're okay."

"The GTO—is it on the *Doria*?" Giancarlo asks.

"Here, Giancarlo. Take a look." Antonio hands Giancarlo the Polaroid pictures. "Il Commendatore is waiting for these pictures. You give them to him, okay?"

Eager to comply and score points with Enzo, Giancarlo says, "Ah, good job, Antonio! You and me—we make the boss a happy man! Maybe we'll both get a raise."

"Listen, Giancarlo. I'll drive the transporter; you take the rental car back to the car rental place in Torino for me. Here, take the car keys."

"Okay, Antonio. You did a nice a job! Ciao," says Giancarlo as he gets out of the transporter.

Antonio is relieved Giancarlo is so agreeable. He carefully drives the transporter away from the cliff back onto the Assietta and heads south. The road is dry and passable, not nearly as difficult nor as dangerous as it was the night before.

Giancarlo sits in the Fiat and wonders why Antonio is travelling in the opposite direction, away from Torino. *Well maybe it is too difficult to turn the transporter around. Antonio—he's a smart man. He knows what he is doing.*

# 7

# Looming Affair

**Fairchester, New York**

*October 21, 2008, Tuesday*

Mike's football team is chomping at the bit to trounce their cross-town archrivals, the Northport Raiders this Saturday. The fifty-year rivalry is the most publicized game in the county, each year attracting thousands of high school football fans to the game. As the last game of the year, it is by far the most important. Mike's team is undefeated. Still, if they lose this game, the season will be considered a failure, and Mike will be a persona non grata in the Fairchester community for several weeks after the game. While his team is in high gear, Mike is stuck in neutral. His mind is on Jaclyn, the Ferrari salesperson from Toronto, not on football.

On the practice field at 3:30 p.m. sharp, Mike has the team doing warm-up drills before they start their formal practice routine. Mike's assistant, Jimmy Boyce, is in the equipment shed on the other side of the field with a couple of players getting the tackling dummies for the next drill. After Mike organizes an intra-squad scrimmage, he walks behind the bleachers and calls Jaclyn on his cell phone.

"I can come up right after the game this Saturday," he says, "and we can go to dinner at Barberian's Steakhouse. I would really like to see you."

"I'm sorry, Mike. I already have plans for Saturday evening." Her voice sounds even more intimate and sensuous on the phone than in person.

"Can you change your plans?" Mike asks. "It's important that I see you."

"You mean you have the nerve to ask me to cancel my plans with the Audubon Society for Saturday? Do you realize it's their annual banquet?"

Mike detects a slightly audible snicker from Jaclyn. "Then it's a done deal! Listen, Jaclyn, we can have a nice dinner this Saturday and discuss a new project I'm taking on. I'm anxious for your feedback."

"Well . . . okay," Jaclyn hesitates. "Sounds good to me, whatever it is."

"Great! Shall I pick you up?"

"How about if we meet at Barberian's at seven thirty?" she replies.

"Perfect!" It really wasn't "perfect." Mike would have preferred to pick her up at her place. Then he could drive her home after dinner and hope that she might invite him in for a "nightcap."

"When I get there we will . . ." Their conversation is interrupted by a loud, painfully piecing scream. Mike knows immediately it is his star senior quarterback and team captain, Bobby Ferre. "I gotta go, Jaclyn. Call you later!"

When Mike reaches Bobby, he is holding his right shoulder with his head back and his eyes squeezed shut in excruciating pain. Bobby looks at Mike and says, "I . . . I can't move my right arm. It hurts so much!"

"Bobby, we have to get this x-rayed. Jimmy call the ER! Tell them we'll be there is twenty minutes."

"I'm sorry, Coach," Bobby says tearfully. "I can still play on Saturday, right?"

They both know the answer but find solace in pretending not to.

"Let's see what the doctor says, Bobby." Mike would rather be injured himself than see one of his players hurt.

A couple of the players carry Bobby to one of the high school vans. Mike gets behind the wheel and heads toward Fairchester General Hospital. "Bobby, you're gonna be okay, buddy. Listen to me. If the doctor says no, then the answer is no and there's nothing you or me or anyone else can do to change that. Understand?"

"Yeah, I guess so. I just hope the pain goes away!"

"Sorry, Bobby. I know how disappointing this can be. If it's physically impossible for you to play you can help me coach. I could use your help! Randall will just have to be the quarterback, and he'll need your support too."

Mike hears Bobby's sniffles and sees his face wet with his tears in the mirror. "Bobby, I would have done anything to have prevented this from happening to you," he says.

"I know, Coach. But why weren't you there?"

Mike strolls into Tommy's office at six o'clock after dropping Bobby off at his home and explaining to his parents that he has a broken right clavicle and will be sidelined for Saturday's final game of the season. The only part he left out is the fact that he wasn't present when the injury occurred.

Mike's usually pristine athletic attire is soiled with sweat. The stretched t-shirt draping over his sweatpants presents a slovenly appearance, and Tommy can tell by looking at him that he feels as bad as he looks. Mike seats himself in one of Tommy's high back chairs, right next to Lilly Brandt, who has been visiting with Tommy for the past hour.

"Hello Lilly," Mike says with obvious despondence. He puts his head back and closes his eyes, attempting to catch up on his thoughts regarding Bobby's injury at practice. He needs to tell Tommy and Lilly what happened, and more importantly, what he has been thinking about the last few days. He wants to tell them before the game on Saturday.

"Hello yourself, Coach! It's good to see you, too," Lilly asserts. After the Sunday breakfast episode at Billy's place, Lilly still harbors a lingering acrimony.

"As I was saying," Lilly continues to direct her comments to Tommy, "just look at that stock market. After all that doom and gloom talk last week, stocks went up 413 points today, one of the biggest all-time point gains! We have one stimulus package, now we're going to have another. No llamas for me! Tommy, I'm giving you all my money to invest into the stock market."

"Well, we can talk about that later, Lilly," Tommy replies. "Just keep it in the bank for now. Having liquid reserves isn't such a bad thing, especially in this market environment—the volatility isn't over yet."

"Oh, life is a big bowl of volatility anyway. But that's just like you, Tommy—always pointing out the downside. You know what I think?" Lilly looks over at Mike.

"Do I really have to answer?" Mike groans. "You're going to tell me anyway."

"Michael, how well you know me!" she exclaims. "Now take you two boys . . . you remind me of the stock market. Mike is the bull. Tommy is the bear. How's that for volatility?"

Mike and Tommy quietly stare at Lilly, not wanting to confront one another with their eyes. Mike repositions himself in the chair, crosses his legs, and finally speaks.

"I know I was wrong on Sunday, and I'm sorry. Are you two still pissed off at me?"

Tommy and Lilly look at one another and say nothing for a few seconds.

"You're forgiven, Bender," Tommy finally says. He isn't smiling. "Just don't ask me to do stupid things with you again."

Lilly shakes her head. "When you were a youngster and things weren't going well, you'd always come to me. It seems like you have been avoiding me lately, Michael."

"I've just been busy coaching, getting the team ready, you know."

"Well, are you ready for Northport this Saturday, young man?" Her comment sounds more like a direct order than a simple question.

"Well . . . it wasn't a very good day today," says Mike. "Lost my quarterback."

"No! Bobby?" Lilly attends Mike's practices on a regular basis and makes highly effective motivational speeches to the team. She is well-acquainted with all the players.

"Broken clavicle."

"Oh, that poor boy! He must be devastated," she says.

"Yeah, so am I. The biggest game of the year and I lose my best player."

"Now then, Coach Bender. We have no room for self-pity on our Fairchester athletic teams. You know that better than anyone else!"

"It's just been a rough day, that's all. I'll get over it."

"You know, Mike, I just read something that really captured my attention and I want to share it with you," Lilly remarks. "*Winning means going as far as you can with all that you've got!* So, even if we lose the game on Saturday, *if our kids have gone as far as they can with all that they've got, they are winners!* Put those boots on and pull 'em up by the straps, Coach. The team is counting on you! I don't like to see you like this."

"I was on my cell at the time," Mike admits, "not paying attention. Well, sometimes I need to make calls."

"Shame on you!" Lilly scolds. "When you're coaching, you should be coaching, not flappin' your jaws on the phone!"

"It was stupid. You don't have to tell me that," Mike sighs. "I messed up."

Tommy wonders why Mike concedes so easily, but feels encouraged by this behavior. Based on recent history, it isn't like him to absorb blame. *Maybe Mike has been doing some self-assessing*, he thinks to himself.

"Tell me something, Mike," Lilly says. "Are you upset because Bobby got hurt, or are you upset because you're worried about losing the game Saturday without him?"

Lilly always has a magical effect on Mike's reality. She reads him so well. Deep down, she knows he really cares, but at times he can come off as totally driven by the number of checks in the win column.

"Mike, forget it," she says. "You can chalk that up as a rhetorical question."

"Maybe that's one he really should answer, Lilly," Tommy says with disdain in his voice.

"Unfortunately, I think we already know the answer," Lilly replies, "and I don't like it one bit!"

"Since you both seem to be such experts on me, I won't even bother trying to answer," Mike mutters gruffly. He stands up ready to leave.

"Michael! I have to go too," Lilly says hastily. "Give me a ride home, will you?"

"I thought you had your car?" Tommy asks her. Then he realizes what Lilly really has in mind.

"It looks like rain. I hate to drive in the rain."

"Hey Grimaldi, we need to talk sometime," says Mike as he displays a woeful smile, like his best friend has just abandoned him.

"About what? I really have to get ready now."

"Tomorrow?" Mike asks.

"Sure . . . tomorrow," Tommy answers. "Tomorrow will work fine."

The downpour starts just as Mike and Lilly leave the office. As he drives slowly down East Avenue, Mike feels the Bentley's tires slip on the wet pavement, so he activates the car's stability control. At first, there is no conversation, only the back and forth sound of windshield wipers, and the loud silence between two people trying to figure out what to say to one another.

Mike is uncomfortable knowing that Lilly, the person he admires most in the world, is disappointed in him. Lilly wants to deliver a tough message, and hopes Mike's defensiveness doesn't spoil it.

"Michael, you know I love you like a son, don't you?" she asks.

Mike nods. "Yes, I do. And I love you too, Lilly." He braces himself. With Lilly, difficult conversations always begin with mutual love confirmations.

"I'm very worried about you, Michael."

"For what reason?" he asks.

"Oh, c'mon, you know exactly what I'm talking about!"

"I'm not sure where you're going with this, but you don't have to worry about me," Mike insists.

"You've been downright rude," says Lilly. "And my God, it's sinful the way you're draining your father's estate. I want you to stop! Do you hear me?"

"But it's my estate now!"

"Damn it, Mike, don't be defensive. Listen to me!" Lilly cries out.

"I don't see what's so wrong with buying an expensive car," says Mike stubbornly. "It's my money!"

"What the hell are you trying to prove?"

"Nothing, absolutely nothing. You're not serious, are you?" Mike retorts.

"You've been arrogant and self-indulgent," Lilly says. "That's not you! Just tell me what's going on, that's all."

There's a long silence. Mike is used to receiving straight talk from Lilly but this time she is striking a nerve. He knows she won't acquiesce until he at least tries to answer her question.

He clears his throat then exhales. "Honestly, Lilly, I don't know what to say," he says softly, almost inaudibly.

"Ever since your dad passed away, you've been acting differently," she remarks.

"He was very successful. I always tried to be like him but never could."

"You're your own person, Mike! Don't you know that by now? Your dad was a very successful business executive. You are a successful teacher and coach. He would never expect you to embrace his style of living."

"No, Lilly. That's not true. The message he pounded into me was: *Those who can do, those who can't teach.* He thought teaching was for those who didn't have the guts to make it in the business world. 'Big' was the most prominent word in his vocabulary. Real men ran *big* successful businesses, bought *big* expensive cars, and owned *big* houses."

"I knew your mother very well. She was different."

"She was the opposite. I remember when she had a big fight with my father and was crying. I could tell the fight had something to do with me. Later, we had a long conversation. She told me to find my own way and not to think I had to be like him. 'Do what's in your heart,' she told me. She was very emotional. I was moved by her words."

"Well then, live by her values!" says Lilly.

"We had a great relationship. I miss her a lot."

"You're still in a great deal of pain. Losing both parents is a horrible loss. Give yourself time, be patient. A spending spree won't bring either one of them back."

"I feel a huge burden." Mike looks at Lilly afraid of her reaction. "Like I need to get rid of the money as fast as I can."

"There are charities all over Fairchester, Mike. I can help you with that."

"I can't give the money away! That would be a major insult to my father."

Lilly shakes her head in disapproval. She realizes just how ingrained his father's influence has been, even if Mike doesn't see it.

"I need a break," Mike says. "I'm getting tired of having all this pressure to win on my shoulders."

"I'm sorry to hear you say that. You've done a wonderful job with the kids."

"I don't know what to say to them anymore," he says. "I've lost my ability to inspire them."

"What's really going on in that head of yours, anyway?" Lilly asks.

Mike pulls over to the curb, turns off the ignition, and places his forehead on the steering wheel. He looks over at Lilly with pain and anger in his eyes.

"It's that damn woman!" he murmurs. "The one who went to Lake Placid with my dad. I have to find out who she was!"

"You're asking for *more* pain," Lilly remarks. "You have to move on and forget that stuff."

"She killed him! They were skiing in Lake Placid, but he left for home without her. Why? The authorities insisted she remain anonymous. Maybe she was married. Who knows? My father didn't care much about things like that, even when my mother was alive."

"Mike, don't go down that road, you never know where it will lead."

"I need to know who she was. I'll bet anything she was after his money."

"You don't know that for sure," Lilly says. "You're just speculating."

"That's all any of them wanted! It was always his money."

Lilly doesn't respond. She doesn't want to discuss Rick Bender's love life with his son.

"That bitch killed him. Whoever she is, I'm sure she killed him!"

# 8

# Jolting Discovery

**Fairchester, New York**

*October 25, 2008, Saturday*

Saturday isn't a good day for Mike. Tommy knew it wouldn't be, as did most of Fairchester's residents. The Eagles don't just lose, they suffer the proverbial drubbing (50-0) everyone feared with their star quarterback, Bobby Ferre, sidelined.

After the game, Tommy visits Mike in the locker room. He is inconsolable. Not only does the loss blemish the team's undefeated record, they lose the county championship for the first time in four years, a terrific blow to the school and the community as a whole.

"We have a live practice. Bobby runs a play I would never have allowed," Mike tells Tommy. "It's a fake pass and hand off where he is supposed to block the defensive end. Unfortunately, one of the linebackers blitzes and flattens Bobby."

"So, why does he run it?" Tommy asks curiously, careful not to trigger Mike's petulant temperament.

"I'm not even there. I'm behind the bleachers talking to Jaclyn, inviting her out to dinner for tonight. The other coaches were in the equipment shed. No one was watching. It's my fault Bobby was injured, and my fault we lost the most important game of the year."

Tommy realizes that no matter what he says or how much empathy he exudes, Mike is determined to blame himself. On those rare occasions when Mike's team loses, his postgame critique is usually spent analyzing the execution of the team and criticizing the players or other coaches rather than finding fault with his coaching performance. Self-incrimination has never been part of Mike's DNA. It especially bothers Tommy when he bolts out of the locker room unwilling to speak with his team or the press. Ignoring the press is one thing, but leaving the kids stranded in a state of misery without words of consolation from their coach, in Tommy's mind, is unforgiveable.

Tommy and Rebecca go to Billy's place for an early dinner after the game. While they feel heartsick over the Eagles' loss, they are more concerned with Mike's state of mind.

"Just wait a few days, then call him," Rebecca suggests. "After he has time to mentally reconcile a few things, he'll be okay."

Billy pours some red wine and brings a fresh loaf of Italian bread to their table.

"Instead of our victory party, the place is like a morgue," he complains. "Last year at this time, there must have been two hundred people celebrating in the place. A losing football team ain't good for business!"

Tommy is not surprised at Billy's cynical, almost callous reaction. His business is dependent on the success of the Fairchester athletic teams.

"It's far from a losing football team," he replied. "They were 9-1 for the season, remember? Now's the time Mike needs our support."

"Support? Did you hear about what he did to that poor Ferre kid?" Billy counters.

"You're not saying Mike did that intentionally, are you?" asks Tommy.

"It's dereliction of duty, plain and simple! He was away from his post talking to some chick on the cell phone instead of coaching the team!"

Tommy doesn't respond. After Billy puts down the place settings, he walks away.

"Mike just lost a friend," Rebecca muses. "That's too bad."

"Over a football game, can you believe it?"

"Small town stuff," Rebecca replies. "Like my father used to say, 'Those who applaud you on Palm Sunday will crucify you on Good Friday.' That's life."

When Tommy phones Mike Saturday evening, there is no answer. He senses Mike is trying to avoid him. As the evening progresses, Tommy becomes more and more concerned. *Why hasn't Mike returned my calls?* At 11:00 p.m., Tommy decides to drive to his home to personally check up on him.

Mike has the most beautiful and expensive home in Fairchester. Mike's dad designed his contemporary palatial mansion mainly for leisure and recreation. Despite its greenhouse, infinity pool, home theater, library, bowling alley, and state-of-the-art gym, other than sleeping there, the only time Mike spends inside the house is when he is throwing a party or hosting one of his many female friends.

Tommy has been a guest at Mike's wild postgame parties on numerous occasions. Most of the participants weren't teachers or even members of the Fairchester community. Business executives and professionals from neighboring towns and nearby cities flowed into his mansion like a crowd pouring into the Super Bowl. Mike loves to hobnob with the well-to-do and the well-connected. Some were well-known television personalities and political leaders. Tommy would become annoyed when they left inebriated and drove home. He cautioned Mike, explaining his potential liability, only to be brushed off with his typical response, "You worry too much, Grimaldi."

The ten-foot-high, black, wrought iron gates in front of the mansion open with slow obedience after Tommy inputs the numeric security code. Motion lights immediately illuminate the long meandering driveway.

A cavernous garage down the road from the mansion contains Mike's private classic car collection. Through a frosted privacy window, Tommy notices the blur of fluorescent lights still turned on. *Bender's up late working on one of his cars.* Tommy opens the front door, disarms the alarm, and walks in.

"Bender, where the hell are you?" he calls. There's no answer. *He must be in the back.* As Tommy walks on the shiny blue epoxy floor between two long rows of pristine classic cars, he notices how perfect they all are. He can't help but think, *This place is a museum, not a man cave!*

Mostly two-seat roadsters are parked perpendicularly along the extended garage sidewalls: Jaguars, Aston Martins, Ferraris, Maseratis, Mercedes, and others. Mike's brand new 1200-horsepower Bugatti Veyron Grand Sport is near the far wall. It's the centerpiece of the collection. Gold stanchions and a red velvet rope surround the car like it's the Pink Star Diamond on display at the 2003 Monaco Grand Prix. Mike always brags that the Guinness Book of Records recognizes it as the fastest street legal production car in the world. Bugatti only made five units. The black carbon fiber body with orange body detailing looks oddly magnificent.

Mike purchased the car six months ago at a Gooding & Company auction. Including the buy premium, he paid $3.19 million. That purchase is another bone of contention between Tommy and Mike.

*I wonder where Mike will place the F12 Ferrari SP1 portfolio car. At a cost of $10 million, it will easily overshadow the Veyron. It will probably just sit here for years, just like the Veyron has. Mike only drives a few cars in his collection.*

Tommy continues his slow walk past a fully restored 1957 BMW 507. It looks less exotic than other cars in the collection, despite its long front hood, wrapped windshield, Rudge-Whitworth alloy wheels, black exterior, and red Connolly leather. Nevertheless, it reminds Tommy of the all-aluminum 2000 BMW Z8 of the same color, built by BMW to commemorate the 507. It is his all-time favorite car. Mike's dad purchased the 507 at an RM Sotheby's Auction in Monterey for $900,000. A 507 article in *Sports Car Market Magazine*, the car collectors' bible, is on the front seat of the 507.

In the British roadster section of the garage, Tommy comes face to face with the 1962 Jaguar E-Type Coupe that was on display at the New York Museum of Modern Art, one of only three car designs to be so honored. Its opalescent silver blue with dark blue interior makes it the sexiest car in Mike's collection. Many argue it is the most beautiful car in the world with its lightweight body and sloped fastback appearance. Tommy calls the car an "XKE" but Mike always sets him straight. All factory literature refers to it as an "E-Type" not an "XKE." More specifically, it is an E-Type fixed head coupe. According to Jaguar purists, Jaguar never made a car called an "XKE." Mike claims that designation is a product of American advertising.

Tommy eventually comes to an oak rolltop desk positioned against the wall with a stack of papers in one of the two wooden trays on the desk. He walks by slowly with his eyes on the mound of papers. *No. It's none of my business*, he says to himself. But he continues to look and begins to sift through some of the paperwork for any clue that might lead to Mike's whereabouts. It appears to Tommy that Mike has never been through any of the paperwork. He notices a bunch of unpaid bills and correspondence addressed to Rick Bender.

A light blue sealed envelope from Placid Days Photography is in the middle of the pile with "CONFIDENTIAL" stamped in big red letters under the address. Tommy considers taking it to Mike. *No. He'll know I've been nosing around in his personal stuff. I'll just open it and see if it's anything urgent that needs to be dealt with right away.* Tommy carefully removes the double tape binder, reaches into the envelope, and pulls out an eight by ten color photograph. A man and woman are holding hands against the backdrop of Whiteface Mountain Lodge and several snow-covered peaks. Tommy looks closer. He recognizes Rick. Who is the woman? Again, he looks closer. His head snaps up as if he has just seen a picture of Satan himself. *Oh my God! It's Jaclyn . . . that Ferrari saleswoman from Toronto!*

Tommy lingers in the garage, sitting on the chair near the rolltop desk, trying to get over the initial shock of seeing Rick and Jaclyn together. Reconciling in his mind that Jaclyn had an intimate relationship with Mike's father, and is now dating Mike, is totally confounding as well as distressing. *So, she's the mystery woman that stayed behind!* He realizes Mike could be in danger and needs to know this right away.

Tommy turns off the lights, keys in the alarm system code, secures the locks, and closes the front door to the garage. Then he drives to the rear entrance of the mansion. When the rear motion detector lights come on, he notices a bright red Mini Cooper convertible parked in front of the rear garage. His first reaction is a bit impulsive. *Don't tell me you bought a Mini, Bender!* Upon a closer look, he notices the license plate is from Canada. *Jesus, what the hell is this guy up to?* he wonders.

Tommy rings the doorbell, then knocks for several minutes. He looks through a bay window facing the backyard. Seeing the lights are out, Tommy wonders if Mike ever returned from Toronto. *But where did the Mini come from?* He quickly jots down the license plate number and walks back to his car pondering the answer. The he stops, turns around, and looks at the Mini again. *I don't believe it! Damn Bender!*

## October 26, 2008, Sunday

Tommy is unable to sleep. He's up at four sitting on the edge of his bed attempting to discover some kind of flaw in his thinking. *Of course, it's his life. If he wants to screw it up, it's his business. No! I can't allow him to self-destruct—no matter what.* He unplugs his cell phone, which is charging on the nightstand near his bed, and calls Mike again.

Mike answers. "Grimaldi, what the hell do you want? It's four o'clock in the morning. Go to sleep!" comes his muffled, worn-out voice on the other end. Then Tommy hears a click.

"Bender? Bender! How dare you hang up on me!"

His next call is to Lilly. She is already up and about.

"Do me a favor, Lil," says Tommy. "Call your friend Mavis at the DMV and see if she has any information on plate number 250-DMD."

"Can I wait until she wakes up?"

"Oh, I'm sorry. I forgot the time."

"For a minute there, I thought I heard reveille!" Lilly says facetiously.

"C'mon, Lilly, cut it out. This is serious."

"Well, what happened? Did Mike buy an island in the Caribbean, or some other stupid thing like that?"

"I'll tell you later. For now, trust me, okay?"

"Okay, Tommy. I'll call you back when the rest of the world wakes up."

A few hours later, Lilly calls. "It's a plate registered to Ferrari Maranello of Ontario, a dealer in Toronto," she says.

# 9

# All In

### Fairchester, New York

*October 26–29, 2008, Sunday to Wednesday*

Tommy is plagued by questions he can't answer: *What should I do about the photo of Rick and Jaclyn? Why didn't Jaclyn return from Lake Placid with Rick? Why didn't she admit to a relationship with Mike's father when we were in Toronto? And, finally, and most importantly, what the hell is Mike doing with her?* Of course, Tommy really knows the answer to that question. Put another way: *What the hell is Jaclyn doing with Mike? That's the real question.*

When he tells Lilly about his discovery, she shakes her head and tells him about her conversation with Mike in the car the other day.

"He is a confused little boy," she says. "His mother's death is taking its toll and he is determined to find out the name of the woman who was with his father on the Lake Placid trip. He's not himself, Tommy. I don't trust that Jaclyn person for a second, especially in Mike's current state of mind."

"So what are we going to do?"

"Let's go to church and pray to St. Ignatius."

"Then what?"

"Then nothing! It's in the Lord's hands."

☆   ☆   ☆

Despite leaving numerous phone messages, by Tuesday of the following week, Tommy has heard nothing from Mike. As best friends, Tommy feels that at the very least Mike can return his phone calls and provide assurances that he is safe. Or that he hasn't gone completely off the deep end.

There are other disturbing developments. What transpired between Mike and his high school principal is just another situation for Tommy to worry about.

"He called in early Monday," Dr. Mitchell explains when Tommy phones him. "He asked me to find a substitute for him for the rest of the week. When I asked 'why' he said there was no particular reason, he just wanted to take the time off. He didn't have any personal days remaining, so I asked if he was sick to which replied, 'Absolutely not.' I mentioned that I couldn't give him the whole week off without some kind of explanation. When I asked him if it had anything to do with Bobby Ferre's injury or that his team lost the county championship, Mike become irate. I could tell he was embarrassed, but I never expected him to respond so harshly. I wanted to help him through it, but he was so rude and abusive, he left me no choice but to fire him on the spot. I'm very sorry it had to come down to this, but Mike has been quite rebellious with me the last few months. When I asked him not to drive his Ferrari to school because it was too distracting to the students, he not only refused, but parked it on the lawn near the bus circle where all the students could see it."

Tommy says to Lilly, "Mike must have been right on the edge for him to respond that way to his principal. I'm convinced it has something to do with Jaclyn."

"Actually," Lilly observes, "I think Mike lost his enthusiasm for the academic world after his father died. When Bobby was injured and the team lost the championship, it only exacerbated an instability that has been brewing in him for months."

"But Lilly, why won't he return my calls? We're supposed to be best friends."

"He won't return mine either," she says.

"Aren't you worried about him?" Tommy asks.

"Mike will get back to you when he's good and ready. He's probably on a weeklong love fest with good old Jaclyn what's-her-name."

"I'm calling the Ferrari dealer right now. It's time to get some answers. This woman is a piranha!"

"Good idea," says Lilly. "Let me know what you find out."

Tommy locates the website on his cell phone and punches in the number.

"May I speak with Jaclyn Le Harve please?" Tommy asks.

"I'm sorry, sir, she no longer works here," the receptionist responds.

"May I have her cell phone number, please? This is important."

"I'm sorry, sir. We don't give out personal phone numbers of former employees."

When Tommy walks into to his office on Wednesday morning, the first thing he does is review his email to look for a message from Mike. He notices a confirmation of a wire transfer from Fidelity Large Cap Stock Fund, one of Mike's conservative mutual fund accounts, to Bridgehampton National Bank of Long Island, New York.

"What the hell is this?" he exclaims so loudly that his secretary Margie charges into his office. "I never authorized this!" he says. "What's the story behind this?"

"Tommy, you don't have to authorize it," Margie explains. "It came directly from the bank to Fidelity's home office with Mike's signature on it. Fidelity has no choice but to honor a liquidation request from a client."

"This is the second time Bender has liquidated money from his account without discussing it with me! Send his damn account to E-Trade, I'm done with him! How much was withdrawn?"

"Fifteen million," Margie says with a tepid smile.

"Fifteen million!" Tommy is in shock. "What the hell is going on with this guy? Is Fidelity sure that's *his* signature?"

"I figured you would ask that question, Tommy. The answer is yes. I've already called Fidelity," Margie replies. "Do you really want me to transfer his account to E-Trade?"

"No!" Tommy jumps up, shaking his head in disbelief. "He's finally done himself in!" he says as he storms out of his office and slams the door shut.

# 10

# The Prince and the Prancing Horse

**Fairchester, New York**

*October 31, 2008, Friday*

Later that week, Rebecca calls Tommy. "How are things going, my friend?"

"Not great," he replies. "Can I see you?"

"Sure. I was calling to tell you I have an appointment at the Center for Public Dissemination and Discourse this evening. Do you want to have dinner first?"

"That would be wonderful."

For their early evening rendezvous, Tommy and Rebecca meet at the best restaurant in downtown Fairchester, Tosca's Italian Bistro. Tommy is handsome in a new navy blazer with a white shirt and lavender tie, and Rebecca is enchanting in a raspberry red dress with a hemline hitting just above her knees and an alluring but discrete neckline.

Tommy remains jittery and upset over Mike. While his stock market performance woes have dissipated, he is gravely worried about his best friend.

"When I stopped at the drugstore, I heard some people say that Mike has been fired," says Rebecca. "It can't have been because he lost the game?"

"He's going off the deep end and I have no idea what to do about it," Tommy replies.

Rebecca listens intently as Tommy recaps the events of the last few days.

"Whatever it is that he's done, he obviously doesn't want to explain anything to you," she says.

"You're right, he knows how pissed off I'd be."

"You're pretty close to him, I know."

"Ever since his mother and father died," Tommy begins, "I've felt like his surrogate parent, like I need to protect him from himself. He's so vulnerable, like a little kid in a candy store with all the money in the world to spend. He's a big, tough guy, but he makes impulsive decisions and I worry about him. After our trip to the Ferrari dealer in Toronto, he arranged a diving expedition to the *Andrea Doria* wreck. He wants to locate the Ferrari GTO that went down with the ship in 1956, salvage it, and then restore it. Can you believe that?"

"Do you think his disappearance has anything to do with that?" Rebecca asks.

"Maybe. But I can't connect the dots. The other thing that's driving me crazy is that Mike had fifteen million transferred from his investment account to a bank in Bridgehampton, Long Island."

"Really? That's weird."

"I've been agonizing my life away over this guy," Tommy grimaces.

"Maybe tonight we can get your mind on other things," Rebecca says softly.

Tommy smiles. "Now there's an enticing thought," he says as he reaches for her hand.

"With all that's been going on, you probably haven't had a chance to read the article about Antonio Grimaldi in the *Prancing Horse* yet, right?" Rebecca asks.

Tommy feels a tinge of hyperacidity and he hasn't even consumed any food yet.

"No, I haven't. In fact, I forgot all about it until you mentioned it. We'd better look at the menu," he says.

Tommy and Rebecca leave Tosca's Italian Bistro around 7:00 p.m. It's a short fifteen-minute jaunt to the Center for Public Dissemination and Discourse at St. Ignatius College. Rebecca is looking forward to researching Tommy's family history, although Tommy is somewhat reluctant. He's afraid of discovering something negative about his ancestry that could have a deleterious effect on his future offspring. But most of all, he doesn't want anything disparaging to come to light that could damage his new relationship with Rebecca. She is quickly becoming a priority in his life.

"Tommy, you're so quiet. Is something bothering you?"

"I don't know. With my luck this guy Antonio will be a serial rapist and I'll be one of his illegitimate offspring," he says.

Rebecca laughs. "Whatever he is, it will be good to finally find out. Don't you agree?"

"Will you still love me?" he jokes.

"Always, Tommy, forever and always!" They both chuckle like a couple of adolescent school kids.

"Why don't we just forget the Grimaldis and go get married right now?" says Tommy.

"We could always have a *morganatic marriage*," Rebecca says as she starts to laugh. She knows Tommy has no idea what she is talking about and waits for his reaction.

"What the hell's an organic marriage," Tommy asks.

"*Morganatic*, Tommy, not organic! It's two people of unequal social rank who get married. It's quite common with the Grimaldi clan of Monaco. It's also known as a left-handed marriage because during the ceremony the groom holds his spouse's hand with his left hand instead of his right one."

"So what's the problem? I'm left-handed anyway," Tommy says with a silly smirk.

"So if Antonio turns out to be a serial rapist," Rebecca grins, "I'll still marry you but you will have a much lower social rank than me—like Prince Philip."

"And Camilla and Diana, right?"

"Very good, Tommy. You have the right stuff for royalty!"

The computer facility at St. Ignatius College contains advanced genealogical software and is considered one of the most inclusive and voluminous genealogical databases in the Northeast. It includes a running public commentary, questions and answers from members, and editorials. The database has become a valuable resource for Rebecca's doctoral studies, especially when she researches European bloodlines and the lineages of the royal families.

Rebecca types in her user ID and password. "Tommy, let's input as much of your personal information as you know," she says.

After inputting the information, Rebecca hits the search button. *Access Denied* blinks repeatedly on the monitor.

"Hmm, strange," Rebecca murmurs. "Let's go in the back door and try a different approach. Let's see. How about if we start in 1850." Rebecca types, *Prince Albert I of Monaco.* Then she types in an even more secure code. A basic diagram of a family tree appears on the screen from The National Genealogy Society.

"Nothing earth-shattering here, Rebecca. Antonio isn't even in the mix," Tommy notes.

"Of course not," Rebecca says. "This is the *basic* lineage of the Grimaldi family during the last 160 years or so. It's what they want the world to see. Look at the footnotes, Tommy. The National Genealogy Society says it's true. So it's true, right?"

Albert I
b.1848
Married Mary Victoria Hamilton

Louis II
b. 1870
Marie Juliette Louvet
Mistress
Louis remained unmarried until age 75

Charlotte
b. 1898
Illegitmate  Daughter of Louis and Marie
Mistress of Pierre de Polignac

Rainier III
b. 1923
Married Grace Kelly
1956

Albert II
b. 1958
Tamara Rotolo
Mistress

Certified 2005: National Genealogy Society

"I usually like to find information the world doesn't see and know by researching the running commentaries, editorials, and op-eds," Rebecca explains. "A word of caution here, Tommy—the information can be entirely speculative or hypothetical. It can come from someone who has an ulterior motive or an ax to grind or worse. Then again, sometimes it can be entirely accurate and reliable."

"So, how do you know the difference?"

Rebecca shrugs. "It's difficult," she says. "Unless the information can be corroborated or verified by objective and reliable sources, you may never know. The problem is that most of this type of information can't be corroborated or verified unless it's certified by a respected institution . . ."

"Like the National Genealogy Society?"

"Yes, like the National Genealogy Society. But more research still needs to be done," Rebecca adds.

"Rumor or hearsay doesn't count, even though it may be truthful?" Tommy asks,

"Hang on. Let's see what we can find on the next few pages."

Rebecca scrolls through several pages. There are plenty of extended family tree diagrams of Grimaldi descendants and relatives.

"Wait a minute!" Tommy demands. "What's that?"

"It's a picture of the House of Grimaldi coat of arms." Rebecca describes a red crown and diamond clustered shield with *Deo juvante,* "with God's help," on a small banner underneath it. It appears on top of one of the pages.

"It looks exactly like the centerpiece on the rosary that my aunt gave me!"

"Where did she get it?" Rebecca asks.

"I never thought to ask. It's onyx and gold. I never paid any attention to the centerpiece," says Tommy.

Then they see something else unusual: an article that has been republished from *The New Yorker* magazine by a journalist named Eaton Stone. It's entitled *The Royal Houses of Europe*. It's an exhaustive study in alphabetical order of more than fifty of Europe's most powerful families. They finally arrive at another Grimaldi family tree diagram. This one is very different. This one is done by Eaton Stone.

They study the tree and after just a few seconds, glance at each other in total amazement. They look at the House of Grimaldi coat of arms, then look at the tree again. They are totally stunned by what they see.

"Rebecca! Does this mean what I think it means?"

"What do you think it means?" She already knows the answer.

"My father is Alessandro Grimaldi, so Antonio is my grandfather! Is that right?" says Tommy.

"And Antonio is born one year earlier than Rainier," notes Rebecca, "so he has dynastic priority and should have been the Prince of Monaco!"

"Then when Antonio dies his son, my father, Alessandro, is supposed to become Prince of Monaco, not Albert. Is that correct, Rebecca?"

"That's right. And guess what, Tommy? That would make *you* next in line!"

"No. This can't be right!" Tommy says.

"When Albert assumed the throne of Monaco three years ago, it should have been Alessandro I, your father," Rebecca explains. "Tommaso I should be next in line. I knew there was something special about you!"

They both look at each other in complete awe. Rebecca is unsure which emotion she will see next from Tommy—sadness, laughter, relief, or all of the above. She will completely understand if Tommy breaks down in tears. Instead, he starts to laugh hysterically.

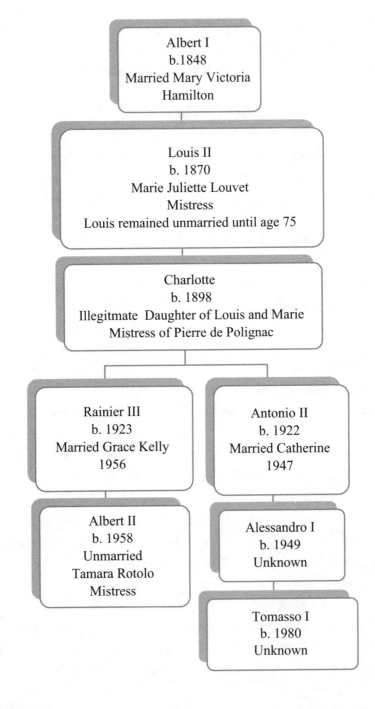

"Tommy, what is *so* funny?" she says.

"Now we can do that organic marriage thing. Would you want to give me your left hand now or later?" he says, nearly choking on his words.

Rebecca laughs politely, but when she focuses on Tommy's cheerless eyes, she sees emptiness. Under the pretext of humor, he tries to project indifference, as if discovering the identity of his father and grandfather is merely routine information. Rebecca is not fooled by his façade. Of course right now, after the initial impact, she understands Tommy's attempt at self-deception. It spares him the pain of reality. But she wants to be close to him when reality finally sets in.

Tommy keeps staring at the tree on the computer monitor. *What the hell did Antonio ever do to get himself disinherited? How did the Grimaldis get away with it? And what about my father, Alessandro? Whatever happened to him? My aunt and uncle must have had the answers. Why were they so afraid to tell me? I have to find out why.*

"Tommy, we've just uncovered information the Grimaldi clan would prefer didn't exist," Rebecca says. "I read Rainier's authorized biography and there was no mention of Charlotte, his mother, or Antonio, his brother. There is something amiss, wouldn't you say?"

"Yes, but the information had to be known when Rainier became Prince," Tommy says. "No one could possibly bury all the records, including birth information, especially with a very public family like the Grimaldis."

"They knew, Tommy. They simply chose to ignore it and did exactly what they wanted to do—like they've been doing for centuries."

"The press must have picked up on it and had a field day," he remarks.

"No, Tommy. Back in the fifties and sixties the press was much kinder and gentler with politicians and heads of state. They tended to protect them from scandal. Look at Kennedy—all his trysts were unknown by the public until twenty years later."

"He had it made, didn't he," Tommy says with an uneasy voice.

"So did the Grimaldis. I remember reading," Rebecca recalls, "that Prince Rainier's father, Pierre de Polignac, as the Duke of Valentinois, wasn't even a Grimaldi. He married Charlotte, who was the illegitimate daughter of Prince Louis II of Monaco and the prince's mistress, Marie Juliette Louvett, a cabaret singer. His mistress's former husband had been a porn photographer. Bear in mind, Tommy, Prince Louis remained a bachelor until he was seventy-five years old when he finally married a French comedy actress named Ghislaine Dommanget."

"So you're telling me that Prince Rainier's mother was illegitimate, and his father wasn't even a Grimaldi?"

"That's what I'm telling you, Tommy," she says.

"Then how did Rainier ever enter into the line of succession?"

"Monaco simply passed a law," Rebecca explains, "recognizing Charlotte as Louis's legitimate daughter and making her a member of the sovereign family. It's still controversial. They just didn't care. In 1944 Charlotte ceded her succession rights to her son, Rainier. That's how he ended up Prince of Monaco. Keep in mind, Tommy, your grandfather Antonio was in the same boat. Charlotte was also *his* mother too."

"This is baffling! I don't know what to say or think."

"One of my professors calls it dynastic manipulation. It's okay for Rainier to assume the Monaco throne as the illegitimate son of Charlotte and Pierre, but he denied that same right to his own son's illegitimate children. When you're the Sovereign Prince of Monaco, you get to control the country's succession policies and the world couldn't care less."

"I can't wait to see what's in that *Prancing Horse* article about Antonio," remarks Tommy.

"I can't either. Let's go back to your place and read it."

☆   ☆   ☆

"God," Tommy groans, "this article is so much longer than I thought it was. Let's sit on my sofa. We can read it together."

"Okay, Your Royal Highness," Rebecca winks at Tommy, folding her legs underneath her.

"And don't forget it," he laughs as he puts on his reading glasses and sits upright with his eyes glued to the *Prancing Horse* article. "This is a publication of the Ferrari Club of America?"

"Yes, every month," Rebecca replies. "My father always had a subscription. I've probably read every single issue."

"Did you ever hear of the author, Rebecca?"

"Eaton Stone. Hmm . . . not that I can remember right now."

"Wait a minute!" Tommy says. "Isn't that the same guy who wrote the article in *The New Yorker*, the one we just read?"

"You're right! Look, here's a full page picture of the GTO," notes Rebecca. "It exudes charisma, doesn't it? In my opinion, no automobile ever had a more beautiful design. The long front hood and fastback—look at the clean, sleek lines leading to the back of the roof. I just love the flared sloping front fenders and the exquisite oval glass covering the headlights. It really is an aerodynamic marvel! Of course, the deep red color makes it the sexiest car on the planet, too! For car collectors, the GTO is the pinnacle. Do you know what GTO stands for?"

"Gas, Tires, and Oil?" Tommy quips. "I learned that in high school. Wait a minute . . . that was for a Pontiac GTO, not the Ferrari."

"You are full of it tonight, aren't you?" she says. "GTO means *Gran Turismo Omolgato,* or Grand Touring Homologated in English."

"Hmm . . . homologated, huh?"

"You're a former English teacher and you're stuck on that word?"

"That's why I'm a *former* English teacher!" Tommy notes.

"In motorsports a car must be approved, or homologated, by the International Automobile Federation, also called the IAF, in order to race," says Rebecca. "Enzo Ferrari wanted the GTO to be a production vehicle that could win on the racetrack. So in 1956, in order to be sanctioned, the IAF initially required Enzo to manufacture twenty-five GTOs that would be for sale to the public. That was their way of making sure they weren't built exclusively for the racetrack. So Enzo started production on the series, the first being the 1956 prototype."

"So now I know what 'homologated' means. What happened to the other twenty-five?" Tommy asks.

"They were never made. That's why this one is so valuable. Enzo had a running feud with the IAF. After the GTO was finished, they changed the rules on him. Instead of twenty-five homologated cars, they insisted on one hundred. Enzo was infuriated and abandoned the project. He had Antonio take the GTO to Genoa for transport to America on the *Andrea Doria*. Of course, in 1962 he resurrected the project producing thirty-nine cars. Actually, the rules still said one hundred needed to be produced, but Enzo tricked the IAF. He numbered the cars out of sequence confusing IAF officials. My father taught me all about the rules and how they were abused when I traveled with him when he was with NART."

"So we're looking at the first GTO," Tommy remarks. "Wow, it gives me the chills!" Some pictures were taken on the dock and others show the car being loaded on the *Andrea Doria*. "It's rather sad," he continues, "a historic car like that decaying at the bottom of the ocean. What a tragedy."

"If it's in a watertight container, it's not been decaying," Rebecca points out.

"Good point. No wonder everyone is after the car."

"That must be Antonio standing next to it." Rebecca looks at the picture for a while, then holds it close to her face. "Tommy! He has a smile just like yours!"

"Good-looking fella, huh? I don't know where the hell I came from, but I have good genes!"

"I do see a resemblance," Rebecca agrees.

"I would love to see a picture of my mom and dad," Tommy remarks.

"I don't blame you," Rebecca says. "I wish you could!"

"Let's take a look at the article, okay?"

"Sure." Rebecca begins to read.

## Antonio Grimaldi—The Prince Who Never Was

Antonio Grimaldi, the lead Formula One technician for Ferrari Scuderia during the 1957 Monaco Grand Prix, encountered an ugly experience at an after-the-race party organized by Formula One to celebrate the victory of Juan Manuel Fangio. An hour into the festivities, a loud voice suddenly boomed across the public address system. A Frenchman named Paul Charone accused Antonio of gross negligence at the Mille Miglia a week earlier. He berated Antonio, calling him a murderer, and telling the crowd that Antonio refused to bring drivers Rene Pelletier and Edmond LaRoche in for a tire change. As a result, their car blew a tire and crashed into the grandstand. Both drivers were killed. Additionally, when their car spun out of control and flew into the crowd, twelve spectators were killed. Five were children.

Charone didn't stop there. "Ask that murdering Antonio to explain what happened to Giancarlo Bandini, one of Ferrari's best design engineers," he continued. "Ask him why the Torino police located Giancarlo's dead body in a red Fiat at the bottom of Satan's Hole on the Strada dell'Assietta. Who do you think rented the red Fiat? None other than the same person who murdered Pelletier, LaRoche, and twelve spectators at the Mille Miglia—Antonio Grimaldi!"

"Rebecca, my grandfather killed all those people at the Mille Miglia plus the design engineer for the GTO, Giancarlo Bandini?" Tommy asks with an empty, forlorn expression on his face.

"Wait, let's keep reading," she says. "I wonder if Antonio had a chance to defend himself. And who is this guy Paul Charone?" Rebecca continues to read.

> Charone made sure to add that Antonio had been arrested eight years earlier for auto theft, a crime for which he was later exonerated. Then he went on to say that given what Antonio had done to Giancarlo, we could surmise that he had really been guilty after all.

"Rebecca, his first arrest in 1949 must be why the Grimaldi family banished him from the line of succession. They must have believed he was guilty, otherwise they would have pulled some strings to get him out of jail."

"You're right," she says, "he was in jail before Rainier became the prince in 1949. Incredible! And he was exonerated in 1954 upon his release. It's like he never existed."

"As far as the world was concerned, he didn't," says Tommy. "But then he was vindicated."

"Yes, but even though he was exonerated, replacing Rainier would have caused a rebellion. They'd have to unravel everything, including the storybook marriage of Prince Rainier and Grace Kelly, the so called 'marriage of the century.'"

"Let's see what other startling revelations this article has to offer."

> After Charone's shattering announcement, he immediately vacated the premises. The damage was irreversible. Antonio later vehemently denied the accusations and proof was never provided. He was

still prosecuted for Giancarlo's murder, receiving a life sentence. The rich and glamorous crowd involved in Formula One turned against him. His friends and acquaintances ostracized him. He was alone in the world.

"It doesn't say where he was imprisoned," Rebecca notes.

"No, it doesn't."

"I wonder why," she muses.

"It's pretty obvious to me," Tommy says, "someone wanted him permanently out of the picture."

"For the second time," she points out. "Do you believe it?"

"This time, though, it's a life sentence probably at hard labor."

"Can you imagine?" she says. "The rightful heir to the Monaco throne doing hard labor in some prison . . . for life? And, no one knows where or even gives a damn."

"And whatever happened to my grandmother Catherine, my father, Alessandro, and my mother? I'm sure I had a mother somewhere along the line. Whatever happened to her?"

"My guess is," Rebecca presumes, "anonymity had to be very important to Catherine. I'm sure she wanted to protect Alessandro. Antonio must be in his eighties by now," she adds.

"After hard labor for that long, he's probably dead," Tommy concludes.

"I wouldn't doubt it, Tommy."

"I have a strange feeling he was really innocent. What a horrendous miscarriage of justice. I feel so sorry for him," he says.

"I hear you. I'd like to know why Charone accused Antonio so publicly. And what possible motive could Antonio have for killing Giancarlo?"

"Great question. Also, I wonder if it's true about him not calling in Pelletier and LaRoche before their tire blew. We have to learn more about this Charone character."

"One thing is for sure, though," Rebecca says. "Back then, those drivers took all kinds of risks. That was the nature of Formula One racing in the fifties. Look at these numbers."

Between 1950 and 1960, thirty Formula One drivers and over a hundred spectators were killed. Finally, in 1960, safety measures were introduced like rollover bars, flag signals, and fire prevention systems. Pit stops in the fifties took about sixty seconds. Today they take ten seconds, so at the time there was much more reluctance to bring a car in unless it was a dire emergency. It could ruin their chance of winning.

"A bad tire *is* a dire emergency, don't you think?" Rebecca asks, clearly annoyed. "So it could very well be true. Antonio could have decided the risk was worth taking. Using up valuable track time with a pit stop could have cost them the race."

Tommy turns the page. "Look—more pictures!" He holds the magazine close to his face as he squints to discern the fine details of the picture. "Hmm . . . this is interesting." He hesitates for a moment. "It's a little grainy, but if I'm not mistaken, it shows a member of the pit crew waving them in. It says here that the 'wave in' occurred right before the accident, and that Pelletier and LaRoche chose to ignore it, staying on the racetrack and crashing into the crowd moments later!"

"That totally exonerates Antonio then," Rebecca asserts.

"It doesn't matter, Rebecca. With twelve people killed, five being children, the racing crowd would have castigated Antonio anyway. To make matters worse, look at this."

A manslaughter lawsuit was lodged by the survivors against Ferrari S.p.A. and Antonio Grimaldi, claiming a worn tire caused the crash and that the Grimaldi team should have insisted that Pelletier and LaRoche come into the pit for a tire replacement.

"Antonio sure had the cards stacked up against him," Tommy says. "He's definitely a scapegoat. What bothers me is *why*."

"I'm inclined to believe the same thing," Rebecca says. "It's awful."

"I hate to think my grandfather was a murderer. We have to get a hold of the author—the guy who wrote this article and *The New Yorker* piece. He obviously did extensive research. Let's take a look at the last paragraph."

> It is the informed opinion of this reporter and a substantial numbers of Ferrari experts and devotees, that the imprisonment of Antonio Grimaldi, first in 1949, and later in 1957, was an act of malicious intent by someone who wanted him blackballed from the world. I pledge to work diligently to prove Antonio's innocence and to ensure his long overdue release from prison.

"See!" Tommy declares. "I knew it! This whole thing reeks. Eaton Stone believes my grandfather is innocent—and I do, too. Rebecca, he's been rotting away in some prison for crimes he didn't even commit. I have to do something, I have to find this reporter!"

While Rebecca is relieved to be able to help Tommy identify his immediate ancestry, she is also keenly aware that he's been concealing his real emotions. She also realizes Tommy won't rest until he discovers the truth about his grandparents and parents. She'd do the same if their roles were reversed.

"Well, so much for the family," Tommy says as he walks into the kitchen and finds a bottle of Dom Pérignon, a birthday gift from Mike. There is an envelope with a note in it. "I'm afraid to read it," he says, as he glances at Rebecca.

Rebecca opens the envelope and reads the note: "May all your ups and downs be under the covers."

Tommy's face turns bright red. "I'm sorry, Rebecca, sometimes Mike can be a real jerk."

Rebecca laughs. "That's okay, Tommy. He's the funny kind of jerk. Let's drink the champagne. That stuff costs three hundred dollars a bottle!"

After Tommy pours the champagne, he walks to the living room and stares out the window into the parking area. The news of his family background is starting to penetrate. Reading his body language, Rebecca walks over to him. Tommy places his arm around her waist and gently draws her closer as she wraps her arms around him. She tilts her head sideways, just enough to see the sadness in his face.

"I'm so sorry, Tommy," Rebecca says, feeling his anguish. "I can imagine how painful this night has been for you."

"Thank you," he says. "I understand better now. My aunt and uncle—they were trying to protect me from this information. Maybe I *was* better off not knowing."

"No. Future generations will be grateful. We're not in the Middle Ages. You don't just erase someone from your family just because you've deemed them 'unacceptable.'"

"Deep down, though, I figured someday I'd learn the truth."

With his other arm, he turns her shoulder toward him so they can be face to face. She leans forward to be closer to him. Her soft smile and gentle eyes dilute his sadness.

"Rebecca . . . Mike was wrong about my being indecisive," he says affectionately.

"What do you mean, Tommy?"

"I mean . . . I'm in love with you," he whispers softly as he bends down to kiss her tenderly. He draws back again to gaze lovingly at her before kissing her again. This time it is a deep, passionate kiss.

The world is slowly disappearing around them, along with the tension of recent revelations. For the first time that evening, Tommy's mind is locked into the present. For him, nothing in his life is more important than this moment of closeness with Rebecca.

# 11

# Ferrari Challenge

**Daytona International Speedway**

*October 31, 2008, Friday Afternoon*

It's one of the hottest days of the year. The tarmac surface at Daytona is close to 120 degrees. Racing tires are hot. As the temperature rises, oil in the asphalt gets warmer and warmer, making the track more slippery. Large wavy bumps start to form on the track near the long chicane. Still, drivers maintain their speeds, oblivious to any dangers the slippery racecourse may tender.

Eaton Stone, a freelance journalist, has gained prominence reporting on everything from Chernobyl to the selection of a new pope, winning the Pulitzer Prize for his nonfiction best seller entitled, *The Imposition of the Inquisition: A Study of European Demagoguery.*

He is also an amateur race car driver. Today, he is driving his Pininfarina designed Ferrari 430 Berlinetta in the Ferrari Challenge, a racing series offering Ferrari owners the opportunity to compete against other Ferrari owners on racetracks across the country. His Ferrari is extensively modified for the racetrack, and has almost 500 horsepower. Its 6-speed transmission, derived from Ferrari's Formula One program, is operated with paddles behind the steering wheel.

Leading the pack from start to finish, Stone has taken the checkered flag in the first two races. Now, just twelve points behind the leader, Robert Fowler, one more win will make him the 2008 Ferrari Challenge Champion.

But Stone's arms feel the stress of attempting to control his car on the slippery track. His race suit is soaked from the 115-degree heat inside the car. His feet boil. Sweat blurs his vision. He is battling for position on the long straight as his speedometer exceeds 200 mph. Then he fights for the inside groove on turn three at the end of the straight. Upon entering the turn, he brakes hard, like he has done several times before during the weekend. He can feel the weight transfer to the front of the car, allowing him to skillfully balance the car as he downshifts the left paddle to fourth gear. Then he accelerates. Suddenly, he loses control. He hears a loud thump coming from the front of the car and feels the loss of tire grip. The car skids violently and becomes airborne. Stone's view into his windshield changes from black road to blue sky. The image of his car turning sideways in the air terrifies him. He lets go of the steering wheel, closes his eyes, and braces for impact.

### Fairchester, New York
*November 1, 2008, Saturday*

The following day, after Tommy drops Rebecca off at Ray's Speed Shop, he arrives at his office with plenty of mixed emotions. The startling revelations of the previous day require further corroboration and research, and he is eager to begin the process.

Tommy clears his computer screen of business items and searches for anything he can find about Eaton Stone. He isn't surprised to find several links with his name listed. *Wait a minute. I need to check out the Ferrari website.* Tommy locates the Ferrari Club of North America's website. He clicks the *About Us* drop-down menu, then clicks *News*. The first item under news releases captures Tommy's attention:

## Daytona International
### Eaton Stone Injured at Ferrari Challenge Event

A frequent contributor to our Prancing Horse newsletter, longtime Ferrari Club member, and international journalist Eaton Stone had a violent crash at Daytona. A wheel broke loose from his 430 Ferrari Challenge car on the short straight just before turn number four. Stone lost control as the car flipped, striking a recently installed tire barrier. His injuries are not life-threatening. This morning he was transferred to Upstate University Hospital in Syracuse, New York, his hometown.

Tommy is jolted. He quickly reaches for his cell phone. "Rebecca! Can I pick you up in ten minutes?"

"Where are we going?" she asks.

"I'll explain later. Just get ready. You won't believe what I just read."

Rebecca is standing outside the speed shop when Tommy arrives.

"How the hell can a wheel break loose?" Tommy asks Rebecca as they drive down the New York State Thruway toward Syracuse. The printed copy of the press release is in her hands.

"Well, it *can* happen," she replies. "Rarely, but it can happen."

"Don't you think it's rather coincidental? Stone just happens to have a horrific accident right after he writes that article about Antonio. Remember his commitment? *I pledge to work diligently to prove Antonio's innocence and to ensure his long overdue release from prison.*"

"Possibly," she says. "You might be overreacting a bit. Those guys always have accidents. That's just life in the racing world. Why would anyone want to hurt him?"

They arrive at Upstate University Hospital in the early afternoon and go straight to the information desk.

"We're here to visit a friend by the name of Eaton Stone," Tommy says in a sober and serious tone.

"You can go right up. It's Room 330," the receptionist responds pleasantly.

They are surprised the receptionist doesn't quiz them for more information. When they arrive at room 330, the door is closed. Peering through a narrow vertical window in the door, they see two men dressed in black suits standing beside Eaton Stone's bed.

A nurse approaches them. "If you're here to see Mr. Stone," she says, "it could be a while."

"How is he recovering?" Rebecca asks.

"He's stable," she says, not wanting to volunteer too much personal information.

"Are family members with him now?" Tommy asks.

"No." She forces a slight smile. "Why don't you have a seat in the waiting area? I'll let you know when they leave."

"Thank you," Rebecca says cordially.

"I wonder why she avoided answering my questions?" Rebecca asks Tommy.

"They're probably cops," Tommy says, "or maybe investigators."

"Maybe they're his doctors?"

"Doctors don't wear black suits and wheels don't just fly off of cars, either. I know that much for sure." His impatience and frustration are becoming more pronounced. Antonio's fate is now a personal matter for Tommy. His trepidations are multiplying by the second.

After about thirty minutes, the nurse gives them permission to enter Eaton Stone's room.

"Who did you say you were?" she asks with some suspicion.

"Friends who want to wish him well," Rebecca replies.

"Well, I'm reluctant to allow any more visitors. He's very tired and quite cantankerous right now, especially after being quizzed by those racetrack officials."

"Racetrack officials?" Tommy asks.

"Yes. They said they represented FCNA or something like that."

"The Ferrari Challenge of North America," Rebecca says. "They're probably doing their postrace due diligence."

"Well, okay," the nurse sighs, "but please don't stay more than five or ten minutes. Mr. Stone has himself all worked up talking to those people."

When Tommy and Rebecca walk into Eaton Stone's room, the two men in black suits are leaving. Their matching attire seems odd to Tommy.

"Are you friends of Mr. Stone's?" one of the men asks with an unfriendly voice.

"Yes," Rebecca says curtly, "we are friends."

"In what way?" the man asks.

"Weren't you just leaving?" she replies, ignoring his question.

They both slowly leave the room, one of the men turning to look back at Rebecca. She turns her head away, avoiding eye contact with him.

"For some reason that guy looks angry," Rebecca whispers to Tommy. "I'm glad they're gone, they give me the creeps."

Eaton Stone looks up at them as they walk into his room. "More company?" he says with a hostile expression. "We having a matinee today or something? Two more private dicks. Lord, give me a freakin' break! I just want to rest."

"Those two men—they're racetrack officials?" Tommy queries.

"Racetrack officials, my ass! From FCNA they say. If they're from FCNA, I'm from Tajikistan!" Eaton's thin body is lying flat on his narrow bed with the white sheets all the way up to his full white beard. His completely bald head shines under the fluorescent lights as if it has been recently polished with a buffer.

"Tell the nurse to turn down the damn heat!" he yells. "The place is a sweatbox!"

"I'll get the nurse," Rebecca says softly.

"Just turn the damn thermostat down yourself," he says. "You don't need the freakin' nurse to do that!"

Rebecca walks to the thermostat near the entrance of the room. "It's locked," she says, dreading another volatile response from Eaton.

"If I could get out of bed, I'd smash the damn thing with a sledgehammer!"

Rebecca calmly smiles at him. "Do you usually carry a sledge-hammer around with you?" she asks. Not expecting Rebecca's comeback, his angst dissolves like salt in boiling water. Her beau-tiful eyes radiate warmth, a great commodity to ease Eaton's self-inflicted gloom.

"Ten thousand comedians out of work—and I have to put up with this! No, I don't have a sledgehammer, sweetie. Do you?" Eaton throws his head back in the pillow, shaking it, as he fights back the urge to smile.

"I can get one for you, or we can call the nurse and get her to lower the thermostat. What would you like me to do?" she asks.

Eaton lowers his head and exhales in a sign of capitulation. "Oh, never mind. Come to think of it, it's really not that warm."

Despite his earlier brashness, Tommy detects affability in Eaton's eyes. He has clients like this—one minute they're raging mad, the next minute they can't do enough for him, especially after they feel guilty for being raging mad in the first place.

"Well, let me tell you," says Eaton, "if a good-lookin' nurse popped in every once in a while, I'd feel a helluva lot better! Most of 'em here are my age and ready for the glue factory. Oh, by the way, did you hear the story about the guy who's in the hospital for three days and takes a turn for the nurse?" Eaton laughs so hard at his own joke, he starts to cough and wheeze.

"Now that's a good one," Tommy says, grateful that Eaton is more relaxed and less ornery.

"You're a nasty old man," Rebecca says with a wide grin. "But I like you."

"A good laugh does wonders for the soul," Tommy smiles.

"A good laugh? Let me tell you something else, my friends," says Eaton. "In my lifetime, I've had many good laughs and many ass aches, too! I've been down-and-out, up and down, and even sideways. Yeah! As a matter of fact, I was sideways when I smashed into that goddamn stack of tires at Daytona! Am I grateful? Yes, I'm very grateful. Do I have any regrets? Not a one! I've seen and done everything in my fifty-nine years and you know what? I wouldn't trade my life for all the gold bricks in Fort Knox!"

"Hope I look as good as you when I'm fifty-nine," Tommy says.

"Tell that to my former wife!" Eaton rejoins. "She ran away with a Volkswagen salesman. Do you believe that? I deserve better than that. I could understand if it were a Mercedes or Bentley salesman. But a Volkswagen salesman! By the way, did you hear about the guy who drove his expensive car into a tree?"

"No, I'll bite," Tommy says.

"He found out how a Mercedes bends!" Eaton laughs hard again, coughing and wheezing. "You know what?" he asks.

"What," Tommy replies obligingly.

"I'm reading a book about gravity. I can't put it down." Again, his laughter ensues.

Rebecca gives him a strange look, wincing and shaking her head. "That's the corniest joke I've ever heard."

"I try, though," Eaton says reflectively. "God knows, I try. Actually, I shouldn't joke about my former wife. I really did love her. Sometimes laughter helps ease the pain."

"What happened to her?" Tommy asks politely.

"After she left me, she died. It wasn't pretty. I was with her when she passed."

Tommy starts to ask another question but Eaton abruptly changes the subject. "Okay! What can I do for you two lovely people—or are you simply lost and came here for directions?"

Once Tommy and Rebecca introduce themselves, they explain how they had read his exposition in *The New Yorker* and his article on Antonio Grimaldi in the *Prancing Horse* newsletter.

"Mr. Stone," Tommy says, "we had some questions about some of your remarks." He hands Eaton a copy of the *Prancing Horse* with Eaton's ending comments highlighted with a yellow magic marker.

"Tell me something," Tommy asks, "do you still want to prove Antonio's innocence, even after your accident?"

"Hand me my cheaters," says Eaton. "They're on the night stand." Rebecca hands Eaton his stylish reading glasses with tortoise frames and oval lenses. "You said your name is Tommy Grimaldi?" he asks as he nods, seeming to know the answer.

"Yes."

"Really now. Let me see . . . you live in Fairchester, New York. You were a high school English teacher. Now you're a financial planner. You were brought up by your aunt and uncle and were told a bunch of lies regarding your ancestry. Correct?"

Tommy is dumbfounded. "How did you know all that?" he asks.

"Well, what the hell do you think I do for living anyway? I research and write! And you, young man, you've been on my radar for a long time. If you read those articles and you're really Tommy, or should I say Tomasso Grimaldi, you can't be very surprised that I know all about you. You've played a rather prominent role in my research projects. Let me say now that I am so very glad to finally meet you!"

Despite Eaton's apparent sincerity, Tommy senses something strange in his words, as if he knows more than he is sharing. *But then again,* Tommy surmises, *he is a writer, and writers do tons of research, much of which they never publish or share with anyone.*

"Okay now," Eaton declares, as if he's a drill sergeant speaking to a group of Marine recruits. "I have some marching orders for you. Turn yourselves around. Go ahead—turn around!" Tommy and Rebecca obey each order and make an about-face. "Now, put one foot in front of the other, walk out the door, and forget we ever met. Just do it!" Eaton pulls the sheets up to his chin and stares despondently out the window of his room.

"Mr. Stone!" Tommy exclaims. "You are the only one in the world who can tell me about my family, please!"

"C'mon, Tommy," Rebecca urges. "Mr. Stone must have good reason for us to leave."

Eaton pushes the call button for the nurse.

"Let's go," Rebecca says. "Let's not create a scene."

"They were just leaving," Eaton tells the nurse when she arrives.

As Tommy and Rebecca leave the room, Tommy notices a wheelchair in the bathroom almost hidden behind a commode. When they reach the hallway, Tommy asks the nurse, "Whose wheelchair is that in the bathroom?"

"Well, it's Mr. Stone's wheelchair, of course. It's in *his* room," the nurse says. "He can't walk. How else would you expect him to get around?"

"He's paralyzed?" Tommy turns around, reenters the room, and walks to the side of the bed so he can be face-to-face with Eaton.

"I thought you had gone," Eaton says with a look of complete dejection.

"What about *your* safety?" Tommy asks empathically. "When you leave here, who is going to protect *you*? After what happened at the track, don't tell me you don't need protection!"

"Sir, you need to leave now!" the nurse says with a firm voice. "You're upsetting Mr. Stone. Leave or I'm going to get security!"

Eaton covers his mouth with his left hand, and makes no sound whatsoever. Tommy can see tears streaming down his face. "I have no one else in my life," he says. "I can't race anymore. It's going to be difficult for me to write. I've really expended my usefulness in this world. But you two . . . you are young and vibrant with your whole lives in front of you. Just go home and leave Antonio Grimaldi to die a quiet death. We'll all be better off, believe me!"

"Listen, Mr. Stone," Rebecca says. She moves a stool near the bed and sits down facing him. "Tommy will never get this meeting out of his head. You must know that. You can't just turn him away and expect that he'll forget everything you wrote about his family. Neither one of us is going to rest until we learn the complete story. Knowing you are incapacitated adds to our concern. We don't want anything to happen to you either. So, please . . . can't we work together?"

Eaton turns his head away from Rebecca. She hears him inhaling deeply. She is patiently waiting for a sign, any sign or indication of his sentiments—one way or the other. After a few long minutes, Eaton turns toward her and extends his left arm out to reach Rebecca's hand. She takes it and squeezes.

"I don't know you, sweetie," he says, "but I must admit you present a sound argument. I'm just afraid that you and Tommy could be drawn into some kind of conspiracy that involves me. I am very grateful that you want to work with me. I have a lot more research to do, and now, after the accident, I could use some assistance. Would you two be willing to help me?"

"Tell us more about this 'conspiracy' against you," Tommy probes.

Eaton pushes the up button on his remote hospital bed controller. As his mattress rises to an almost vertical position, he says,

"Sometimes as a journalist, some of my revelations damage lives. People I've offended sometimes seek retribution. Those characters in black suits got me all stirred up."

"Like the so-called accident at Daytona?" Tommy asks.

"All right," Eaton sighs reluctantly. "Ever since I wrote that article in the *Prancing Horse* making the pledge to exonerate Antonio, I've been receiving threatening phone calls. One such call warned me that I would have a serious accident at Daytona. The Ferrari 430 Berlinetta that I race in the Ferrari Challenge has titanium wheel bolts. They don't just break by themselves. But that's what happened to the right front wheel. Not only were they replaced with inferior bolts, all the threads were stripped. The wheel couldn't handle the stress around the curves."

"How do you know that?" Rebecca asks. "Are you sure it wasn't just an oversight by a member of the pit crew?"

"I can tell, young lady, you know something about racing. I'm very sure about what I am telling you."

"How can you be so sure?" she asks.

"Listen, after several years of participation, you take things for granted, you know, like trusting your pit crew. I received a call from my crew chief after I was admitted. He found broken bolts still in the lugholes. There was also a message on my cell phone with someone claiming responsibility for the accident. How much more evidence do you need? Now, do you still want to help me? Because—"

"Wait a minute, Eaton!" Rebecca exclaims. "Who was the person who called you?"

"I don't know. I have my suspicions, but I can't say right now. I need to do more research."

"Can you tell us who you think it is?" Tommy pleads.

"We can handle the truth," Rebecca adds.

"Yes," Eaton agrees. "John 8:31-32. 'If you abide by my word, you are truly my disciples and you will know the truth, and the truth will set you free.'"

"I've heard that before," Tommy smiles. "I had a remarkable catechism teacher. Hopefully, you will have an opportunity to meet her someday."

"Discovering the truth is why I do what I do for a living. The truth is: I don't know the truth yet. I'm sorry."

"May I ask another question?" Tommy treads cautiously.

"And your next question is where can you find your mother and father, right?"

"Yes," Tommy replies. "Lately, I've been totally preoccupied with it."

"I can certainly understand why," Eaton replies, "but I'm sorry again. I don't know the answer. Let me tell you what I *do* know. Your grandfather and grandmother, Antonio and Catherine, eloped. It appears that both of them were rebellious by nature and, for some reason, already on the outs with the Grimaldis. European royal weddings have always been grand spectacles and headlines for the international news media. Theirs was secret, and I suspect the Grimaldis did their best to keep it that way. I did learn that your grandmother was from a rather ordinary family from Milan who were in the construction business. My research regarding Catherine ends there. It's very difficult, especially in Europe, to find people who don't want to be found. I still have a lot of research to do."

"You're not very encouraging," says Tommy as he sits down on the chair near the bed. "Did Antonio really kill Giancarlo?" he asks.

"I'm working on it," Eaton replies succinctly. "We should arrange another time to meet."

Just then the nurse enters the room. "I'm sorry but you must leave now. Mr. Stone needs his rest."

"Go away for five more minutes!" Eaton demands. "These people are very important to me and I would like them to stay longer."

"In five minutes I'll be back!" she says. "I mean it—five minutes, not one second more!" She storms from the room with long, angry strides.

"There's no question about 'sweetie's' punctuality either, so listen up! I'll be out of here in a few days. I'll call you. I already have your cell numbers."

"Don't you have several weeks of rehab scheduled?" Rebecca asks.

"Again? Oh, God no. I've been paralyzed for most of my life. Look!" Eaton raises his bandaged right hand. "It was crushed in the accident. No more driving. Writing will be out of the question for several weeks, too. With your help, I'll get through this, just like I did when I was paralyzed."

"May I ask how you became paralyzed?" Tommy asks.

"Tommy!" Rebecca admonishes.

"It's okay, sweetie. I had a bad boating accident when I was seven years old. Now you two don't worry about me. I'm used to being a paraplegic. I get around fine. My van and even my Ferrari have been modified with a special apparatus that allows me to do everything with my hands. By the way, Tommy, do you have a pistol permit?"

"Yes," Tommy answers. "I applied for one right after I was released from the service. I have a .32 caliber Beretta."

"Keep it with you at all times and make sure you carry enough ammunition, too."

"How much is enough?"

"Just make-believe you're still in the Rangers," says Eaton. "*Be prepared* is the best advice I can give you. You know, like in Afghanistan, a firefight can erupt at any moment."

"What else?" Tommy asks. He feels intensity similar to how he felt just before going out on a patrol. "I saw a lot of action in Afghanistan."

"Like I said, make believe you're still there. *Rangers lead the way,* remember?"

"Yes, very well, in fact," Tommy replies.

"When I'm released, which should be in a few days, we'll sit down and I'll explain in greater detail. We also must formulate a strategy."

"Offensive or defensive?" Tommy asks.

"Both! I'm not the kind of person who sits back and takes the shit. I can dish it out too!"

# 12

# Satan's Hole

## Italy

### *July 17, 1956, Tuesday*

Giancarlo is still nervous. His high-strung nature has been put to the test the last few days. As he sits in the red Fiat and contemplates his next assignment, he can easily picture Il Commendatore's wide smile as he thumbs through the pictures of the GTO being loaded onto the *Andrea Doria*. Still, Giancarlo finds it difficult to understand why Il Commendatore doesn't want to keep the car, even if the IAF did increase the homologation requirement from twenty-five to one hundred. Antonio is right, though. It isn't their job to second-guess the most beloved person on the continent. *I'd better get going*, he says to himself with his usual sense of urgency.

The Assietta is rather easy to navigate in the Fiat, especially without any traffic. Nevertheless, Giancarlo has to keep the Fiat below thirty, especially when he reaches the next turn, right above Satan's Hole. People call it the Bermuda Triangle of the Alps, since so many vehicles have ended up at the bottom of it. He knows he has to be careful. The mere thought of making the turn at all frightens him to death.

Giancarlo is anxious to return home so he can begin work on Enzo's next design project. More importantly, he needs to return to therapy. His bouts with traumatic stress have been more frequent lately, and if Antonio ever tells Il Commendatore about his recent meltdown, it will be curtains for his career with Ferrari. He simply has to get a better grip on his condition.

A black Citroen DS sedan is parked just before the turn. Giancarlo wonders why so large a vehicle would be on the Assietta and, of all places, parked near Satan's Hole. As he moves closer, he notices a tall man behind the steering wheel. When the man exits the car, he motions Giancarlo to stop. *Who is this man wearing a red tie, black suit, and black fedora hat? He must be from Maranello, an emissary from Il Commendatore,* Giancarlo assumes.

The man walks up to the Fiat, takes out his French made 9 mm Luger, and before Giancarlo can react, he fires three shots point-blank into Giancarlo's upper chest, and a final shot into his head. Giancarlo slumps sideways on the seat with the blank stare of a dead man on his face. He never knew what hit him. Opening the door, the man searches Giancarlo's dead body. Finding the pictures of the GTO, he places them in his coat pocket. Then he cranks the steering wheel hard to the right, turns on the ignition, and places the car in gear. He watches as the Fiat slowly approaches the precipice and falls over the steep cliff, crashing to the bottom of Satan's Hole. The man lights up a cigarette and inhales deeply. His assignment complete, he returns to his Citroen and drives off.

Antonio lowers the driver's side window on the transporter so he can enjoy the cool air coming from the Ligurian Sea. He is on the Corso Giuseppe Assereto heading for Chiavari, a coastal town southeast of

Portofino on the Italian Riviera, where he has to stop and pick up two important items. Then he'll continue on to the coastal town of Piombino, midway between Genoa and Naples. After one more stop, he'll return to Torino. A brand-new Ferrari GT Berlinetta Competizione awaits his arrival. His instructions are precise: bring it to Maranello and prepare it for the Tour de France Automobile, then the Mille Miglia.

Despite his lack of sleep, Antonio is pleased with his progress. He was able to see the GTO loaded onto the *Andrea Doria* and find Giancarlo safe and sound. He wishes he could be present when Giancarlo gives Il Commendatore the pictures of the Berlinetta being hoisted onto the deck of the *Andrea Doria*. A smile from him is like a citation of honor, an acknowledgment that would stay with him the rest of his life.

Antonio has a lot of affection for the many small seaside villages and fishing ports he passes through. They are, after all, the stomping grounds of his youth, where he could get far enough away from Monaco to roam incognito—that is until he and a few of his friends got caught conducting a panty raid at the Rapallo School of Nursing. Once it became known that he was a member of the Grimaldi family of Monaco, his extracurricular activities were severely stifled. It wasn't until he was expelled from the University of Bologna's School of International Studies for cheating on a final exam that he incurred the unforgiving wrath of his family. After that incident, Antonio found it impossible to win back their favor. That's when he phased into the melancholic stage of his life, where his daily inebriation became such an embarrassment for the Grimaldis that they send him away to an expensive treatment center in northern Milan. However, it wasn't until he met and fell in love with Catherine, a volunteer at the treatment center, that he totally recovered.

It is mid-afternoon when Antonio reaches Chiavari. The transporter scarcely fits the narrow, twisting streets that meander around tall, stately buildings. Painted in warm pastel colors, he can see the

considerable medieval influence of the numerous arcades and buildings from the thirteenth century, including the castle, several man-
sions, and the Church of San Salvatore di Lavagna. For Antonio,
Chiavari is the most beautiful town in the Liguria region

It was also one of Antonio's favorite locations for pleasure boating
on the forty-foot Vagabond staysail ketch that had been given to
him by his father when he was still in good graces with the family.
Its white hull, teak decking, and brass bright work, not to mention
its speed, were perfect for Antonio when, as an eligible bachelor,
he sailed the coastal towns of the Tigullio—from Portofino and
Rapallo, to Santa Margherita and Chiavari.

Soon after he met Catherine, they decided to live on the boat
together in a quiet cove in the Portofino Marina known as the Giardino
dell'Eden, or the Garden of Eden. In 1947, they secretly married on
a small terrace in Castello Brown overlooking the center of Portofino
Bay and surrounded by the jet-set's most luxurious villas and yachts.
It was a quiet wedding. The civil registrar of Portofino married them,
and a couple they had befriended from the marina served as witnesses.

Those were good years. Reminiscing about them is still very painful
for Antonio. Five long years in prison has taken its toll. While in prison
in 1949, he learned of the death of his grandfather, Prince Louis, and
how Rainier, his younger brother, had been crowned Prince of Monaco
instead of him. That news plunged Antonio into a deep depression that
he didn't overcome until he was transferred to an agricultural penal colony on Gorgona Island in 1952, two years prior to his release.

In April of 1956, the much-heralded marriage of Prince Rainier to
Grace Kelly, the American movie star, reinforced the fact that he could
never return to Monaco. His son, Alessandro, was two years old when
he went to prison. To this day he still isn't sure why his wife Catherine
disappeared, even when he had pleaded with her to wait for him.

He's been angry for a long time. Losing his station in life, along with
his wife and son, all for a crime he didn't commit, has been impossible

for him to accept. Yet for the first time in several years, he's getting tired of being angry. He just wants to remove the latest threat to his life and be reunited with his wife and son. He has finally accepted the fact that reclaiming his regal status with the Grimaldis is hopeless.

As he drives by Castello Brown high up on a hill, he can see Portofino Bay in the distance. He squeezes the steering wheel tightly and fights back tears. As feelings of worthlessness and shame overwhelm him, he removes his foot from the accelerator and pulls into a vacant parking lot.

He still doesn't know why he was accused of stealing Enzo's 1948 Ferrari 166 Spyder Corsa, also known as the Tipo 166. When the car was recovered from the real thief, it was sent to America. The 166 became the first Ferrari to be imported to America. After Antonio was vindicated in 1954, Enzo felt compelled to help him get back on his feet and hired him. That's when Antonio's life began to change for the better. Nearly every day he would say to himself, *I'd be selling pencils on some street corner if it weren't for Enzo's benevolence.*

During his first two years with the Ferrari organization, Antonio worked hard cultivating a reputation as a highly skilled and trusted employee. He became a lead technician traveling to Formula One races with Scuderia, Ferrari's factory racing team. Few other techs could match his proficiency at tuning the V12 racing engine. Many of Ferrari's Grand Prix victories during the mid-1950s were due to Antonio's ability to tune the Colombo V12 to perfection.

Despite Antonio's acclaim at Scuderia, his pay level was the same as any other Ferrari technician. Nevertheless, he saved enough money to hire a private investigator to locate his wife and son. But the investigator ran into one dead end after another, finally suspending all activity until Antonio paid the $10,000 in fees and travel expenses he was owed. Tormented by his obsessive desire to locate Catherine and Alessandro, Antonio made the most critical mistake of his life. He joined a French secret organization known as the Charbonneries, and thus his life began to spiral downward into a chasm of inescapable terror.

Antonio met their leader, Paul Charone, who was also a member of the French racing team, at the French Grand Prix. Two Ferrari Scuderia entries, Luigi Villoresi and Alberto Ascari, withdrew their cars because of unresolved engine problems. Charone and some of his technicians volunteered their assistance. Unnerved by the prospect of letting Il Commendatore down, Antonio welcomed their help.

After working on the car, Paul Charone invited Antonio to dinner. He said he had a proposal for Antonio, and it would be in his best interests to accept his invitation. So many times Antonio had wished he could turn back the clock and decline that dinner invitation.

☆   ☆   ☆

Charone is a tall man, over six feet and slender as a nail with bony, hunched shoulders. His droopy, half-closed, steel gray eyes make his complexion look pasty, and his short, thinning white hair lies flat, parted on the right side. His closely shaven face conveys a clean-cut appearance, while his beaky thin nose protrudes conspicuously out of proportion with the rest of his face. Yet he has an infectious smile and possesses a surprisingly charismatic way about him. Even with his conservative dress—a long-sleeved gray shirt and gray trousers— there is something magnetic and alluring to his personality.

"Did you know," Charone asks Antonio, "that Monaco's borders had always been protected by the French armed forces until de Gaulle rescinded the defense alliance between the two countries? With the Algerian War consuming France's military resources, Monaco has become an afterthought. They are defenseless and vulnerable."

"I wouldn't know," Antonio responds with indifference.

"How would you like to return to Monaco as its leader?"

Antonio places his napkin on the table and gets up to leave.

"No damage done if you merely listen, right?" Charone says before Antonio can walk away.

Antonio sits back down. "I'm listening," he says reluctantly.

"I've organized an anonymous group of wealthy business entrepreneurs from all over the world, and set up the Charbonneries as a *Société Anonyme,* or 'French corporation,' with an executive committee and president director general. I will chair the executive committee. My vision is for Monaco to become the adult playground of the world. Guess who I've nominated for the PDG position?"

"You want *me* to run it?" Antonio asks, totally astounded by Charone's offer.

"Why not? You are a Grimaldi and the true prince of Monaco, aren't you? I will begin paying you three hundred and fifty million francs, that's one million dollars per year, immediately after you accept my offer."

Antonio's thoughts digress immediately to Catherine and Alessandro. *Financing the investigation will take more money than I could ever earn with Ferrari.* Now Charone has Antonio's undivided attention.

"What happens to my brother and the rest of my family in Monaco?" Antonio asks.

"They continue as symbolic heads of state. I think they call it titular leaders, like the Queen of England, who has no real government power."

"Are you sure nothing will happen to them?" Antonio asks again.

"Absolutely not," Charone assures him. "We need them."

"When can I let you know my answer?" Antonio asks.

"Right now," Charone answers. "You can keep your job at Ferrari until after we accomplish our objective. I'll write you the first check when you say yes . . . right now, for instance."

"Yes, then. I'll do it!" Antonio exclaims with a degree of impulsivity.

Charone pulls out his checkbook and pens Antonio a hefty check. "One more thing." Charone glares at Antonio and asks, "Have you ever heard of the Greek poet Archilochus?"

"No, I haven't."

"He said, 'I have a high art: I hurt with cruelty those who would wound me.'"

★   ★   ★

Within minutes, a black Citroen DS sedan pulls up alongside of the transporter. A tall man wearing a red tie, black suit, and black fedora walks over to the driver's side where Antonio has rolled down the window waiting for him.

"Bonjour, Monsieur Grimaldi. Here are two briefcases and an envelope I was told to deliver to you. The tan briefcase is for you. It has thirty-five million francs, worth one hundred thousand dollars, inside. The black briefcase is for Lorenzo. Mr. Charone's specific instructions are in the envelope along with a personal communiqué to you."

Antonio reaches down from the cab of the transporter to accept the items.

"Merci," he says. The man returns to his Citroen as Antonio backs out of the parking lot and points the transporter south.

Antonio is about to execute the most felonious thing he has ever done. He struggles to fight off his feelings of deep shame. Then he rationalizes. *I've already served the time, I may as well commit the crime. They owe me! Not only that, I can finally get Charone and the Charbonneries off my back for good.*

# 13

# Mystery in Montauk

**Fairchester, New York**

*November 1, 2008, Early Saturday Evening*

Rebecca and Tommy leave the meeting with Eaton Stone perplexed and unsure what to do next. Were they really in danger? Eaton's words lacked clarity. Nevertheless, they are frightened by the implications of their visit. Who were the men in black suits? Was Eaton imagining the reasons for his accident or did someone intentionally cause it? Who was the mystery person that called him to take blame for the accident?

Tommy has experience in combative situations. The firefights in Afghanistan recur often in his memory. The Beretta he now carries in a shoulder holster, including a double magazine pouch, is in the same location as it was when he fought the Taliban in Kandahar. Tommy works hard to forget that part of his life. The number of times he engaged in hand-to-hand combat, or when enemy fire killed his close friends, are painful recollections. He would just as soon keep them tucked away in a back chamber of his mind.

Rebecca also cannot stop thinking about Eaton Stone, despite Tommy's comforting embrace as they cuddle on his sofa. *Why was*

*Antonio framed? Why is Eaton so committed to his exoneration?* She intends to learn more when Eaton visits them tomorrow morning.

"Tommy," she asks, "I'm curious. What is the first question you're going to ask Eaton tomorrow?"

"That's easy," he says. "'Can you help me find my parents?' If I come out of this thing knowing that answer, it will all be worthwhile."

"I guess I already knew your answer," Rebecca says softly. "The 'how' part has me baffled, though."

"The truth about Antonio's imprisonment will lead us to them," Tommy responds.

"I hope so. Learning more about Paul Charone is a good place to start, don't you think?"

"I do. You know I was thinking that maybe you should go away someplace where you would be safer. I really want to untangle this conundrum, but my first obligation is your safety." He brings her closer and looks directly into her eyes. "While I want you near me, being around me may place you in danger."

She places her head on his shoulder. "Remember 'alea iacta est'?"

"The die is cast? Julius Caesar?"

"Yes. We've crossed the Rubicon, Tommy. I don't want to be away from you. I just wish I hadn't stirred the pot and inflamed this situation."

"You have, that's true. But I wanted you to." Tommy embraces her and they kiss.

"Tommy . . . I couldn't possibly feel safer than when I'm in your arms."

"I'm sorry for all this drama in our lives."

"I'd do it all over again," she says softly.

"I love you." Tommy lifts her chin and looks into her eyes.

Just then a ring from his cell phone interrupts their moment. Tommy shakes his head in disgust and answers the phone.

"Hey, Grimaldi!" comes Mike's voice. "How the hell are you, old buddy? I just called so you could congratulate me!"

"Bender, where in hell have you been? Everyone on the planet is looking for you!"

"Well, I got hitched. Can you believe that? Me, a married man?" There's a long pause. "You still there, buddy?"

"Yeah, I'm here. And cut the baloney," Tommy adds, pretty sure Mike is kidding around. "Just tell me where you are. You've upset a lot of people."

"I'm in beautiful downtown Montauk—on Long Island, that is. We're staying at a bed and breakfast right near the point."

"Montauk!" Tommy exclaims.

"Yeah, Montauk!" says Mike. "Remember that strange dude in the movie *Jaws* called Quint? His real name was Frank Mundus and he has the record for the largest fish ever caught with a rod and reel. His good friend Jim Crowley took us out on Mundus's boat, the Cricket II, and we caught a bunch of hammerheads."

"Shut up for a minute, who the hell is 'we'?"

"Remember that gorgeous saleswoman who waited on us at the Ferrari dealership?"

"Oh my God, Michael, you didn't!" Tommy groans.

"Say 'congratulations,' she's my wife!"

Tommy grapples with an obvious dilemma: tell him how stupid he is and alienate both of them, or say 'congratulations' and pretend to be sincere.

"Well, Bender, congratulations and the same to Jaclyn. I wish both of you the best."

A million things are spinning through Tommy's head: *Why did they get married so soon after meeting one another? Does she really care for Mike or is she just after his money? Oh, yes—and was he smart enough to have her sign a prenuptial agreement?* Then he recollects

Mike's mercurial behavior over the last several weeks, his vulnerability, especially his spur-of-the moment decision making. *It probably didn't take much to get him to the altar, assuming that was her motive from the beginning. Bender, what the hell did you go and do?*

"Thanks! Make sure you let Lilly know, okay?" Mike says.

"Don't you think Lilly might deserve a personal phone call from you? She's been like a mother to you and she's been wondering where the hell you are—like everyone else!"

"I'll try and call her later this week. You still dating that Ricci girl, the broad that thinks she's Mario Andretti?" Mike asks.

"Yes," Tommy replies. "She's right here. You want to say hello?"

"No, no, that's okay. Oh, I almost forgot. Check on my cars, will you? Just make sure everything is locked up and the alarms are set."

"When are you coming home?" Tommy inquires.

"Not sure, buddy. We may stay down here awhile."

"Tell me Bender, why did you withdraw fifteen million from your account?"

"We're looking at a summer bungalow in Bridgehampton."

"Bungalow! For fifteen million? Did you really say 'bungalow'?"

"Things cost a lot down here," says Mike.

"You're gonna be broke!"

"Not to worry. Tomorrow we're going after the GTO Berlinetta. Once we raise that treasure up from the *Andrea Doria*, the whole world will take note. Once it's restored it will be the new wonder of the modern world!"

"You're losing it, Mike," says Tommy. "Get your ass home. You, Lilly, and I can sit down and discuss everything you're thinking about doing."

"You aren't listening, you never listen to me! It's a done deal. Jaclyn and me—we're doing it tomorrow. Our diving expedition to the *Andrea Doria* wreck leaves at 6:00 a.m. and we'll be gone for a week on the *Ocean Diver*. Al Adelman, the captain, is a good friend of Jaclyn's."

"The captain is a good friend of Jaclyn's? Oh, I see. Isn't November pretty late to be diving off Nantucket? What about all the storms this time of the year? Have you checked the weather reports?"

"No problem," says Mike. "The captain says it's as safe as diving in my backyard swimming pool."

"Please, let's talk before you go on this expedition," Tommy pleads.

"You want to know something else? Captain Al says that millions are still on the *Doria*. There's another safe like the one they raised back in the nineties. But locating and salvaging the GTO is my first priority. Have to go now. We have to prepare. Tonight Captain Al is hosting a dinner at Ron's Crabby Cowboy Café. He says those pearl oysters they serve are supposed be the best in the world! Oh, yes, I almost forgot. He's invited someone who has actually *seen* the GTO inside the *Andrea Doria*! Take care, Grimaldi. Will call you next week, buddy, and don't worry about me. I'll be just fine!"

"Bender, wait!" Tommy hears a beep. "That's it. He's gone." Tommy slams his fist on the armrest of the sofa, then places his forearms on his knees. He leans forward and says, "My God, what in hell has Bender gotten himself into?"

## November 2, 2008, Sunday

All night long Tommy sweats blood. He agonizes over the kind of danger Mike may encounter. He can't help but think that things just don't add up. Early in the morning he lumbers downstairs to the TV room. Rebecca is already there sitting upright in the recliner, her feet firmly on the floor, her hands locked together, and an expression of absolute fear on her face.

"Mike's walking into an ambush," she says. "I'm sure of it!"

"I know," Tommy agrees. "I've been stewing about it all night long."

"What bothers you most?" she asks.

"His reckless decision making! My best friend getting married without telling me, to a woman he has only known for a few weeks. If I could get my hands on him, I'd shake him until his teeth rattle!"

"And no prenuptial?" Rebecca says. "We need to check this woman out."

"The damage is already done, Rebecca. If he isn't going to listen to us, the game's over. She's got him figured out and has pushed all the right buttons."

"It doesn't take a shrink to figure him out," she remarks. "His face is like an open book, it leaves nothing to the imagination."

"What concerns you the most about Jaclyn?" Tommy asks.

"I think she's a highly skilled con artist. I felt like a Mack truck hit me when you told me about the picture of Rick and Jaclyn at Lake Placid. She smells dollar signs. Also, you'd have to be crazy to dive that area of the North Atlantic at this time of the year. It's always cold and stormy. Everyone knows that! The captain making light of it bothers me a whole lot."

"Hmm . . . good old Captain Al," Tommy muses. "In Toronto Jaclyn mentioned her former boyfriend is running a dive business in Montauk."

"And someone really saw the GTO inside the *Andrea Doria*?" Rebecca scoffs. "C'mon, I saw Noah's Ark once, too!"

"Rebecca, I'm about ready to panic. If Mike doesn't return to the surface after a dive, she stands to inherit around $50 million."

"Call him back, Tommy. Call him right now."

"It's four in the morning, so he'll probably ignore the call."

"Then keep calling until he answers!" Rebecca urges.

After several rings, Mike answers. "Now what the hell do you want, Grimaldi?"

The signal is weak so Tommy talks fast. "You're up and about—good!"

"Yeah, I'm up!" Mike says with an angry voice. "We're walking out the door now."

"Bender, listen to me. It's a setup. Get the hell out of there! Tell them you're going for a short walk, then call a cab and leave . . . NOW!" Tommy hears static indicating an unclear connection. "Bender!" he hollers.

"Stop yelling, will you? You asked if we're set up? Yes, we're almost set up, not quite, though. Why the hell does that matter to you, anyway?"

"No, I said, 'it's a setup.' Your life is at risk!" More static obscures the call and it's dropped. "Son of a bitch!" Tommy cries out.

"Call him back right away," Rebecca shouts. "Hurry before they leave!"

"It's ringing," he says. "C'mon Bender, answer your damn phone." Tommy grits his teeth. A look of desperation blankets his face. He grimaces and tries again.

"Cell towers are scarce around there," Rebecca notes. "Once they get out on the water, forget it. The only communication they'll have is their VHF radio."

"It dropped again. It's not going to work. Now what?"

"Try again. We have to convince him, Tommy!"

Tommy tries five more times. "It's no use."

"We can try to contact their marine radio by calling the Coast Guard."

"They'd ignore it. Not only that, what the hell would we say?" Tommy points out.

"We need to call the police," Rebecca insists.

"And tell them what? No crime has been committed."

"What are we going to do then?" Rebecca groans.

"I'm calling Lilly," Tommy announces.

"Call Eaton, too. Get them both over here ASAP!"

After calling Lilly and Eaton, Tommy and Rebecca await their arrival restlessly. When Lilly finally arrives, she gets to work preparing breakfast while they wait for Eaton. Later, Eaton arrives in his Chrysler van with a steel lift gate and electric powered wheelchair. The threatening possibility that Mike will be devoured by the North Atlantic trying to locate the GTO on the *Andrea Doria* has them all on edge. As they eat, they attempt to sort out the details.

"It's about a hundred miles to the *Andrea Doria* wreck from Montauk, about an eight to ten-hour boat trip," Eaton says. "Of course, everything depends on the weather, and this time of the year the weather is unpredictable, but usually very bad in that area."

"I'll check the Northern Atlantic Weather Satellite on my phone," Rebecca says.

"The *Andrea Doria* is about fifty miles south of Nantucket Island," Eaton explains. "Do you know that the *Stockholm* was lodged in her starboard side for several minutes, like a cork in a bottle? When it pulled away a teenage girl from the *Doria* was on the *Stockholm*'s crushed bow. She actually survived. They called her the 'miracle girl.'"

"We're going to need more than a miracle to figure out how to handle this situation," Tommy grimaces. He's noticeably on the verge of panic. "I can't eat, I can't think, and I can't relax knowing my best friend might be murdered."

"Okay," Rebecca says as she reads the Atlantic offshore marine forecasts. "It shows strong wind warnings—thirty to forty knots veering northwesterly to sixty to eighty knots by tomorrow."

Eaton shrugs his shoulders. "The boat can handle it, but I sure as hell wouldn't want to be diving in that. Not unless I was a sea cucumber. Do you know that those things were found seven miles down at the bottom of the Marianas Trench?"

"You're a real encyclopedia, aren't you?" Lilly remarks with a degree of rankle.

Eaton looks at Lilly and smiles broadly. "It's all part of the territory, sweetie," he replies.

"I'm not your sweetie," Lilly shoots back with a frown, though the twinkle in her eye is impossible to hide.

Eaton gives her a sly, devious look. "Sorry. Just adding a little mirth to the situation, that's all."

"People need to work very hard to gain *my* affections. A 'little mirth' won't cut it! But it's okay if you try harder."

"Well okay, sweet—I mean Lil!" Eaton smiles and winks at Lilly.

"Listen," Tommy says, "if anything happens to Mike, they'll just blame it on the weather."

"Believe me," Eaton points out, "there's plenty of danger out there without needing to blame an accident on the weather. Twelve people bought the farm diving the *Doria* wreck, and they were all experienced divers. If Mike were lost during the dive, no one would question it. They'd just chalk it up to another *Andrea Doria* diving casualty, that's all."

"Yes, I know there are plenty of excuses to commit murder out there," Tommy mutters.

"Listen Tommy," Eaton replies, "I don't know where to begin, but let me ask you this. Did Mike ever investigate the reason for his father's accident?"

"Strange that you would ask. Everything was blamed on the weather," Tommy answers.

"The weather again . . . hmm," Eaton pauses. He places the bowl of his bulldog pipe deep inside a tobacco pouch and scoops with his index finger. A cherry cavendish aroma fills the room. "Nothing like the scent of Admiral's Choice."

"Yeah, if you like the smell of cow dung," Lilly retorts.

"Lilly, mind your manners!" Tommy chides, finally laughing.

"Just tell me who the hell this Jaclyn woman is anyway, will you?" Lilly asks with obvious agitation. "I know Mike can be naïve, but I have trouble believing he could get sucked in this badly."

"Jaclyn Le Harve," Eaton replies. "She's a saleswoman at the Toronto Ferrari dealership. Of course, she's been a saleswoman at several other Ferrari dealerships, too."

"She fits the bill and can sell the goods, that's for sure," Tommy adds.

"She's a rather conspicuous member of the Ferrari Club, too," Eaton notes. "I've seen her and her husband at several club events."

"Wait a minute," Tommy interrupts. "Her husband?"

"Yes, I'm sure he is her husband. The guy doesn't say much when he's with her. He's like one of her appendages. He just hangs around. When he's not with her, he's behind a table selling dive trips to the *Andrea Doria*. He touts the missing safe, artifacts like china and jewelry, but mostly he talks up the Ferrari GTO, the prototype that's supposed to be in one of the watertight cargo containers on the *Doria*."

"She's a polygamist!" Rebecca asserts, as she looks over at Tommy. "Can't your friend do anything right?"

Tommy shakes his head in disbelief. "Rebecca, we don't know that for sure. We *do* know that this guy is operating the *Ocean Diver* and Mike could very well be his prey."

"And this Jaclyn woman—she's obsessed," Eaton adds. "At every one of our Ferrari club meetings she gives an impassioned presentation about raising money to salvage the GTO. Members are starting to complain about her, but she's pretty tight with the club president. She's an operator, I can tell you that for sure."

"So why would anyone want to give *her* money to raise the ship?" Rebecca asks.

"Good question," Eaton replies. "Every once in a while she picks up a hot lead. She uses her physical attributes quite well. You know what I'm saying."

"Her 'attributes'?" Lilly asks.

"You can add 'seductive' to 'attributes,'" Eaton replies. "She met Mike's dad at one of those meetings. I think she sold him a few cars, too. Then they started to show up together at all the shows."

"Seductive is the perfect word," Tommy agrees. "The woman is definitely seductive!"

Eaton lights his pipe with a compact torch lighter. "Oh, and another thing. She confronted me at a recent show after I wrote the *Prancing Horse* article. She thought it was wrong for me to draw attention to Antonio and the GTO. When I asked her why, she said that finding out what really happened to the GTO would hurt many people. When I asked her to explain, she walked away with the angriest look on her face."

"Do you think she's dangerous?" Lilly asks.

"Dangerous? If you're asking me if I think she would do *anything* to sell GTO dive trips, I would have to say yes, although I can't say if there was any foul play involved in Rick Bender's accident. She didn't stand to gain anything, unless they had a major argument and she got pissed off at him and wanted revenge. Maybe she asked him for money and he refused. I have my suspicions that she's the one behind the threatening phone calls I've received, and I can't help but think she also had something to do with my accident at Daytona. I can't prove it, but I'd bet on it! She's definitely hiding something."

"Well then," Tommy says firmly, "let's put it all together. Couple your suspicions with the fact that she eloped with Mike without a prenup and then he deposited $15 million in some bank in Bridgehampton—it's enough for me. I shudder when I think of Mike being with that woman in dangerous weather on the North Atlantic. We have to come up with something and fast!"

# 14

# Find the GTO!

**The North Atlantic, South of Nantucket Island**

*November 2, 2008, Late Sunday Afternoon*

Towering walls of water driven by powerful winds slam the bow of the *Ocean Diver*, the fifty-foot dive boat owned by Captain Al Adelman, a certified dive master and master dive instructor. From his enclosed pilothouse, Adelman is able to skillfully maintain forward momentum with enough power to steer the vessel through the turbulent sea. He keeps the bow pointed into the waves, since one massive wave striking its side could capsize and sink it. Nearly thirty years of storm experience in the North Atlantic has taught him well.

In the heated cabin below, Mike and Jaclyn are standing up hanging on to a support pole with both hands, trying to maintain their balance as the boat climbs and plunges through the steep canyons of the sea. The Velcro on their life jackets is fastened so tightly they strain to inhale. Two crewmembers in raincoats are seated outside on the u-shaped gear-donning bench located on the large stern platform. The torrential rain and violent wind whip their raincoats, yet they seem unperturbed by the turbulent conditions. The grim look on Mike's face has not changed since the early morning when they first encountered stormy weather. He is embarrassed to show his fear, but his shivering is not because the cabin is cold.

"I'm getting sick to my stomach," Mike moans. "I can't let go of the pole."

"Hang in there," Jaclyn urges. "If you get sick, we'll both be booted off the boat—without a life raft!"

"Really, I'm getting nauseous, Jackie," Mike says with a troubled voice. "I always thought I could handle rough water, but this is beyond brutal!"

"The North Atlantic can get vicious, especially this time of the year." Jaclyn places her hand on his shoulder. "Just think about the GTO and how excited you'll be when we find it. You'll be a famous celebrity, even more famous than Richard Branson! I can't wait to see the look on your face when we open the shipping container. Won't that be sensational?"

Jaclyn's sales pitch is not as effective as she thought it would be. Not even an inspiring pep talk from her can calm Mike's queasiness.

"That's if I survive," he says, "which at the moment, I seriously doubt. Jackie, why the hell didn't you tell me about how bad the weather could be?"

"Calm down, Mike, we have an experienced captain and this boat can handle bad weather very well. I've told you that several times already."

"Tell it to my stomach!" Mike groans. Then he looks up at the charcoal sky and shakes his head. "I sure as hell don't want to be in this stuff at night. What are we going to do?"

"The only thing we *can* do—ride it out. Do you have any other suggestions?"

"Yeah, let's go home!"

"C'mon, Mike, you don't mean that. It would be more dangerous to turn back now. Anyway, we're only a few miles from the wreck, just relax!"

The *Ocean Diver* is equipped with all the latest safety devices: chart plotters, GPS, sonar, radar, VHF radios, first aid kits, life jackets, flares, and a six-person life raft. The large cabin area has v-berth bunks for six people, a head with a shower, and a small galley area, which has a microwave, stove, and refrigerator. For Mike, it doesn't matter much; even air bags and antilock brakes wouldn't ease his tension.

Jaclyn steps away from the pole. "I'm going up with Al to check on things. You stay here, I'll be right back."

She walks up the stairs to the pilothouse where Al is navigating the vessel and sits next to him on the large bench seat. Both synchronize their body movements to the gyrations of the boat as if they have done it hundreds of times before.

"I'm getting concerned about our passenger," Jaclyn says. "He's really wimping out on me. I thought he was a pretty macho guy, but now I'm wondering if he's going to choke when it comes time to dive."

"Everyone you bring out on the boat is a damn wimp!" says Al. "You need to improve your selection process. Next time, listen to me when I tell you it's too dangerous to travel out here this time of the year. Why I allowed you to talk me into this trip, I'll never know!"

Dressed in jeans and a blue windbreaker, Adelman is a middle-aged man of medium build. Not more than five foot eight inches, his salt-and-pepper hair is curly and tight, as if the top of his head is full of round knots. The shallow wrinkles that cover his tan face are more from sun and wind exposure than from aging. His muscular physique is about what one would expect of a dive boat captain, someone who needs stamina to maneuver his vessel in stormy seas and dive the wrecks of the North Atlantic. Adelman is known for his ruggedness and his skill. Even with all the instrumentation, it takes great physical endurance to navigate a boat this size through a storm of this magnitude.

In 1981, in his early twenties, he was selected as a crewmember when department store magnate Peter Gimbel led an expedition to the *Andrea Doria* wreck using a diving bell and saturation diving techniques. Divers cut away a 28-foot entrance door to the first class foyer lounge. Their goal was to raise the purser's safe, which was purported to hold millions of dollars in valuables. The opening of the safe was a major television event, but it only yielded a few hundred dollars. The hole cut in the side of the ship became known as "Gimbel's Hole," and was the main gateway for divers entering the *Andrea Doria* in search of artifacts—until recently when a portion of the front bow collapsed.

Adelman pushes the throttle forward to gain speed to climb over another wave crest.

"We've had too many failures," he says. "After this I'm done. Sooner or later, someone's going to catch on. Do you hear me, Jackie? I'm done!"

"Things are different now—way different," Jaclyn responds firmly. "You're forgetting about the large opening now in the bow. It's a new ballgame! We'll have access to Decks B and C, both forward and aft. We can advertise that and people will buy in."

"You are on notice, Jackie. This is the last time. I'm shutting down the operation permanently. I've had enough! You're going to have to find yourself someone else." Captain Al stiffens his arm on the wheel as the *Ocean Diver* descends down another large swell.

"Look, Al," she says, "we both know that going into Gimbel's leads through too many blind alleys. It's always been unproductive and discouraging. We walk a few hundred feet and the silt and mud make visibility impossible, and then they give up and want to return to the boat."

"But, that's what you want, you already have their money! It's really starting to bother me. Don't you feel any responsibility or guilt?"

"Hell no! Having the bow open will only create more business for us." Jaclyn stands up and props her elbows on the ledge under the salon windows. "This time will be very different," she smiles. "Anyway, we've had *some* success diving the wreck. Remember when we discovered the wine cellar? The dinner china and wine bottles look terrific on display in my china cabinet." The boat lurches down another trough.

"Maybe we'll find the other safe this time," Captain Al says. "That'd be a real jackpot. Regardless of what we find, this will be our last expedition to the wreck."

"So be it! But Al, listen to me, with the $15 million that my new husband deposited in my account, we've already hit the jackpot."

"And that 'new husband' scam you are operating really pisses me off!" Al retorts.

"Don't complain, Al. That'll buy you your own boat—it will be the best ship in Montauk harbor. After all our trips, you've earned it!"

Jaclyn turns and staggers toward the stairs as the ship sways. She never anticipated Al's abrupt reversal or his ultimatum regarding future trips. But then, he has vacillated before and all it required was a few martinis and a hot tub to change his mind. Yet, somehow, she thinks this time is different.

As dusk turns to darkness, the boat's engines throttle down and they arrive at the site where the wreck of the *Andrea Doria* lies 240 feet below in ghostly silence. Although slowed considerably by the rough seas, they've been traveling for almost nine hours and are weary from all the turbulence. Moderate winds allow them to open a few portholes. The waves oscillating along the sides of the boat pacify and soothe, even though the late evening air is a bit chilly

Captain Al still has work to do. Since the three moorings that are usually on the surface are gone, Al wants to hook onto the wreck so the North Atlantic drift won't move his boat during the night. After one hour and four passes over the hull, using his expert seamanship, Al latches the white nylon anchor line to the top of the wreck at the stern. It is several hundred feet away from their ultimate dive destination, but Captain Al wants to swim the entire length of the wreck, from the propellers to bow.

Crewmates and brothers, Craig and Sean Holloway, throw down an umbilical line to the front of wreck, then dive down and secure both lines. After they return to the surface, Captain Al turns on the masthead lights so other boats will see him anchored. Then he shuts down the engines and turns off the running lights.

It's midnight as they gather around the cabin dining table adjacent to the galley. With the engine noise gone, an uncommon silence fills the cabin. In the distance, they can see running lights of freighters. The major international shipping lanes have their usual traffic, the same lanes navigated by the *Stockholm* and the *Andrea Doria* before their fateful collision.

"Good weather news for tomorrow!" Al says as he descends the stairs from the pilothouse. "Supposed to be only a light chop with temperatures in the low fifties."

Al opens the refrigerator, serving baloney sandwiches with one quart of water to each person at the table. "This isn't the greatest combination," he says. "I want you to be fully hydrated when we dive. In the morning, I'll have you drink two more quarts before the dive."

"How can I be hydrated if I'm up all night peeing?" Mike asks curtly.

"Just drink the water and don't ask so many questions," Captain Al responds.

"That's fine," Jaclyn says with a big grin. "Tomorrow we'll have champagne!"

"I'm just glad as hell the goddam trip is over," Mike exclaims. "What's our plan for tomorrow?"

"Eggs at six o'clock, two more quarts of water, a recap of the diving instructions, and equipment checks. Then we dive." Al gets up from the table stretching and yawns. "I'm hitting the rack," he says. "I suggest you all do the same. Believe me, you'll need every ounce of energy you have for tomorrow's dive."

After Mike kisses Jaclyn goodnight, he wastes no time dropping his tired body on his v-bunk. He peers out the side porthole and sees ship lights moving in the darkness, as if they were suspended in midair. He watches as they converge from opposite directions.

*What a horrific collision it must have been between the Stockholm and the Andrea Doria. The passengers must have been petrified!* he thinks. Unable to see land, at the complete mercy of the North Atlantic, and not knowing if the ship would sink at any moment must have been a terrifying experience. While 51 people were killed, fortunately 1,700 were rescued. It was the greatest sea rescue in history. Once the fog lifted, the passengers must have seen the same evening sky beset with the same shining stars. They blink like marker lights, as though communicating in Morse code.

The *Andrea Doria* lies on its starboard side 240 feet below the surface. When Mike realizes its uppermost point is only 160 feet beneath his bunk, half the length of a football field, the tragedy becomes even more close and personal. In his prime, Mike could run the entire football field in ten seconds. The dive down will take about fifteen minutes. They plan to spend around an hour on the wreck, and it will be more exhausting than eight hours of work on land.

Mike is painfully aware divers have died inside the wreck. He rolls over on his side and sees Jaclyn in the bunk in front of him and Captain Al, Craig, and Sean against the wall on the other side of the cabin. His eyes scan the dive gear hanging in the cabin. Behind him is a long, gray object that looks like a torpedo tube from a WWII submarine. Two notebook computers are resting on its top. He looks more closely. "Hyperbaric Chamber" is written on the side. He feels a degree of solace. *Having a portable decompression chamber on board is good insurance—just in case.*

As his eyes get heavy, he becomes nostalgic. His life has changed so much over the last couple of weeks. It feels funny, although not in a comical sense, more in a curious or strange way. He recalls his strong resolve when he first met Jaclyn at the Ferrari dealership. *I had to possess this woman,* he thinks to himself. *I thought she'd be a perfect complement to my new lifestyle. Things have sure changed.*

He feels his abdominal muscles tighten and his heart pound. He sits up on the edge of his bunk. *It's indigestion, because dinner was so late,* he assures himself. As he wipes the perspiration from his forehead, he can't help but notice how much his hand is trembling. *The kids . . . did I really need to go and get myself fired?* The lump in his stomach feels bigger. It seems like light-years ago when he and Tommy were rollicking around town in the F40. *I miss my good buddy. I miss Lilly, too. All right, go to sleep Bender!*

## November 3, 2008, Monday

At the crack of dawn, a cowbell clangs so loudly Mike jumps up from his bunk. Acclimating his mind to the unfamiliar surroundings takes him some time. Captain Al's wake-up routine annoys him. A simple alarm clock would do but *there's no question who's captain of this ship. I just hope this guy knows what he is doing underwater!*

After breakfast, Captain Al calls the group together for a briefing. He'll lead the dive down to the *Andrea Doria*. Mike and Jaclyn will follow. Craig and Sean, both certified divers, will provide surface support on the large stern platform. Craig will be "dive ready" just in case any one of the three divers runs into trouble.

"Let's do a quick review of what we learned last week." Captain Al is standing next to an easel with a long white flipchart with a blueprint of the inside of the *Andrea Doria* wreck. He has a pointer in his right hand. The others are seated on the u-shaped bench on the open stern.

"Well, first of all, the ship is big, longer than two football fields. When you see it for the first time, you will be amazed by its size, Mike. It still looks like a ship, not a pile of indistinct debris. Okay, here are her guts. This is Gimbel's Hole." He points to the arrow on his blueprint about 180 feet down on the hull just below the Belvedere deck.

"Stay the hell away from it!" Captain Al continues. "As soon as you start walking inside the wreck, the swirling mud and silt in the water is like a blinding snowstorm. I don't want you going in there, under any circumstances, and getting lost in the dark rooms and corridors. The sharp twisted metal can cut your breathing lines, then you're dead! Divers have lost their lives trying to match a saucer with a teacup. Anyway, all the china and collectible stuff is mostly gone. Go right to the break in the bow and follow me into the lower decks. The watertight shipping containers holding the GTO and the Norseman should be in cargo hold one and two on Deck C right here." Al points to the bottom front section of the ship, where the bow is partially collapsed.

"We'll be the first divers in there," Al says. "Let's hope the cargo holds haven't caved in yet. We won't know that until we get inside. As I mentioned before, Deck C has recently become accessible because the bow has rolled slowly onto its keel and the break is much wider now. So let's take advantage of it! In the near future, the whole ship might implode and we may never have another chance. Another thing . . . underwater weather around the ship can change suddenly from clear and calm to a ripping current filled with sediment. The sediment can lacerate your body and you can bleed to death in minutes. So if you notice any change in the current, go for the granny line and wait there for me. Do not, I repeat, do not attempt to return to the *Ocean Diver* without me! We have a staged decompression routine that is absolutely essential to avoid getting the bends. There are also fishing nets draped all over the hull, but what's even more dangerous is the invisible web of tough monofilament fishing lines. Your fins and tanks can easily get tangled up in them. If you get caught in them, don't use your knife. Use the nail clippers I placed in your tool belts."

Mike isn't afraid of the dive itself. Bouncing on the waves getting there was much more daunting. Having dived the Bermuda Triangle wrecks with his father gives him confidence. He knows all about nitrogen narcosis. Jacques Cousteau called this physiological phenomenon "the rapture of the deep." Mike's father compared it to having too many martinis, a state of intoxication, something Mike could relate to when he was in college. But when that happens at depths below a hundred feet, it can have deadly consequences.

Diving the *Andrea Doria* requires a different gas mixture. In place of some of the nitrogen normally breathed by divers, Captain Al requires the use of other breathing gas mixtures containing helium such as trimix and heliox. Helium has no narcotic effect, but plenty of nitrogen is still present in the tank.

"Now listen to me," Captain Al says forcefully. "When you arrive at the wreck, pay attention to your state of mind. If your eyes can't focus, or you experience feelings of euphoria or claustrophobia, stop swimming. Concentrate totally on your breathing. If that doesn't work, rise to a more shallow depth. Like everything you do down there, do it damn slow! The longer you experience those symptoms, the more difficult it will be to recover and make the decisions necessary to save your ass. For most of the twelve people that died down there, they waited too damn long. Some suffered decompression sickness from ascending too fast, and then they went into cardiac arrest. So pay attention to what I am telling you. Don't tempt fate!" Jaclyn and Mike look at each other and nod.

"I've dived with Jackie before," says Al, "so she knows the routine. Mike, you are in great shape. Have faith in your abilities, but follow my lead, okay?"

Excitement glows on Mike's face. "I'll be right behind you," he says. "I'm ready to go!"

"Okay, then. Any questions?"

"Tell me one more time how we can identify the shipping container with the GTO in it," Mike says with lust in his eyes.

"Nine passenger cars were placed in the garage section on Deck B," Captain Al explains. "The GTO and the Norseman were very special and treated differently. Two watertight metal containers, one holding the GTO and the other holding the Chrysler Norseman, were placed in two separate cargo holds. They should be right about here." Captain Al points to the forward Deck C on the starboard side.

"Before the collapse of the bow," he continues, "this area was inaccessible. I think we can get in there now. While these cargo holds were spared the brunt of the collision, much of the internal superstructure has collapsed, so you will find a pretty large debris field. I'm sure the containers suffer from corrosion with barnacles and decay on the outside. The cars inside should be unmolested, especially since the containers were specially made to be waterproof. Strong, high-grade steel cargo chains were also used to restrain the cars. Jaclyn showed me the pictures of the GTO being loaded.

One picture shows the GTO being lowered by crane onto the deck. Then it was lowered to Deck C into the shipping container by a cargo elevator."

Captain Al pulls his flipchart closer. "Here is Deck C," he says, pointing to a spot adjacent to the chapel. "Now with the bow opened by the break, we should be able to locate the containers."

"How do we tell them apart?" Mike asks.

"Good question, Mike. If we find the two containers in that area, we find the GTO! We also find the Norseman. We can recover both cars."

"That works for me!" Mike says.

"I'll take the Berlinetta!" Jaclyn exclaims.

"Okay. Any other questions?" Captain Al pauses and looks at each one of them.

"What about sharks?" Mike asks tentatively.

"What about them?" Captain Al responds.

"What if one bites me?"

"If a shark bites you, you're dead. It's that simple."

"Oh, I was just asking," Mike says, as he winces in make-believe pain.

# 15

# Andrea Doria Dive

### North Atlantic, Andrea Doria Wreck
*November 3, 2008, Monday Morning*

Mike, Jaclyn, and Captain Al are fully equipped. In addition to their regulators, air hoses, swim fins, and swim masks, each has two pressure and depth gauges, two bright yellow scuba tanks, one emergency or "bail-out" tank, a buoyancy compensator device, and an inflatable lift bag. They also have tool belts with assorted chisels and hammers to remove barnacle-like sediment. Fifty-watt lights are secured to their chest harnesses. Visibility will vary depending on how much silt they stir up.

It's cold. While summertime water temperatures are in the mid-forties, today the temperatures are in the mid-thirties. Unlike the first *Andrea Doria* divers who shivered in quarter-inch wetsuits, Captain Al provides dry suits for much improved insulation against the icy chill of the November water.

During their descent down the anchor line, their breathing is slow, deep, and relaxed. Rapid breathing can overwork their high-performance regulators. Shallow breaths can cause a buildup of carbon dioxide in their systems, which can lead to panic. Also, to

169

ensure against embolism—when air bubbles escape into the chest cavity from the lungs—they never hold their breath. Captain Al closely monitors their movements, especially their rate of breathing. As the current tugs at them, their eyes strain through the dark waters to catch a glimpse of their destination. Soon they see shadows and an ominous dark shape. Mike reads his depth gauge at 150 feet. When the back of the wreck appears in his light beam, the first thing he sees is the sixteen-foot, brass-coated propellers. They look like magnified outboard motor props. His heart pounds. He feels like a tiny insect next to the giant, rust infested blades.

Captain Al motions them to follow him. They begin to swim the 697 feet to the bow. Mike is startled by the sheer size of the ship. There is so much to take in. It somehow still looks majestic, even though along the base of the ship is a long pile of rubble. It is surprising to see how much the wreck has fallen apart. Yet strangely, as they pass the Promenade deck and the three swimming pools on the Boat, Lido, and Sun decks, Mike is glad to see all their diving boards still in place. As they swim side-by-side in the direction of the bow, they see thickets of overgrown anemones encrusted on the portholes where the windows used to be. Rust has assaulted anything metal. Mike is in absolute awe. *What an incredible adventure!* he thinks to himself. *This has to be the most exciting experience of my life. Just wait till Tommy finds out what we've discovered.*

Upon reaching the open break in the bow, ocean currents roar around them. They shine their lights directly into the break, hoping to see a way forward. It merely magnifies the sediment swirling in the water, restricting their visibility to around twenty feet. When they turn off their lights, they see nothing but squalid blackness. They slow their pace to a crawl. Captain Al secures two strobe lights to the umbilical line dropped by the crewmates above on the *Ocean Diver*. Then each diver unclips their two smaller decompression tanks and ties them on the same line. They will need them when it's time to ascend.

With the strobes on, the area around the break becomes more distinct. Mike and Jaclyn follow Captain Al to the open area of the bow, attempting to circumvent the littered debris piled high below them. They carefully swim for about a hundred feet through the mouth into the twisted wreckage and rotted-out bulkheads.

Remembering Captain Al's blueprint, Mike realizes they must have entered the forward portion of Deck C. He sees a broken, contorted, and deeply sloped concrete floor beneath them. It seems out of place amid the crumpled passenger cabins it has crushed on both sides. Mike points to a pulverized hunk of metal in the corner of the floor. *My God, that's a mangled gantry crane. It's huge! Have the floor and the crane fallen from Deck B above them?* Captain Al points to the bottom of the slope, about fifty yards away. All three of them swim down closer to the floor. What they see next looks more like the aftermath of a tsunami than a shipwreck. Ruins scatter the bottom corner of the floor with dissimilar piles of debris rising to peaks spaced about ten feet apart. It's like Mother Nature decided to "rake the lawn" and place the rubble into hundreds of organized stacks.

As they slowly meander through the angular fragments of masonry, Mike shines his light on the far end of the slope. His eyes nearly bulge out of his swim mask and his breathing accelerates. Captain Al moves closer to him. He slaps his shoulders and motions him to slow it down. Piles of iron and steel loom in front of him. A veritable automobile recycling center comes to mind. Rusted hubcaps, headlights, broken mirrors, exposed engines, and transmissions, all barely discernable, are resting in one big hulk in the deepest corner of the floor. *We are on the garage floor! Nine cars were in the garage when the ship sank.* Mike's heart races again. *We must be getting closer to the containers!*

Suddenly, Mike's breathing becomes labored. Captain Al warned him of this. He experienced it one other time while diving the wrecks in Bermuda with his father. His ears start to ring with intensity. With each exhale, he hears bubbles and then a popping sound. As the sounds get louder and more rhythmic, they become mesmerizing. It is easy to become disoriented in the mire of blackness and silt. His entire body wants to drift to the bottom, lie on the rubble, and fall into a deep sleep. *No, this isn't happening! Deep-water blackout! I can't lose mental control. Sharpen your focus, Bender. Think about the GTO. We're so close. Don't blow it now! Think about how it will be when it's salvaged, when the whole world will want to see the most valuable car ever made!*

Dizziness forces him to drop to his knees. His eyes close. He tries to control his breathing and refocus on the task, their ultimate goal. Captain Al motions to him not to move. Jaclyn kneels next to him. She points to the surface. Captain Al shakes his head. "Not now," his lips say through his mask. Mike lowers his head and concentrates. Sixty seconds later, his head begins to clear. He gives them a thumbs-up signal.

They move deeper inside the wreck. A shadowy outline of what appears to have been a double door entranceway comes into view. Captain Al folds his hands together as if he is praying. Mike concludes it must be the chapel. They swim with short, gentle kicks to avoid stirring up the silt and obscuring their path forward. They proceed through the passageway into the chapel, staying low in the corridor to avoid the dangerous sharp metal edges of cables strewn above them.

Mike points to the crude remnants of an altar with a twisted kneeler on the floor and a battered metal crucifix embedded in a nearby wall. He lifts his index finger signaling them to "wait a minute" and kneels to say a prayer. When his knees touch the dilapidated, rot-infested kneeler, it collapses and creates a blizzard of sediment, making any kind of visibility impossible, with or without lights. Ironically, he can still see a haunting silhouette of the crucifix, and when he attempts to move closer to it, he stumbles on a protruding pipe on the floor and, weighed down by his heavy gear, falls twelve feet downward into a canyon cushioned by a thick bed of muddy grime. Next to him is a ten-foot high slab of steel with about twenty corrugated grooves facing him. The length extends twenty feet toward the rear of the ship. *An automobile shipping container,* Mike concludes, *like those used by father for shipping and receiving cars from Europe.*

Despite being on the verge of uncontrollable jubilation, he remembers to maintain his "cool" and his breathing remains even. Identification marks or labels will confirm his belief. *But where are they?* Side labels have worn off decades ago, but Mike remembers when he and his father picked up cars shipped from Italy at the Port of Newark how he identified the contents by their customary foot-high white letters stamped on the lower left near the access door. *Could it be possible those white letters are still legible?* He would only need to recognize one or maybe two letters side-by-side.

Mike maneuvers himself gingerly to the lower left side of the container, removes a chisel and hammer from his tool belt, and carefully begins to scrape off some crust until he reaches flat metal. He is astonished at the condition of the metal. It is only slightly rusted as if the barnacles acted as some kind of preservative. Chipping away near the bottom, he sees significantly faded white letters. His adrenalin skyrockets. The first letter he sees is an "I." *It can't spell "Ferrari" because no letters are before it.* He continues to gently scrape. The next two letters are "O" and "R." *Wait a minute. The "I" must be a "T." Torino! Oh, but both the Norseman and the GTO were designed and manufactured in Torino.* Mike's determination intensifies.

When he begins to scrape directly above "Torino," he sees more withered letters. He notices an image of a heart with a crown resting on top. He shines his flashlight on it. Faded letters "G H I A" appear. *Ghia! Carrozzeria Ghia. Of course, the company that designed the Norseman!*

Mike feels like doing one of his characteristic somersaults that he use to do with his physical education students, but he knows better. *Now I have to locate the GTO.* His eyes glow with excitement as they gloss over the immediate area. There are no more containers, at least not here. Before he searches for a way out, he checks his metering equipment. He has only forty-five minutes left in his tanks. He has to find Jaclyn and the captain. Suddenly, a powerful current wallops him. He falls backward. Silt congests the water again like too much confetti at a wedding. As he positions his hands to get up, he feels a groove in the floor. He leans forward to his knees, groping the surface and poking around for more corrugated grooves.

*Holy shit, I'm standing on another container!* The left side is flat up against a wall. *This has got to be the GTO! What else could it be?* He checks his gauges again, then locks in the coordinates on his GPS wristband. He needs to swim to the umbilical line and hook into a decompression tank. The ascent needs to be staged, and will take one hour. He keeps telling himself not to panic as he swims up through the opening from which he fell. He surveys the area for any sign of Jaclyn or Captain Al. When he sees none, he begins to swim toward the break in the bow section, the place where they entered about an hour ago.

Still, he sees no one. The prevailing currents have kept the passageway relatively clear of sediment, and using his compass and GPS, he has no problem with his bearings. All is well until he feels a familiar intoxication returning. *No! Not now. Not while I'm alone!* His mind nearly anesthetized, his body feels like an empty shell in a deep abyss. He tells himself, *Don't panic! Where the hell are they? Why did they leave me stranded?*

He breathes slowly, rhythmically, measuring each inhalation. He orders his mind to function as if it's some kind of telepathic device apart from his body. It's useless. He drops to his knees. A modicum of logic returns, just long enough for him to distinctly remember Captain Al saying not to try and ascend without him. He can die waiting for Captain Al or Jaclyn, or he can die attempting to rise to the surface alone. He has to choose. But now every breath is tired, heavy, and short; his world is a shapeless blur. He begins to hallucinate, then loses consciousness. A fast moving current sweeps him up then deposits him face down onto the debris field at the base of *Andrea Doria's* bow.

Three great whites gather above him and are swimming gracefully in tighter and tighter concentric formations. Every now and then one wanders deeper to probe the lifeless body resting near a pile of rubble.

# 16

# Mortal Threat

## Piombino, Italy

### *July 18–19, 1956, Wednesday and Thursday*

The day is cool, crisp, and sunny. Antonio parks the auto transporter near the Vista del Canale in the coastal town of Piombino on the west coast of Italy, a midway point between Genoa and Naples. A light meal at La Rocchetta is followed by a short phone call. Then he walks in a westerly direction toward the water's edge with the briefcase he received from the tall man in the black Citroen, his Polaroid in the other hand. Antonio sits down on a concrete bench on a wide balcony on the terrace of Piazza Bovio, directly above an outcropping of large gray rocks. Looking out on the Ligurian Sea, he takes in the stunning view of Elba Island, part of a group of islands known as the Tuscan Archipelago.

When he peers to the northern panorama, the day is so clear he can see the small island of Gorgona, the northernmost island in the archipelago. Antonio is well acquainted with Gorgona. Due to the intervention of his famous family, he spent the last two years of his prison sentence at the Gorgona Agricultural Penal Colony on grounds next to the Gorgona Abbey, an archaic Benedictine monastery. Despite having to work several hours each day on a farm, he was allowed to interact with area residents, including police officers and the few remaining Benedictine monks at the abbey. Antonio smiles as he recollects how he would secure permission from one of his police officer friends and spend several days in the abbey with Father Nicholas making wine and olive oil. They also worked in the greenhouse behind the villa harvesting rhubarb by candlelight, a practice that produces a sweeter, tenderer stalk. But the pièce de résistance was always the homemade rhubarb pie Antonio learned to make under Father Nicholas's tutelage. *It was good to see him last year at the Rome Grand Prix. He is a true friend.*

Antonio's thoughts are interrupted by a flyspeck on the northern horizon. In a few minutes, just southeast of Gorgona Island, the *Andrea Doria* comes into full view. Antonio is enraptured by her appearance. Even at a distance of several miles, the ship looks regal and proud, a floating palace in total harmony with the open ocean. Owing to favorable weather, Captain Piero Calamai will steer his vessel through the channel between Elba and Piombino, always a scenic delight for the passengers. Soon Antonio will have a picture-perfect view of the ship. He can't wait. His Polaroid is loaded with film and he is ready.

Antonio shields his eyes as the sun drops down closer to the peak of Monte Capanne, the highest mountain on Elba Island. He leans back, folding one leg over the other, and his thoughts turn to Catherine and Alessandro, his wife and young son.

Just then someone taps him on the shoulder. "Prototype 0000GT," a man says with a nervous voice that lacks cordiality.

Antonio turns his head so he can see the man and says, "Pininfarina number one."

"Okay. Do you have the briefcase?"

"Let me see some identification," Antonio says firmly. The man walks around the bench and sits next to Antonio.

He is a portly man with an officious, overzealous appearance. His tailored black business suit with matching tie seem incongruous with the informal surroundings. His slick brown hair has been professionally styled, giving it a wet, glossy look with a part down the middle.

He hands Antonio a small accordion file folder with the pockets tied together. "Everything is in the first and second pocket," he says.

Antonio extracts official looking papers from the first pocket and reads: Lorenzo Prinzi, *Directtore delle Operazioni, Autorita Portuale di Napoli.* Antonio looks at the man's face and compares it to the picture in the second pocket.

"So you're the one who makes all the decisions, the Manager of Operations at the Port Authority of Naples?" he asks.

"Well, that's why I'm here. I'm the man in charge. Did you expect one of my subordinates instead?" he asks in a sardonic tone. "Can I have the briefcase now—the key too, if you please? I'd like to get out of here before someone recognizes me."

Antonio hands him the briefcase and the key. At the same time, he wonders if he can really trust Lorenzo or anyone associated with Charone. Lorenzo carefully scans the area, making sure there are no onlookers. He inserts the key, opens the briefcase, and starts counting the money. Fifty wrapped piles of ten one hundred-dollar bills are evenly lined up in the briefcase.

"Looks like $50,000—all in American currency. Good!" he says after he finishes counting. "Don't come before dark. Everything will be ready. You have the envelope. You know where to go and who to see."

"I understand," Antonio nods.

Lorenzo stands, looks around, and lights up a cigarette. Antonio remains seated and notices a holster bulge on the side of his right hip. He turns and watches Lorenzo walk back toward the parking lot near the restaurant holding the briefcase.

When he turns back around, the sight of the *Andrea Doria* passing so closely before his eyes startles him. He quickly reaches for his Polaroid. *What a great picture against the backdrop of Elba Island.* He clicks the camera and quickly reloads the film. *My God, she is so graceful!* By the time he is ready for the second picture, the ship's stern passes by. Lifeguards sitting on their towers are the only inhabitants of the three heated swimming pools as passengers crowd the observation decks to have a close-up view of the enchanting scenery. Antonio leans back and watches the quiet energy of the great ship's white-water wake as it disappears into the Tuscan Archipelago. Then he hears waves crest on the shoreline. He remains there for the next hour, anxious to return to his thoughts of Catherine and Alessandro.

## Naples, Italy

It isn't easy driving a 35-foot auto transporter through Naples. In addition to trolleybuses, small cars and scooters congest the narrow streets. But Antonio isn't in a hurry. He'll need the cover of darkness to complete his mission and right now, it's too early to do anything except wait.

Antonio drives to the Port of Naples, then to the mooring location for passenger ships. He parks the transporter in a parking lot in front of the terminal and begins walking toward Maschio Angioino, a medieval castle in the heart of Naples. He feels dwarfed by the unmistakable shape of Vesuvius hovering on the horizon as he passes numerous cafés and ice cream parlors, finally arriving at the passenger terminal.

Antonio climbs the stairs to the passenger level and sits down in an observation lounge. He takes a free copy of the Naples newspaper *Il Mattino* from the information counter and begins reading the headlines. *Prince Rainier and Princess Grace Host President René Coty at a Reception in Monte Carlo.* He folds the paper and tosses it into a nearby trashcan. Then he remembers the envelope from Charone that he placed in his back pocket. He opens it and finds a typewritten letter. The first few paragraphs outline Antonio's instructions while in Naples. The last paragraph is a threat.

> I trusted you. You betrayed me. Your brother Rainier had to be assassinated for our plan to work. You knew that. You still went to INTERPOL. **If you fail me this time, your wife and son will be dead within twenty-four hours. But first I will subject them to unthinkable torture. You know I always do what I say.**

Antonio crumples the letter in his clenched fist and leans forward, placing both hands on his knees. He inhales deeply. His entire body shutters and shakes. *That bastard, he never said anything to me about my brother being assassinated! I had no choice. I had to go to INTERPOL.* At that moment he knew the meaning of the word anger: unadulterated, unfettered, abject anger. *If anything happens to them, I will kill myself. But first—Charone will pay!*

The *Andrea Doria* usually arrives at the Port of Naples around 9:00 p.m., the first leg of its voyage to America. Departure is the next day at noon. After a brief stop at Gibraltar, it will steam to New York City, arriving on Thursday morning, July 26.

Antonio stands and moves closer to a railing overlooking a vast diorama of maritime activity. The *Doria* sits a few miles out from port awaiting tugboats to carefully guide her in. She looks invincible surrounded by an aircraft carrier, three destroyers, and two submarines anchored nearby. It seems like the only reason the American Navy's Mediterranean fleet is outside the harbor is to protect the *Andrea Doria*.

Large overnight ferries unload passengers at the Molo Beverello
ferry port. All new *Andrea Doria* passengers will need to identify
their luggage with terminal customhouse personnel, verify the tags,
and retain the ID numbers for arrival in New York. Then their luggage will be transferred to the ship on a long conveyer belt.

It is 8:50 p.m. when the *Andrea Doria* is securely berthed, towering over a smaller white ship, the *Conte Biancamano*. It is taking Italian immigrants to South America. Both ships point toward
Mount Vesuvius, as though their destinations are the peak.

Antonio waits until all the new passengers board the ship and
virtually no one is around the wharf or on the pier. It's 12:30 a.m.
He heads for a small dockside cantina frequented primarily by dockworkers. Not far away is a loading and unloading quay for the *Andrea
Doria*. Antonio sits at the empty bar and orders a Bloody Mary.

"Extra Tabasco?" the bartender asks.

"No thanks," he answers. "Just give me three extra ripe limes."

The bartender gives him a thumbs-up and smiles.

"Glad you made it, Antonio," he says, and walks out from behind
the bar to shake Antonio's hand. "Okay. Bring your trailer to holding area twenty-five. It's right on the side—over there. See it?" He
points out the door to a small black brick building adjacent to a
gantry crane attached to an elevated rail system.

"I've had armed longshoremen guarding the area all day long,"
the bartender says. It is apparent that he is well pleased by his
performance.

"Thank you," Antonio responds. "I'm glad I'm working with people I can trust."

Two longshoremen with hard hats and safety vests direct Antonio
as he backs the transporter into the black brick building. Antonio is
somewhat relieved but not completely. Not yet. At the far end of the
building, the Ferrari Prototype GTO Berlinetta sits in resplendent

glory, like a racehorse that has just won the Triple Crown yet doesn't understand what all the fuss is about.

"That's a pretty nice sports car," says one of the longshoremen. "Ever since I was a kid, I've always loved Fiats."

Antonio laughs a little too loudly. It's been a stressful day. He isn't sure if the remark is a joke. He doesn't really care. He just wants to load up and get out of there. Once the car is strapped down inside the transporter and the rear gate closed and locked, Antonio makes an audible sigh of relief.

"One more thing," the bartender says. "The map. You almost left without it."

"Thanks very much for your assistance." Antonio places the map behind the sun visor.

"Don't mention it," the bartender says. "Thank *you!*"

Antonio smiles and nods. He is quite sure the "thank you" is sincere, even if it does come from the bottom of the bartender's wallet.

Antonio drives out of the building and merges into the northbound traffic on Spaccanapoli Street. It's very slow going on the narrow road, but because it's early morning no one's around. He'll be on the main highway soon, and on schedule for his last stop.

Antonio's mindset is now irreversible. Any second-guessing about betraying Il Commendatore vanished when he read Charone's malicious letter. He must do everything he can to save Catherine and Alessandro; even if means betraying Il Commendatore.

Antonio attempts to analyze the situation. *By the time Enzo discovers Luigi Chinetti hasn't received the car at his Manhattan garage, they will be safe. Then I can blame the theft on the Port of Naples dockworkers. Everyone knows they are corrupt as dirt. After all, Il Commendatore must have the Polaroids by now, so he has the evidence that I did my job in Genoa.*

The next day at noon, three large tugs pull the *Andrea Doria* to open water. Passengers crowd the port deck to wave goodbye to friends and relatives. Three long horn blasts blatantly announce her departure. A strong vibration on the ship indicates the powerful engines are coming to life. The seven-day voyage to New York City is underway. Soon, the tugs leave and return to port. One more horn blast concludes its farewell departure routine.

# 17

# Deadly Agreement

**Tommy's Apartment, Fairchester, New York**

*November 3, 2008, Monday Morning*

Eaton relights his pipe. Wisps of white smoke curl in the middle of the Tommy's kitchen table. The combination of pipe smoke and caffeine from four cups of coffee makes it impossible for Tommy to remain in his chair. He begins to nervously pace the kitchen floor.

"A gentleman would park the pipe!" Lilly says, as she fans the ribbons of smoke away from her face. "It's starting to look like a damn poker game in here."

Eaton smiles. "Sorry, sweetie." He takes out a nickel and forces it into the pipe bowl, extinguishing the burning tobacco.

Lilly frowns. "I've told you before, I am not your sweetie, but thanks for getting rid of that disgusting chimney."

"So tell me again," Tommy interjects, "what's the connection between this guy Charone and my grandfather?"

Eaton leans back in his chair. "Tommy, I've always been fascinated by your grandfather. He's becoming a top priority in my research. As much as he created many of his own problems, I have to admire his courage. I also feel sympathy for his predicament. I'm sure Antonio will go down in history as one of Monaco's most heroic figures."

"Huh . . . that's interesting. I can understand 'tragic,'" Tommy reflects. "I don't quite get the heroic part."

"Then let me explain some things to you. You grandfather saved the principality of Monaco. It's that simple. If it weren't for him, Prince Rainier would have been assassinated and who knows how many other family members would have been killed. The entire region would have been thrust into major turmoil."

"So what about this Charone character?" Tommy asks.

"First of all," Eaton answers, "he was the smartest and definitely the deadliest French operative that ever existed."

"He actually worked for the French government?" Rebecca asks.

"Initially, yes. He was involved with special ops, but he was mostly a rogue agent. Back in the fifties he founded the Charbonnerie Universelle, a French cloak-and-dagger society that was once a clandestine appendage of the French government. Unfortunately, he channeled his energies to overthrowing the Monaco government and took advantage of your grandfather's vulnerability."

"Monaco was also vulnerable back then," Rebecca explains. "Rainier used low business taxes to lure hundreds of French companies, private banks, and wealthy individuals to Monaco. France lost millions in tax revenue. It wasn't long before this little principality of Monaco was among the most financially successful countries in Europe."

"So why is that such a bad thing?" Tommy asks.

"Because Monaco's good fortune was at the expense of the French government," Rebecca replies.

"And that opened the door for Charone and his Charbonneries," Eaton adds.

"So what's all this have to do with my grandfather?" Tommy queries.

"Imagine you're Antonio Grimaldi," says Eaton. "Every day of your life you're in agony, longing for your wife and son, unable to afford money for an investigator, ostracized by the royal family, and humiliated throughout Europe. You save almost every cent you earn. It's never enough. Then, someone approaches you with an opportunity. He offers you a chance to find your wife and son. You have hope again. And you will do just about anything to make that happen."

"Pandora's box!" Lilly declares. "There has to be strings attached."

"Sure. But would you at least listen to an offer?" Eaton asks.

"Yeah, I guess I would," Lilly admits.

"So what was Charone's offer?" Tommy asks.

"He offered Antonio a chance to return to Monaco as PDG of a French corporation, that's the same as a CEO of an American corporation. That corporation would seize control of Monaco. Charone would chair the executive committee."

"How could Charone possibly finance such a takeover?" Tommy inquires.

"Charone secretly sold certificates of ownership to wealthy people all over the world," Eaton explains. "He retained 51 percent for control. Certificates could be transferred privately so no one, including the government, would know who owned the shares. This led to money laundering and other concealed business practices that adversely affected France's economy. People started to call Monaco 'a sunny place for shady people.' Charone agreed to start paying Antonio a million dollar stipend per year as soon as he said yes to his proposal. Under the circumstances, can you see how difficult that would have been for Antonio to refuse?"

"Yes, I suppose so," Rebecca replies. "What about the Grimaldis who were already in power in Monaco?"

"Charone claimed they would be unharmed and would continue as titular heads of state, without any real power."

"And Antonio didn't challenge that crap?" Lilly demands.

"He was a very desperate man," Eaton says. "All he ever really wanted was to be reunited with his wife and son."

"Sounds like a coup," Tommy remarks. "What happened? Why didn't it work?"

"Your grandfather!" Eaton taps a metal ashtray to remove the dead ashes from his pipe. He separates the stem and runs a pipe cleaner back and forth to clean it.

"Tommy," he finally says, "this is where everything comes to a screeching halt. Antonio blew the whistle on Charone, the Charbonneries, and the entire sinister plot. The grand scheme was exposed on the front page of *Le Canard Enchaîné*, France's popular investigative newspaper. However, INTERPOL was never able to prove anything conclusively, so Charone was never arrested."

"Don't tell me the bastard got off scot-free!" There's fire in Lilly's eyes.

"Not exactly," Eaton asserts. "Learning about Antonio's plan to foil the plot, Charone attempted to sell his certificates to a few of the entrepreneurs who were anxious to buy him out and gain control of the project. But having been made aware of Antonio's intentions in the nick of time, they refused and tried to unload their own certificates. After the article was published, the certificates owned by Charone and his cohorts were worthless. Charone lost everything. Guess who he blamed for the collapse of his plan and the loss of his fortune?"

"Antonio, of course," Rebecca states with absolute certainty. "So that's the reason he accused Antonio of negligence at the Mille Miglia and had Giancarlo murdered—revenge! It always comes down to revenge, doesn't it?"

"Not quite, Rebecca," Eaton cautions. "There's more to the story."

"But wait a minute," Tommy interjects, "that was a good thing Antonio did. I would think the Grimaldis would have accepted him back into the family fold."

"Are you kidding?" Eaton answers. "He was damaged goods—much too blemished for reinstatement into Monaco's elite royal family."

"Too much dirty water flowing under the bridge and they didn't have the guts to swim through it, it's that simple," Lilly declares.

"You've got that right," Eaton agrees.

"Okay, so now we know why Antonio got his butt in a sling," Lilly says. "What does this have to do with Mike and his GTO fishing trip?"

"Another good question!" says Eaton. "Maybe you can help me. I suspect that Antonio made a second deal with the devil. There's more research to be done, but this will be the most interesting part."

"I have to admit, Eaton," Tommy says, "just based on what you've told us, my grandfather saved the lives of the Grimaldis. He also saved Monaco's monarchy."

"The word I used, Tommy, was 'heroic.'"

"That brings us back to Montauk," Rebecca reminds everyone.

"I can't take it any longer," Tommy bursts out with exasperation. "I have to go to Montauk."

"So what are you going to do once you get there?" Rebecca asks. "Their boat won't be back for another six days."

"Ask questions. Find out about Adelman and the *Ocean Diver*, see if the Coast Guard has any information. At least I'll feel like I am doing something constructive instead of sitting around here twiddling my thumbs."

"I can't let you go alone, Tommy," Rebecca says.

"Well, then, let's pack and get cracking."

"I'd be happy to drive you there," Eaton says. "We can all fit into my van. It's very comfortable."

"Well, then, I'm going too!" Lilly chimes in.

"All right, all right!" Tommy sighs.

# 18

# Decompression

### Montauk, Long Island, New York
*November 3–4, 2008, Monday Evening and Tuesday*

They arrive in Montauk just before dusk. Eaton had made a few phone calls on the way down and arranged lodging at his writer friend's Leisurama prefab on Culloden Point.

"My friend bought the Leisurama prefab on the ninth floor at Macy's. During the late 1950s, they were a hot commodity in Montauk. I think about two hundred of them still exist down here. The company had a display in Moscow that was the scene of the famous Kitchen Debate between Nixon and Khrushchev."

"How interesting," Lilly says. "I remember that debate. Nixon did well."

Eaton glances out at all the fishing docks they are passing on the Old Montauk Highway.

"We have just arrived in the sport fishing capital of the world," he notes.

"Most of the tourists have left by now, so it shouldn't be too crowded," Tommy says. "Let's drive over to the point."

They swing past Montauk Point Lighthouse and catch a glimpse of the open sea.

"You know, when I look out from the point at the vastness of the ocean, I feel so incredibly small," Eaton says. "Nothing compares to the colossal bigness of the sea."

"Please don't remind me," Tommy shrugs. "My best friend is out there. I still can't believe he would do such a damn foolish thing. But Mike is Mike."

"Who is the guy we are renting from?" Lilly asks.

"Miles Cantor," Eaton answers. "He's a lousy writer but a real kind-hearted guy. We did a few articles together for *Autoweek*. He did the research, I did the writing. Good thing, too. He writes like an EKG machine." Eaton starts to laugh. "And you wouldn't believe the color-ful plaids and stripes he wears. When he gets dressed up, he looks like a walking kaleidoscope! Sometimes I think he has more screws loose than a Studebaker. I can't figure out what makes the guy tick. Either he doesn't understand what proper attire looks like, or he's just being a rebellious twit. Last year I stayed down here with him at his place for a few days. His pajamas, get this, they were his permanent uniform every day of the week—night and day! And he only showered and shaved on 'odd days' of the week. It was like living with a cave dweller. I did all the shopping and cleaning up. It's tough to do in my wheel-chair, but I managed. I was never so glad to finish a story in my life!"

"Just curious," Tommy asks, "when you say 'odd' you mean like 'odd and even'?"

"Yeah, that's right."

"So this guy only showered or shaved on the 'odd days' of the week based on the calendar?"

"No, he never looked at a calendar."

"Tell me something, then," Tommy continues. "Which days were 'odd days' and which days were 'even days'?"

"It depended on which day of the week he started counting," Eaton explains. "Most of the time he didn't bother."

"You must have kept the doors and the windows open all the time," Tommy laughs.

"He won't be there, right?" Rebecca asks nervously.

"No, Miles is working on some big event at Radio City Music Hall called NART: A 50 Year Salute. Miller's Motorcars is sponsoring it. He's also been helping me with my research project on the Grimaldis, too. I'm anxious to see him and learn what else he has uncovered. You'll have to meet him sometime, Lilly."

"No thanks," Lilly says firmly. "I have enough strange characters in my life! I just hope this place is habitable."

"If it looks anything like it did the last time I was there, we're going to have to fumigate it," says Eaton. "Believe me, he's one big disorganized slob."

"You can drain the swamp for us in the morning, Eaton. Sounds like you've had some practice," Lilly smiles. She's beginning to enjoy ribbing Eaton.

"Anything for you, sweetie, anything in the world. You name it!"

"Eaton," Rebecca laughs, "you're pressing your luck!"

"I think I'm making some headway," Eaton grins.

"Hey, let's head over to the Coast Guard station before we settle into our place," Tommy suggests. "Maybe we can find something out."

"Sure," Eaton agrees. "Maybe we can speak with someone who has information on the *Ocean Diver* and Captain Adelman."

Eaton proceeds south on West Lake Road past Snug Harbor toward Lake Montauk and then drives north on Star Island. Three white colonial style dwellings with dormers, red window shutters, and red roofs face the northern channel to the open sea. Eaton parks behind the largest building. After he lowers his electric wheelchair, they proceed up a sidewalk surrounded by a beautifully manicured lawn.

A Coast Guard seaman opens the main entrance doors for them. They approach a reception area with a group of six waiting room chairs with dark blue cushions and teak frames. A seaman apprentice, a young man about twenty-two years old, is seated behind a rectangular table, an American flag draped proudly behind him.

"How can I help you, sir?" he asks politely.

Tommy responds, "We would like to know if any reports have come in regarding the *Ocean Diver*, a dive vessel out of Montauk?"

"Yes, sir. One moment, please." The young man rises and walks down a narrow hallway toward the back of the building. After a few minutes he returns. "Please come with me," he says. He brings them to an administrative area with copiers, computers, satellite equipment, and other tracking devices. A petty officer and two seamen are seated behind the computer monitors. He leads them to an oak paneled office with framed citations on the wall. A tall, thin man stands and greets them. His dark blue operational uniform matches the somber look on his face.

"Good afternoon," he says cordially. "I'm Captain Holloway, commandant of this Coast Guard station. May I ask why you're concerned about the *Ocean Diver*?"

"We have a close friend on the boat," Tommy replies. "We've noticed the weather is acting up quite a bit and want to assure ourselves that everything is okay."

"I wish I could provide that assurance," the captain says. "We are monitoring an emergency radio distress call from *Ocean Diver* received by our Brant Point Station on Nantucket about two hours ago. Since the *Ocean Diver* is out of Montauk, we've dispatched our cutter, the *Ridley*, to pick them up."

"May I ask what kind of distress call?" Eaton queries.

"They notified the Nantucket harbormaster that they were in a bad storm and couldn't control their boat. Then their VHF radio went dead. We checked their position with our satellite, and they are dealing with some collateral effects from Tropical Storm Paloma." He looks at his computer monitor. "It's just been upgraded to Hurricane Paloma with winds up to 120 miles per hour."

"Oh my God, their boat can't handle that, can it?" Rebecca asks.

"Probably not. But they won't feel the full strength of the storm. Still, eight-foot waves are not out of the realm of possibility." Captain Holloway leans forward. "What the hell are they doing out there, anyway?" he asks with a puzzled look.

"Diving the *Andrea Doria* wreck," Tommy replies.

"In November? Incredible! That borders on insanity. People need to stay away from that area this time of year. I continue to be amazed," the captain declares with displeasure. "When it comes to that wreck, for some unknown reason people never understand the risks. On twelve occasions we've had to retrieve victims. They get tangled in the web of wires and sharp metal or get totally disoriented. Most of the dead divers get nitrogen narcosis or die from the bends when they ascend. A few years ago, we lost one of our best officers when he attempted to locate a missing diver inside the wreck. I'm getting very reluctant to continue placing my people in jeopardy."

"What about *Ocean Diver*?" Tommy asks. "Any incidents with that boat?"

"Yes, unfortunately." Captain Holloway pauses, somewhat hesitant to answer.

Tommy sits motionless. His lips tighten and his eyes connect with Captain Holloway's.

"That boat has lost three divers," Captain Holloway continues. "More than any dive boat in Montauk. Most dive boats take people to the wreck for a fifteen-minute dive to see or touch the ship or just look for artifacts. They gave up on the GTO a long time ago. The *Ocean Diver* is the only one that sells dive trips to find it. I think they're operating a scam. My efforts to suspend Adelman's dive license always fail, though. I can't prove there was any negligence."

"But three people lost their lives on his boat," Tommy asserts.

"I know. Another nine or so lost their lives on other dive boats, and they weren't even looking for the GTO. Everyone just blames the inherent perils of diving the *Andrea Doria* for the deaths. It's a convenient scapegoat."

"I don't know if you can answer this question," Rebecca says, "but were the divers lost on the *Ocean Diver* wealthy?"

"Interesting question," says the captain. "I found that to be a strange coincidence. All of them were wealthy business executives who had a penchant for adventure and the money to pay for it."

"And what greater adventure could there be than to dive the *Andrea Doria* in search of the most valuable car ever made?" Tommy looks at the others, shaking his head in disgust. "They were probably Ferrari owners, too!"

"Hang on a minute." The captain peers at his computer monitor again. "One of our Hercules air rescue planes en route to Boston just did a low altitude flyover and spotted the *Ocean Diver*. Apparently, other than lunging on the waves, it isn't moving in a forward direction." The captain taps his keyboard and grimaces. "Hmm," he says. "On the stern they saw what looked like a body covered by a canvas."

Tommy presses the heels of his palms into his eyes so hard he feels pain. "I'll kill that vile woman!" As he drops his hands to his lap, he feels Rebecca's warm touch on his face as she presses his head to her shoulder. He feels nauseous and clammy and tries recalibrating his thoughts. Then he puts his head back and stares at the ceiling, trying not to break down in tears.

Lilly walks to the corner window and watches several fishing boats return to their berths. Tears stream down her face. Eaton sits with his head down. No one says a word except Captain Holloway.

"I'm so sorry," he laments. "Our cutter will arrive early in the morning with the *Ocean Diver* in tow. Would you like to meet me on the dock?"

It's a sad evening. The Leisurama home is as disheveled as it was the last time Eaton saw it. No one cares, though. After the bad news at the Coast Guard station, they plunk themselves on whatever living room furniture they can find and remain there until morning. Every now and then a quiet sniffle interrupts the eerie silence of the evening.

"This place is a rathole!" Lilly blurts out as she makes coffee early the next morning. She has tissues in her hand and periodically wipes tears from her eyes. "Eaton, you should be ashamed of yourself having us stay in a place like this!"

Receiving the brunt of Lilly's grief is okay with Eaton. Thankfully, he's sensitive enough not to call her "sweetie." He thinks to himself, *Even a fool, when he holdeth his peace, is counted wise.*

"I'm sorry," Eaton says with sincerity. "I'll clean it up while you guys go down to the pier."

"No, I want you to come with us," Tommy says, "and see if you recognize Jaclyn."

At 9:00 a.m. Tommy receives a call from Captain Holloway. "We're ready," he says.

"Can you come over now? We're at the long pier."

Tommy trembles as he is suddenly overpowered with a combination of sadness and bitterness. His heart pounds as he thinks about Jaclyn and what he will say or do to her.

"Yes, Captain. We'll be right over," he finally responds.

Eaton advances his wheelchair slowly down the long pier. Tommy, Rebecca, and Lilly walk beside him. When they reach the *Ridley*, Senior Chief Petty Officer Mary Wagner, officer in charge of the 87-foot long cutter, greets them.

"It was a rough ride," she says. "The weather deteriorated by the minute last night. We made headway this morning when things calmed down a bit. Looks like we're going to get hit pretty hard again as Paloma moves further north."

No one responds. They are petrified at what they may see on the *Ocean Diver*. They move closer to the bow. Black rubber fenders between the boat and the dock make ominous binding sounds as if someone is rubbing their thumbs over a large balloon.

A body covered with a dark blue blanket lies in the middle area of the *Ocean Diver*'s stern. Captain Holloway is standing there with Craig and Sean. He leans forward to assist everyone on board. Craig helps Eaton as he wheels his chair up the gangplank.

"I'd like to introduce my two sons, Sean and Craig," he says proudly. "One of these days, I'm going to convince them to become coasties."

The two smile politely. "Please excuse us," Craig says. Then they disappear into the cabin.

Tommy, Rebecca, and Lilly gaze down on the body. Then they look up and see Jaclyn walking out of the cabin toward them in striking contrast from the way she looked the first time Tommy saw her at the Ferrari dealership. A brown blanket covers her body, her hair is towel dried, straight, and full of knots, and her bloodshot eyes are half-opened. She's been crying and is clearly very upset. Tommy is frozen like an ice sculpture.

"Where is Adelman," Tommy asks intently.

Jaclyn recoils. "Is that some sort of sick question?"

Tommy is surprised by her reaction.

"You mean you don't know?" she asks sharply. She points to the blue blanket.

"They both drowned?" Tommy chokes out, catching Jaclyn off guard.

"Tommy," Rebecca interrupts, "allow her to explain herself, okay?"

"Go ahead," he says, confused, angry, and extremely impatient.

"Mike has decompression sickness," Jaclyn explains. "He's in the onboard compression chamber. Craig is a trained and licensed chamber operator and has been with him the past several hours. Captain Holloway had a doctor waiting for us when we arrived. Thankfully Al invested in one of those transportable chambers, God rest his soul." She begins to weep.

Tommy feels an incredible relief that he finds impossible to disguise. "Will Mike be all right?" he asks, disregarding her emotional state.

"I don't really know," Jaclyn says as she catches her breath.

"What the hell happened out there?" Tommy asks.

"Craig and Sean—they saved both of our lives," Jaclyn stammers. "I can't remember everything. I'll try, though. Mike, Al, and I—we were on Deck B. Based on Al's blueprints, the cargo holds were on Deck C, below the chapel. Once we found the chapel, we went inside. Mike attempted to kneel on a wooden kneeler that had rotted away. He fell backwards into one of the cargo holds below the chapel on Deck C. So much silt was stirred up that Al and I were lost for a while. Once things settled, Al motioned me to follow him through the hatch to Deck C. When we made it through the hatch, Al's foot got wedged between two pieces of sharp metal girders."

Jaclyn sits down on the bench seat near the cabin. "Can I have some water, please?" Captain Holloway hands her a bottle of water.

She continues, "We both struggled to move the girders and manipulate Al's foot to set him free. Blood was in the water. Each time I turned his foot I could hear him scream through his mask. His hand motioned me to stop. I'm sure his leg was cut pretty badly, maybe broken. He started pointing at his gauges and signaling me to leave." She sobs and wipes her eyes. "Our air supply was running dangerously low. I couldn't leave him there. Then I felt the onset of narcosis and became faint. I knew from my diving experience that nitrogen bubbles would soon be blocking off my blood flow. I kept trying to free Al, though, until a horrible and helpless fatigue came over me. All I can remember is someone's arms reaching around me and taking me to the umbilical line near the bow."

"Someone else was down there?" Tommy asks.

"Sean and Craig. Sean rescued me. Craig had Mike, who was in much worse shape than me. I was thrown into a state of total confusion. It seemed like an eternity to ascend to the surface and it was all I could do to maintain control of myself."

"It's the standard decompression procedure," Captain Holloway interjects. "They are supposed to stop every ten feet or so and remain at the final decompression stop for seventeen minutes."

Jaclyn continues, "That's when my head cleared and I tried to break away and go back down and get Al. Sean was too strong, thank God. He forced me to stay. Once on board, Craig placed Mike into the chamber immediately. He was still blacked out and was going into deep shock. I was okay except for being devastated over Al. Sean dived right back down to the wreck to find Al. How I prayed that Sean would save him."

"I'm sure it was too late," Captain Holloway adds. "It had to be an hour since they left Al. There's no way he could have survived that long."

Jaclyn covers her eyes with the towel. "I'm sick," she says. She drops the towel and runs inside the cabin.

Tommy, Lilly, and Rebecca sit on the bench seat. "I want to talk to the doctor," Tommy says.

"Not now," Captain Holloway advises. "He's monitoring the oxygen flow for Mike. We can check with him when the cycle finishes."

Meanwhile Jaclyn returns with a heavy jacket and another towel around her neck.

"Are you feeling better now?" Lilly asks, as she stands up and walks toward her.

"I'm not as nauseous anymore, thanks," she answers.

"You've been through a lot, Jaclyn, I'm very sorry."

Jaclyn slowly nods.

"Let's get you off your feet," says Lilly.

Tommy jumps up from the bench seat as Jaclyn sits down. His confusion and fear eclipse any empathy he may have for Jaclyn or her story.

Lilly hands her another bottle of water. "Keep drinking the water," she says. "We don't want you to get dehydrated."

Jaclyn sits motionless. "I keep going over it and over it asking myself if there is anything I could have done differently. I will never forget the look on Al's face when he motioned me to leave."

"Close your eyes and just rest for a while," Lilly says. She places her hand on Jaclyn's shoulder. "You'll be all right, honey. Don't blame yourself, now. There's nothing you could have done to change what happened down there."

"I have to go inside," Tommy says. He looks through the window on the door to the cabin. A silver-haired doctor sitting on a three-legged stool waves him in. Tommy sits down on the chair next to him. The doctor, a man in his fifties dressed in whites with his sleeves rolled up, his collar open, and his blue tie loose, scrutinizes two portable computer screens on top of the chamber. A raised door on the side reveals six gauges and a maze of copper tubing. *I'd absolutely die if I had to be in that thing,* Tommy thinks to himself.

"Would you like to say hi to Mike?" the doctor asks.

"You mean we can actually talk to him inside that tank?"

"Sure. Go ahead."

"Just a minute. Does he know what happened to Adelman?"

"Not yet. I told him Jaclyn was okay but decided to wait and let someone else tell him about Adelman."

"That's good, Doctor, thanks."

"Are you ready?" the doctor taps a key on the computer. "All set," he says.

"Hey Bender! You in there, buddy?" says Tommy.

"Well, hello Grimaldi. It's about time you got your ass down here," comes Mike's voice.

Profound relief overcomes Tommy and he has trouble controlling his emotions. With tears filling his eyes, he smiles broadly.

"So how are you doing inside this here tube?" Tommy asks.

"Now I know what a torpedo feels like before it gets fired! Hey, Doc—this thing work for hangovers?"

The doctor laughs. "You're getting out in an hour or so. You can try it out tonight."

"How long have I been in this damn tube anyway?" Mike asks.

"About twelve hours. Thanks to Craig, you were placed inside just in time."

"My ears are still popping, but not as bad as they were."

"Hold you nostrils together, move your jaw, and blow through your nose," the doctor advises.

"Yeah, I know the drill," Mike says.

"It'll take a while for that to clear up completely," the doctor adds.

"The doc already told me Jackie is okay. I was so out of it, I forgot to ask about Al."

"He didn't make it," Tommy answers. "He was trapped inside the wreck. Jaclyn says she tried everything to free him."

"Ah . . . yes. I'm sure she did. I'm so sorry," Mike says, as he takes time to process the bad news. "Did they find him?"

"Yes," Tommy says, not wanting to elaborate.

"What's Jackie's state of mind?" Mike asks.

"She's very upset," Tommy says.

Mike is quiet for a few seconds.

"What are you thinking, Bender?" Tommy asks.

"I only remember a little bit about what happened down there. After I fell into the cargo hold, I was alone for about fifteen minutes. I remember swimming out of the bow, but then I was overcome with divers' sickness and blacked out."

The doctor looks over at Tommy wondering how to respond. Tommy places his index finger vertically on his lips. The doctor receives the message and remains silent.

"We have to talk, Grimaldi. Just you and me, buddy. We have to talk," Mike continues.

"Just relax for now, Bender. We'll sort it all out once you're feeling better."

"That was one lucky fall, though! Guess what I found in the cargo hold?"

"I know. You found the Starbuck's mermaid!" Tommy quips.

"Very funny. I'd still be down there if I found *her*!" Mike laughs.

"Well then, what the hell *did* you find?"

"Brace yourself! Are you sitting down?"

"I'm sure at some point in the future you're going to release the information," Tommy says.

"Grimaldi!" Mike pauses for effect. "I found the GTO! That's right, did you hear me? I found the GTO!"

# 19

# Painful Revelation

### North of Naples, Italy
### *July 19, 1956, Thursday*

At three in the morning, the traffic is sparse on the Via Ripuaria, a highway that runs north from Naples. It's a good thing. Antonio is having great difficulty concentrating. The arrangement Charone devised to transfer possession of the GTO is scheduled to take place at Lucca, a town in Tuscany a few miles northeast of Pisa. Charone will meet Antonio in one week, on July 26, next Thursday, at the Guinigi Tower, easily recognizable by the hanging garden on the roof.

As he continues to dwell on Charone's inflammatory message, the bitter hostility brewing inside him penetrates every fiber of his being. How had Charone found his wife and son, and for how long had he been holding them hostage? Suddenly Antonio is aware of the fact that nowhere in the message does Charone say anything about releasing them.

Antonio's anger intensifies. Some of it is directed at himself for getting involved with a monster like Charone in the first place. He is also angry with himself for not negotiating the release of Alessandro and

Catherine. For some reason, he just assumed they would be returned to him at the Guinigi Tower after the GTO was transferred to Charone.

He should have known better. *The chaotic events of the past few days have impeded my thought processes. Even if I deliver the GTO to Charone, there are no guarantees. Charone could still torture and kill them.* Antonio asks himself, *I wonder if Charone really even has them to begin with?* The answer is irrelevant. He simply can't take the chance of assuming otherwise—the safety of Catherine and Alessandro must come first. Any departure, no matter how small, from the agreed upon plan would put them at risk.

Antonio is mindful of the Beretta M1951 semiautomatic pistol he placed inside the center console before leaving Torino. He expects to use it on Charone. *Once I'm confident Alessandro and Catherine are safe, that bastard will receive a bullet right between the eyes.*

A pair of fast-approaching headlights reflected in his rearview mirror interrupts his thoughts of retaliation. Antonio accelerates. The vehicle quickly follows suit and comes closer. The driver blinks his high beams. Antonio slows down and moves over, giving the vehicle enough room to pass, however, it remains behind him.

Antonio opens the console, removes the Beretta, and holds it in his right hand. *It has to be one of Charone's henchmen coming to finish me off. . . or maybe it's Charone himself.* Then it occurs to him. *Those bastards, they've already sold the information! Lorenzo Prinzi and his dockworkers are the only ones who know the GTO was unloaded from the* Andrea Doria, *and they are notoriously bribable.* He slows down and drives the transporter under a bright streetlight on the side of the road, places the shifter in neutral, and mentally prepares himself for a confrontation. Despite the tremors traveling through his body, he tightens his grip on the Beretta.

A light blue Peugeot 403 Limousine parks behind the transporter. Under the streetlight, Antonio identifies it as a belonging to Monaco's Compagnie des Carabiniers du Prince, the security force that protects the prince and the royal family. A man in a white uniform exits the limo and begins walking toward the transporter. Antonio braces himself, rolling down the window with his left hand and pointing the gun toward the open window with the right. As the man approaches, Antonio recognizes the Carabiniers insignia on his shirtsleeve patch and the three stars and crown on his shoulder boards indicating the rank of colonel. Still, Antonio points his Beretta at him ready to pull the trigger at any sign of trouble. Trusting anyone has been difficult lately, and the last thing he expects is an emissary from Prince Rainier to find him on the Via Ripuaria in the wee hours of the morning.

"Monsieur Grimaldi. Please don't be afraid. Here are my credentials."

Antonio reads an official communiqué with a seal of the familiar Monaco coat of arms, a red crown and diamond clustered shield with *Deo juvante,* with God's help, on a banner underneath it. Prince Rainier's signature appears on the bottom.

"Okay," Antonio says, as he stows the Beretta back inside the console. "Please, Colonel, step inside the cab." Antonio opens the passenger side door. The colonel enters and sits down.

"I have an important message for you from His Royal Highness, Prince Rainier. To demonstrate his gratitude for saving his life, he enlisted our services to locate your wife and son. I am happy to report, Monsieur Grimaldi, that Alessandro and Catherine have been found."

Antonio looks into the colonel's eyes, unsure of what he just heard. "You said you have found my wife and son?" he asks in a soft, inquiring voice.

"Oui, Monsieur."

"Please, just tell me they are safe." Antonio's heart is pounding.

"The prince directed me to personally deliver them both to the *Andrea Doria* in Genoa two days ago for the trip to America. Arrangements have been made for them to live in a community in New York State."

Antonio slumps back in his seat and exhales. Never in his life has he felt as much relief as he does now. The mental strain of the last few days is drifting away like dark clouds after a thunderstorm. *Alessandro and Catherine are safely aboard the* Andrea Doria. *Thank God!* Then his relief turns to disappointment. *I could have gone with them. I was right next to the* Andrea Doria *twice!*

"There is something else the prince wants you to know, Monsieur."

"Something else?" Antonio asks, believing whatever else the colonel has to say will be insignificant compared with what he just told him. The important thing is that Alessandro and Catherine are away from the evil clutches of Charone.

"Catherine has remarried," the colonel says, his eyes reflecting sadness.

Antonio is speechless. Despite the goods news of their safety, he feels as if a long spike has been driven straight though his heart. Every moment of his life, ever since he was sent to prison, he has done nothing but think of the day when they would be reunited. His head slumps with grief.

"Why would she do that?" he utters under his breath. "Why?'

"The prince wants you to know how sorry he is, but he also wants you to know that Alessandro and Catherine are doing well and are out of harm's way."

Antonio regains a degree of his composure. "Who did she marry?" he asks.

"I'm sorry, I'm not at liberty to mention his name."

"Alessandro and Catherine—they're alone in New York? What about her husband?"

"Monsieur, I have been instructed by the prince not to discuss her husband, only that he did not accompany them to New York. I can assure you that their passport names have been changed to protect their true identities. While the prince deeply appreciates your revelations to INTERPOL that saved his life, he is very concerned about Paul Charone's continuing hostility toward you. Catherine is still very much afraid and wants to protect Alessandro from harm. That's why she asked that their names be changed, and their exact location in America remains undisclosed. The prince hopes you will understand and not attempt to find them. He realizes you would never want to place her life or your son's life in jeopardy. May I assure him that you will not attempt to contact them?"

As the colonel speaks, Antonio's eyes freeze on the road ahead. He is thankful for what Prince Rainier did by arranging their passage to America. But he always believed she would wait for him; she would be there for him when he was released from prison, no matter what. *I was naïve. It's just another example of how I ruined my life. Rainier is right. Catherine and Alessandro's safety is more important. They're definitely better off without me in their lives.*

"Monsieur Grimaldi, what should I tell the prince?" the colonel asks.

"The answer is yes. You may assure him I will not try to find them."

"Thank you, Monsieur Grimaldi. The prince will be delighted with your answer. And now, if there is nothing else, I need to get back to Monaco."

"Wait. Can you tell me a little about Alessandro?" Antonio asks.

"Ah, oui, Monsieur. You would be proud of him. At seven years old, he is quite the gentleman, very active and always helping his mother, always at her side."

Antonio clears his throat. His voice quivers and his hand trembles as he extends it to the colonel. "I appreciate your efforts, Colonel," he says cordially.

"Merci," the colonel acknowledges, as he extends his hand.

"Please tell Prince Rainier I am grateful for what he has done."

"Of course, Monsieur Grimaldi. After all, Alessandro and Catherine *are* Grimaldis."

"Yes, of course they are," Antonio agrees. "Grimaldis."

"Bonne journée, Monsieur."

"And to you, Colonel."

An hour has passed since the colonel's departure. Antonio still has not moved the transporter. He revisits the colonel's words over and over again. *Catherine has remarried! She must have been very scared. That's the reason. She was angry and not thinking straight. And I wonder why her husband did not go to New York with her. Are they even still together?*

Self-incrimination continues to drag Antonio farther down into the abyss. As relieved as he is that Catherine and Alessandro will be safe in America, far away from the diabolical Charone, he blames himself for all their distress.

*Charone was bluffing all along!* That realization doesn't remove the bottomless pit he feels in his stomach. Hope is the one thing that has kept him going. It's been his lifeline, his ticket for renewed family togetherness, which is the only thing Antonio has ever really wanted. That's gone now, and he is heartbroken.

*Exactly where do I go from here?* he wonders. *The restaurant bar in Piombino—that's where I'll go and drown my troubles, maybe find a charming woman who would love to spend the evening with a famous member of the Grimaldi family. That's exactly what I need!* Then Antonio's body and mind finally yield to nearly twenty-four hours of sleeplessness.

At around 7:00 a.m., bright sun and highway noise awaken him. Thirsty and hungry, he immediately heads north until he finds a roadside restaurant where he stops for breakfast. Later, drawn by the promise of an alcohol-induced escape, he checks into a motel in Piombino. The thought of killing off a few million overactive brain cells is simply irresistible.

He hides his briefcase with the thirty-five million francs under the bed in his motel room and places a bottle of Italian brandy on the nightstand. He will anesthetize himself for the rest of the day and make the rounds to his favorite bars in the evening. *The perfect plan!* He immediately consumes two full glasses of the brandy. *This will take the edge off.* He's right. Within five minutes, he blacks out. His muddled brain is unable to function, but the pain is gone—for now.

# 20

# Megamouth Attack

### Montauk, Long Island
*November 4, 2008, Tuesday*

When the East Hampton coroner arrives at the USCGC *Ridley* to pick up Al Adelman's body, Lilly asks if an autopsy will be performed.

"Anytime someone dies from an accident, injury, or in an unnatural way, we do an autopsy," the coroner replies. "It's standard procedure."

"Is the information made public?" Tommy asks.

"A copy of the report will be available to the next of kin or anyone authorized by the next of kin to receive it." Tommy and Lilly look at each other. They realize they are both thinking the same thing. *The next of kin will never share the information.*

As they disembark, Captain Holloway and his sons, Craig and Sean, extend their sympathies to everyone. Their condolences focus more on Jaclyn than anyone else. Just prior to leaving, as they stand in the parking lot, Tommy asks Captain Holloway a question.

"Mind if Rebecca and I stop over to see you tomorrow? We have a few questions about some things."

"Not at all. Early in the morning is best for me," he replies.

"Will eight work?"

"Absolutely."

Jaclyn and Mike walk to his Bentley. Mike says, "We're going to rest for a few hours. Maybe we can catch dinner together tonight. I'll call you later."

Mike leans on the fender of the Bentley for a few minutes, still queasy and unstable. His time spent in the decompression chamber, an action necessary to save his life, spawned some sobering thoughts. He'll never forget the debilitating feeling when he fell to his knees near the bow of the *Andrea Doria*. An overpowering sense of loneliness and abandonment consumed his disoriented mind. As he recovered in the chamber waiting for the pressurized oxygen to remove gas bubbles from his bloodstream, he remembered how much he valued Tommy's friendship and how close he came to losing it.

The ride back to the Leisurama is so quiet they can hear every little rattle in Eaton's van. But mostly their minds are rattled by Jaclyn's depiction of the underwater events inside the *Andrea Doria* wreck. Each person wonders what to say, how to think, and what to do next. Yet in all probability, they are all thinking the same thing. Oddly, the person who has been the most unassertive throughout the experience on the boat has been Eaton Stone. Once they arrive at the cottage, however, Eaton makes sandwiches, and as they sit in the living room, he is first to initiate conversation.

Eaton repeats the remarks Jaclyn made on the boat. "*I keep going over it and over it asking myself if there is anything I could have done differently. I will never forget the look on Al's face when he motioned me to leave.*"

"How much I would love to know the answer to *that* question," Tommy says. "I think her entire story is a fairy tale! It's the manner in which she said it. It sounded so artificial."

"I think you guys are being way too critical of her," Lilly says bluntly. "After all, Al *was* her husband. Isn't that right, Eaton?"

"Al Adelman was the man I saw her with at the shows. He was always trying to drum up business for souvenir diving trips to the *Andrea Doria*. But she was the one who made the most noise about salvaging the GTO. She managed to get on the docket for every Ferrari event. I went to one of her presentations. She had slides with diagrams of the inside of the *Andrea Doria*. She's a very persuasive lady."

"Mike needs to know about this," Lilly says. "If you don't tell him, Tommy, I will."

"Of course I plan on telling him, Lilly." Tommy nods as he says to himself, *Mike needs to know some other things, too.* Then he remembers Mike's remarks: *I only remember a little bit about what happened down there, Grimaldi. After I fell into the cargo hold, I was alone for about fifteen minutes. I remember swimming out of the bow, but then I was overcome with divers' sickness and blacked out.* Tommy wonders, *Why was he left alone for so long? They saw him fall. Why didn't they go right after him?* Tommy can't wait to speak with Mike privately, to discover what's going on in his head, and to see if he has a different view of things after his harrowing experience on the wreck. But Mike never calls about dinner. Neither does Tommy. There is simply way too much tension for a relaxing dinner.

## November 5, 2008, Wednesday

Breakfast the following morning is ready at six thirty. Eaton has been in an avid conversation with Lilly over coffee since six. Rebecca and Tommy arrive at the table late, rush through breakfast, and then prepare to leave for their eight o'clock appointment with Captain Holloway.

"Hope you had a good night's sleep," Tommy says to Eaton.

"I was so tired last night I threw myself over a chair and put my pants to bed!" Eaton replies.

"Well that must have been quite a sight!" Lilly snorts as she just about falls on the floor laughing. "Do something with this guy, will you please, Tommy?"

"He's *your* problem!" Tommy says. "But it's great to start off the day with a good laugh for a change."

"Eaton and Lilly—would you like to come with us to speak with Captain Holloway?"

"No," Lilly says. "I'll stay here with Eaton. I still have a bunch of questions for him."

"Good. He's a mystery man—that's for sure. Let me know what you find out! Can I borrow the van, Eaton?"

"Of course," Eaton responds. "The 'mods' aren't hard to figure out."

"Thanks," Tommy smiles as they leave.

When Tommy and Rebecca arrive at the Coast Guard station, Captain Holloway greets them in the reception area and leads them into his office.

"Coffee?" he asks.

"Sure. Cream and sugar please," Tommy says.

"No thanks," Rebecca says. "God, I'm already too wired."

They are seated on two armchairs facing Captain Holloway's desk.

"Would you like to ask the questions or would you like me to tell you what I know?" the captain asks.

"Both," Tommy says attentively. "I want the whole biscuit."

"How long have you been stationed here, Captain?" Rebecca asks.

"My family and I have been here four years. We've been fairly active in the community and try to fit in. Coasties are treated pretty much like tourists—probably because they come and go so frequently."

"Tough to establish roots when you're in the service," Tommy says. "It was like that for Mike and me when we were in the Rangers—until we got shipped to the Middle East. Then we didn't want any roots, we just wanted to get the hell out!"

Captain Holloway nods. "I can understand that," he says. "You know Montauk is a small town. You can learn a lot about what's going on around here over at Meggie's Bar. I stop there for a drink a few nights a week after I finish up here."

"May I speak bluntly, Captain Holloway?" Tommy asks.

"Yes. I learned a long time ago at the academy that the shortest distance between two points is a straight line."

"What's the scuttlebutt around here regarding Captain Adelman and Jaclyn?"

"That *is* the question, isn't it?" Captain Holloway smiles.

"Yes, and somehow I believe you have the answer," Tommy remarks.

"There's no scuttlebutt. They're husband and wife. Everyone knows it. Those two have been the topic of conversation over at Meggie's for some time. I'll bet they're already drawing conclusions about Captain Al's death."

"Sometimes the grapevine yields good fruit," Rebecca says.

"Sometimes," the captain agrees. "Sometimes it turns out to be sour grapes. You can taste the grapes yourselves if you go over there right around lunchtime. It should be less rowdy than at night. The owner is Al Adelman's sister. She sits at the end of the bar and never stops talking. As you may have guessed, her name is Meggie. She could get rich writing a weekly gossip column around here."

"Meggie?" Rebecca asks. "Short for Margaret?"

"No, it's short for 'big mouth.' She was nicknamed after a very rare species of shark called the 'megamouth' by her husband. He divorced her and moved to Montana. Guess he just wanted some peace and quiet. Now she just hangs at the end of the bar and spouts off. She's a rather interesting woman and believe me, she really does have a megamouth. She never leaves the place, so I'm sure you'll find her there."

"Well, meeting her ought to be an interesting experience," Rebecca notes.

"Yeah, I can't wait," Tommy says. "How do you know what to believe around here?"

"You really don't," says the captain. "She has a pretty good track record, though."

"Well, that's good," Tommy replies. "That could turn out to be a great lead. Thanks."

"Be prepared, though," the captain warns. "She can be quite volatile."

"We'll tread cautiously," Tommy responds.

"Tell me, Captain Holloway, what do you think really happened out there?" Rebecca asks.

"We'll find out. I'm the one who called the coroner."

Meggie's Bar isn't very crowded when Tommy and Rebecca arrive at one o'clock. The first thing they see when they walk through the front door is the curved end of a smoke-filled bar that extends all the way back to the far wall. It has bar stools for about ten people. An attractive young barmaid is serving beverages. Behind the bar area, in a separate room, is a small dining area with about eight tables.

Chilled amber colored beer bottles strew the top of the bar and four overweight older men in work clothes sip the frothy white foam as it rises in their beer glasses. At the far end, a brawny woman in her sixties, her gray hair in a ponytail secured with a thick red rubber band, is gazing at a flat-screen TV. CNN News is on, but she doesn't appear to be watching it. She is dressed in blue jeans with a t-shirt that says "Meggie's Bar" across the front. She is quiet and looks angry, somewhat inconsistent with Captain Holloway's description. Tommy and Rebecca sit on two of the three vacant bar stools next to Meggie.

"Ain't seen you two mates in here before," she says loudly as she sips Guinness dry stout and removes the foam on her lips with her hand. "Can't be tourists. Too late in the year for that." She holds her head high, takes a long drag on her unfiltered Lucky Strike, and exhales through her nose, snorting like a horse. "You probably come down here for the funeral tomorrow. She murdered him! That vampire bitch he married killed him, sure as shit! If she ever shows her ass in here again, she ain't never gonna walk out with it! That's for goddamn sure. He was one helluva good dude until he got mixed up with that slimeball wife of his!"

"Did he come in here much?" Rebecca asks, attempting to move the conversation along.

"Did he come here much? He's my brother, or should I say, he *was* my brother." She lowers her head close to the bar as if she is having stomach cramps. "I really did love him."

"We're sorry," Tommy says.

She looks up. "So what really brings you jokers to town?" She takes another drag from her Lucky Strike and exhales right into Tommy's face.

Tommy coughs, then waves away the smoke.

"We're here with Mike Bender, her second husband," Rebecca says, wondering how Meggie will interpret the remark.

"Second husband? You say second husband, huh? She ain't never been divorced from the first one."

"So do you have any idea what's going on?" Tommy asks.

Meggie looks over her shoulder. "I'm all done keepin' my big god-damn piehole shut! They been runnin' a scam business down here. Jaclyn trolls for suckers at some Ferrari dealer up north. Her and my brother—they attend all the big Ferrari shindigs. A few times a year she hoodwinks some fool Ferrari owner into investin' to raise up that GTO that's suppos'd to be in the *Andrea Doria* someplace. They don't never find it. But they rip off the damn nitwit for thousands. This time that bitch hustler—she screwed herself royally. When she shacked up with that friend of yours, Mike—that lit a firebomb under my brother's big ass. I know. He told me! I ordered him to shut the scam down and get rid of the damn bitch. He finally used his thick head as something other than an ornament and took my advice. This would be his last trip, he told me, and he was gettin' a goddamn divorce. Guaran-damn-teed, he told that bitch that too, that's why he's toes up at the morgue! That woman—she'll burn in hell! I'll see to that."

"Why don't you go to the police?" Tommy asks.

"Police? You kiddin' me? Montauk ain't got no cops. No one never does nothin' bad 'round here. When they do, the Easthampton 'county mounties' shows up. But you don't really think I'm bird-brained enough to squeal on my own brother, do you? When they're here, I just play like I'm a dumb ole broad. Down here, my rules work best for bitches like that."

"Don't you think Jaclyn ought to be interrogated by the appropri-ate authorities?" Rebecca asks. "If she's guilty, she'll pay."

"Please!" Meggie gives Rebecca a disgusted look. "Interrogate, you say? We let the tin snips do the interrogatin' . . . one finger at a time! Oh yes, that bitch will pay. So will that schmuck she been livin' with! He's gotta have elephant balls to be showing his ugly mug in this town." Meggie reaches behind the bar. "This here newfangled *magnauseum* bat will work just fine on him." Meggie points the bat directly at them. Tommy and Rebecca realize it's time to make a quick exit. "And you two," she adds, "get your asses out of Dodge right now! Go on, get the hell out of here!"

"Thanks for the information, Meggie," Tommy says awkwardly. "C'mon Rebecca. Let's go!" He pushes Rebecca forward as they dash toward the door.

"You better find your chum quick. My brother has a lot of pissed off friends in this here town!"

A tall, full-bearded man with muscles bigger than truck tires slides off his stool and blocks Rebecca's path. She attempts to walk around him but he moves his big-barreled chest in front of her.

"When folks show up here and piss off my Meggie, that's when I get involved," he says with an angry smile.

Tommy moves Rebecca to the side and stands in front of the man.

"Listen," he says firmly, "we don't want trouble. Would you please move so we can leave?"

"Let 'em go, Carl!" Meggie yells, as she spits on the floor. "They ain't worth the goddam bother."

"Sure, Meg," he says. "But first . . ." He arches his right arm back to deliver a punch to Tommy's face. "First, I have to—"

Before he can thrust his arm forward, Tommy intercepts it, wraps it behind his back, and kicks him in the butt knocking him to the floor. His head hits the bottom of the bar with a thud and he's out cold. Two men sitting at the bar turn and look at their friend on the floor, then look at each other. They're either too drunk or too scared to mess with Tommy. They shake their heads and return to their suds.

Suddenly, Meggie grabs the neck of a full bottle of beer, smashes it on the lip of the bar, and runs toward Tommy swinging it at him like a wild woman with a bayonet.

"You son of a bitch!" she yells. The razor-sharp, jagged end of the beer bottle narrowly misses Tommy's face.

As Tommy dodges his oncoming assailant, he clutches her wrist, jerking it downward, and the bottle falls to the floor. Now she's desperate and runs behind the bar.

"You're a dead man!" she hollers as she seizes a pistol from under the bar.

"C'mon Rebecca, let's get out of this madhouse!" Tommy shouts.

They bound over Carl's outstretched body on the floor and sprint out the door. As they enter Eaton's van, Rebecca looks in the side mirror. "She's coming after us!" she cries.

Tommy thrusts the shaft with the hand accelerator backward. The crack of gunshots behind them causes Tommy to swerve the van from left to right as it speeds down the street.

"Tommy, that's not a woman. It's a wild animal!" Rebecca exclaims.

"Yes, a thoroughly demented, mad dog!" Tommy responds.

"She's actually firing a gun at us! Can you believe it?"

"Let's find Mike and get the hell out of here before someone else gets killed."

"Yeah, you just have to convince him of the mess he's gotten himself into," says Rebecca.

"Do you have Mike's address?" Tommy asks.

"Not exactly. I know it's a B&B near the marina."

"Why don't you try calling him?" Tommy suggests.

She taps his number into her phone pad.

"The call doesn't go through. Maybe Jaclyn destroyed his phone!" Rebecca says.

Tommy drives Eaton's van at breakneck speed. "Let's find him before it's too late!"

# 21

# Collision Course

### Piombino, Italy
#### *July 20, 1956, Friday*

*Ten years of sobriety down the drain!* Antonio stares at the empty bottle of brandy on the nightstand. His head pounds like a jackhammer. His mouth feels like a dirty ashtray. Unable to keep his eyes open, he rolls over and returns to a deep slumber. A few minutes later, the telephone rings.

"It's 8:00 a.m. and this is your wake-up call," says a jovial voice.

*Now why in hell would I put in a wake-up call?* Antonio wonders. *Never waking up would have been perfectly fine with me.*

Water is running in the bathroom. He sits up, placing his legs over the side of the bed. Then he starts massaging his face with his hands, attempting to revive his foggy brain. He feels shame. *What the hell did I go and do now?* When he looks up, he sees an attractive, fully clothed, middle-age woman standing beside the bed.

"Good morning, whatever your name is," she says. "Things were slow last night at the club." She is visibly frustrated. "I tried to leave before you woke up."

"The club?"

"Yeah, Amore's strip joint, down the street." She sits down on the bed.

"Oh."

"You were a real dud last night. I should have accepted the bartender's offer. Not only that, you snored like a steam engine!" She starts to laugh.

Antonio's too disoriented and bleary-eyed to say anything and merely stares straight ahead.

"Here's your money back," she says, and throws a stack of bills on the bed, "unless you change your mind right now? Hurry up and decide. I've got other appointments."

"Change my mind for what?" he mumbles.

"Maybe another time, huh?" she says and gets up, heading for the door.

Antonio waves goodbye without raising his head. *Good riddance,* he says to himself.

"You know what, buddy? You should see a shrink," she says as she leaves, shaking her head.

After she leaves, Antonio quickly falls back asleep.

It is early afternoon when Antonio finally sees the light of day again. He drags his emaciated body out the door of the motel and climbs into the transporter. Later, he stops at a corner cafe for espresso. His stomach is too upset for anything else. As he sips the espresso, he feels his sanity returning, as well as his memory.

He views the map given to him by the corrupt bartender at the Naples pier. He is near the port city of Livorno, where he can catch the two-hour ferry to Gorgona Island, the place where he spent two years as a prisoner in the agricultural penal colony on the island. Most of his time, however, was spent with Father Nick at the Benedictine Monastery near the penal colony making wine, olive oil, and Antonio's favorite, rhubarb pie. Father Nick, always a good listener, helped Antonio put his life back in order at a time when he was filled with hatred and revenge.

Antonio decides to order a light breakfast and continues to assess his options. *Do I really need to meet with that bastard Charone next week? My son and wife are safely onboard the* Andrea Doria *headed for America. I have a valuable Ferrari in my possession. I also have $100,000 worth of cash in my briefcase.* Suddenly, he is jolted. *Oh my God, where the hell is my briefcase? I brought it inside my motel room yesterday!*

Antonio runs back out to the transporter, combs the inside of the cab, then frantically drives back to the motel. First, he looks under the bed, the place where he hid the briefcase the previous day. *It's not there!* Then he scours every inch of the motel room. *It's gone. That bitch! As usual, the only one I screwed was myself!*

## Gorgona Island, Italy

There is only one entrance to Gorgona Island: Cala dello Scalo. It's an ancient fishing village facing the northeast and the emerald green waters of the Ligurian Sea. Most of the Tuscan style farmhouses stacked on the steep slopes and terraces are now uninhabited, their stucco exteriors cracked and chipped, the tiles on their terracotta roofs in total disrepair. However, the sixty prisoners who live in the farmhouses are not complaining. They roam freely in the village performing their agricultural chores during the day. Only prisoners serious about rehabilitation are accepted. Mafiosi and sex offenders are banned from the penal colony.

At first, police officers guarding the entrance refuse to allow the transporter onto the island. Then one of the officers remembers Antonio as a prisoner on the farm and provides a police escort to Father Nick's residence. Driving on the narrow, unpaved road through the steep hills and mountainous terrain, Antonio passes through acres of olive groves. Picking by hand with burlap nets with the help of plastic rakes and sometimes long wooden sticks was the only acceptable method to harvest the olives.

Father Nick and two other friars occupy a country house adjacent to two other freestanding buildings: a small chapel, and an infirmary used primarily by the prisoners. Pirates drove out most of the Benedictines hundreds of years ago.

Father Nick dedicates his life to the prisoners and meets with them frequently, in small groups and individually. He wants them to know God is present in their lives, even at a penal colony isolated from the rest of the world. He teaches them how to pray and prepare for a spiritual life upon their release. Antonio's time with Father Nick gave him insight and strength. After his release, Antonio was doing well—until he was seduced by the devil, Charone.

Father Nick's one-story country house, about the size of a two-car garage, has a dirty gray stone exterior and thatched gable roof. It is several hundred years old and was formerly used as a barn until the prisoners remodeled the inside just before Father Nick moved in. Several houses just like it, although not remodeled, surround it.

Antonio is anxious to see his old friend. The last time they saw each other was last year at the Rome Grand Prix. Father Nick travelled all the way to Rome to see one of Antonio's Formula One cars race. Not that he really cared much about Formula One, he just wanted to see and support Antonio's new life.

"Padre! Padre! Are you here?" Antonio calls out loudly as he enters the house. When no one answers, he walks to the back of the house. He sees Father Nick in the middle of a small grotto on a ladder reaching up to a birdhouse with a bag of birdseed. About thirty feet away, two prisoners are cultivating the soil. Antonio sneaks up on Father Nick and taps him on his side.

"Antonio! *Oh mio Dio!* Antonio!" he exclaims as he nearly falls off the ladder. Antonio grabs his arm and helps him down. Father Nick smiles broadly as he embraces Antonio.

"Tell me, *caro amico,* dear friend, are you back in town as a prisoner or just visiting?" asks Father Nick.

"I came here to see you, *mio padre!*" Antonio laughs.

*"Fantastico!"*

Father Nick, a man in his late sixties, is about five foot six with a grey brush cut and large black eyeglasses that make him appear scholarly. His thick, enquiring eyebrows, the first thing people notice about him, accentuate his expressiveness. His traditional black monastic tunic, confined by a waistcloth, suggests a stocky but sturdy build underneath.

While sipping wine and eating Italian bread made from the flour of a gristmill built by the prisoners, Antonio and Father Nick get reacquainted. The brief interlude from Antonio's stressful odyssey is refreshing. He enjoys dipping chunks of warm Italian bread in olive oil and drinking Italian wine with his old friend.

Father Nick finally asks, "What about Catherine and Alessandro? We've been talking for two hours and you haven't mentioned them. How come?"

"It's painful, Padre." Antonio's relaxation slowly reverts to anguish.

"You didn't come here just to have wine and bread. Tell me, what's so painful?"

"I made the worst mistake of my life last year."

"Oh, my dear Antonio, I know. You joined an organization called the Charbonneries run by Paul Charone. You bought into his plan to take over Monaco and it backfired when you discovered he planned to assassinate your brother."

"I should have known," Antonio remarks. "Nothing gets by you, Padre."

"Yes. You should have. It was a very distressing thing for me to hear that." Father Nick shakes his head and places his wine glass on a nearby table.

"What do you mean?" Antonio asks.

"I am troubled, Antonio. You never came to me."

"I knew what you would tell me," Antonio responds.

"Of course you did. But why didn't you come to me anyway?" asks Father Nick.

"I was desperate. Charone offered me a million dollars. I owed the investigator thousands. I was obsessed with getting my family back. Look at this message I received from Charone."

Father Nick adjusts his glasses and reads the message threatening Antonio's family. Then Antonio explains the plan to deliver the GTO to Charone in Lucca in six days, and the communiqué from the prince indicating that Catherine and Alessandro were on board the *Andrea Doria* and would soon be safe in America.

"I appreciate what the prince has done, but I still don't trust Charone," Antonio says.

"You have good reason not to trust him," nods Father Nick.

"Now, all my choices have grave consequences."

"Choices always have consequences—good or bad."

"I'm afraid, Padre," Antonio sighs. "No matter how difficult my life has been, I fear the worst is yet to come. Whatever choice I make, it will inflict a staggering blow to the rest of my life. So if I do the right thing and return the car to Enzo, I'll be fired and thrown back in prison. If I don't deliver the car to Charone, he will kill me. Look at it this way, Padre. I've already spent five years in prison for car theft, a crime I didn't commit. If I keep the car, it'll be like an even trade. If I keep the car, I'll have something to pass on to Alessandro. I already lost the $100,000 Charone paid me to some hooker in Piombino. At least he'll remember me for something good other than being a criminal. Maybe it's time I stopped being the victim."

"The car still belongs to Enzo Ferrari," Father Nick points out. "I hope you remember that, my son."

"Yes, but if I give the Ferrari back to Enzo, I'll have to explain why the car is not on the *Andrea Doria*. The most important expectation of Il Commendatore is trust. He'd press charges on someone for stealing a pencil off of his desk. I can't return the car to him, I just can't. More jail time will kill me!"

"Ah, yes. You do have quite a dilemma. Give the car to Enzo and go to jail, maybe even die before then, or . . ."

"Or keep it myself!" Antonio interrupts. "Once Enzo discovers Luigi Chinetti hasn't received the car, he'll focus blame on the Port of Naples dockworkers. Everyone knows they are dishonest snakes. Not only that, Enzo must have the Polaroids of the GTO being loaded onto the *Andrea Doria* by now. So he has the evidence that I delivered the Berlinetta in Genoa. I did *my* job."

"Yes, you did *your* job." Father Nick gets up and walks to the backyard window.

Antonio smiles somberly. "You still bounce when you walk," he says.

"Comes from all the ups and downs in my life around here," Father Nick laughs.

"I'm very sorry, Padre. I didn't mean to unload my problems on you." Antonio walks to the window and stands next to Father Nick.

"See those prisoners tilling the soil?" Father Nick asks. "Do you know what they are doing?"

"Planting flowers?" Antonio asks.

"Not yet. They're preparing the earth for a small cemetery. The two other friars and I will be buried there some day. Then there will be no one left to take care of all the prisoners."

"That would be a big mistake. Won't the order replace you?" Antonio inquires.

"We're independent, Antonio. The order closed the abbey years ago," says Father Nick.

"I'm so sorry."

"Don't feel sorry for me, my son. Feel sorry for the prisoners." Father Nick points to the birdhouse in the grotto not far from the prisoners. "Do you know that Gorgona Island is one of the very few places in the world where you can find the Corsican finch? It never ventures far from its native habitat and is rapidly becoming an endangered species."

"They're very colorful," Antonio remarks.

"Only the males. They are the ones who defend the nest."

"That's good to know," Antonio replies politely, struggling to sustain his interest.

"It's a wonderful songbird," Father Nick continues. "I wake up every morning hearing its silvery twittering. Did you know that when the chicks reach a certain age, even though they resist, their parents push them out of the nest, forcing them to fly into the big, bad world?"

"No, Padre, I didn't know that," Antonio responds, unable to see the relevance. "It sounds like tough love to me."

"Yes. The very toughest kind of love."

"Do any of them survive?"

"Very few. As they fall through the air attempting to fly, sparrow hawks swoop down to devour them."

"Is that why their species is endangered?" Antonio asks.

"That's why," Father Nick replies.

Father Nick looks at Antonio and hesitates for a few seconds. Then he looks back at the finch and says, "But Antonio, the finches that survive always sing much better than all the other birds."

Antonio quietly ponders Father Nick's message, unsure of its underlying meaning. He nods respectfully, hoping Father Nick will decipher it.

"So the ones who escape from the sparrow hawks are able to sing better? What does that mean, Padre?"

Instead of answering him, Father Nick asks another question.

"So, Antonio, what are you going to do about the sparrow hawk?"

## July 25, 1956, Wednesday

Despite the emotional drain of having to make the most important decision of his life, Antonio has been able to relax for a few days in Gorgona with Father Nicholas. They spend most of their time walking through the olive groves and sitting behind the house engaged in avid conversation regarding everything except the choice Antonio needs to make. As the end of his visit approaches, Antonio's anxiety is ignited once again.

"Tomorrow is July 26, Antonio," says Father Nick. "Charone is expecting the GTO to be delivered to him in Lucca at the Guinigi Tower. Have you made a decision, my son?"

"No. But Catherine and Alessandro will always be in my heart." Antonio avoids eye contact with Father Nick. He *has* made his decision. "Thank you, Padre, for everything," he adds as they embrace warmly.

"Are you sure you haven't made a decision?" Father Nick asks one more time.

"No, not yet, Padre."

Just as Antonio steps into the transporter, a courier from the mainland delivers the Naples newspaper *Il Mattino*, a task he performs daily for Father Nick. The headline astounds them:

**The Italian Liner Andrea Doria and Swedish Liner Stockholm Crash Off Nantucket! Andrea Doria Sinking! Stockholm's Bow Crushed! Fog Hampers Rescue!**

"Oh, my God!" Antonio shouts. "Catherine and Alessandro are on that boat!"

Father Nick reads the article out loud:

The Andrea Doria lay helpless in the thick fog. The Italian Line ship reported she was listing very badly. She gave no other indication of the extent or nature of her damage, nor was there word whether she could remain afloat. The Stockholm reported that the Andrea Doria's main deck was dipping to the surface of the water. The 29,000-ton vessel apparently was listing so severely that she could launch no more than two of her lifeboats.

"I have to leave!" Antonio says frantically. "I have to leave now!"

# 22

# Cunning Gambit

**Fairchester, New York**

*November 5, 2008, Wednesday*

Tommy keeps calling Mike's cell until he realizes it is an exercise in futility. Unable to find Mike and Jaclyn, they leave Montauk, hoping they'll find Mike back in Fairchester.

"I'm sure glad we got the hell out of Montauk when we did!" Rebecca exclaims. "A lynch mob was forming, and the way things were going, Tommy, you were going to be the first one at the end of the rope!"

"I'd be the second, Mike would be the first! And you'd be close third," Tommy replies.

"I'm damn glad to be home, too," Lilly says. "Things were getting a little dicey in that hellhole!"

"Usually it's a pretty sedate community," Eaton remarks.

"Yeah, as long as you stay the hell out of Meggie's joint," Tommy says. "I'm going to have nightmares about that banshee woman shooting at us tonight."

When they arrive in Fairchester, at Tommy's request Eaton drives by Mike's house. They see the Bentley parked in the driveway

"Well, that's a relief!" Tommy exclaims.

"I'm sure Jaclyn realizes Meggie and the gang have her number," Rebecca chimes in.

"I'm sure she does, too," Lilly responds. "I'm not that sure about Mike."

"Go ahead, Eaton, pull up to the front door," Tommy says. "Maybe I can get Mike out of the house for a while."

When Tommy knocks, Mike opens the door almost immediately.

"Grimaldi, am I glad to see you! C'mon in," he says. Then he waves everyone in the van to come inside.

Once inside, they sit on red leather upholstered furniture in a cherry-paneled family room off the foyer. Lilly embraces Mike.

"I'm so glad you're safe, Mikey," she says.

Everyone is quickly seated. A warm fire is crackling in the hearth.

"I don't have a land line and I lost my cell phone somewhere in the North Atlantic and had no way of contacting anyone," says Mike. "I didn't know you had returned from Montauk. Anyway, I'm damn glad you guys showed up!"

"Where's your wife, Bender?" Tommy asks.

Mike stands and starts pacing the floor. "She left me."

"What do you mean?" Tommy inquires.

"After we got back to our B&B that day, she insisted that we leave Montauk immediately. She never said a word all the way back to Fairchester. When I initiated conversation, she gave me one of her sassy attitudes. As soon as we got home, we had a vicious argument. I mean, it was really bad, Tommy. Look at floor." Mike points to a pile of broken ceramics littered in a corner on the floor. "It got so bad I couldn't take it any longer. In the heat of our argument, I almost physically threw her out the door. Believe me, if she had a gun, *I'd* be dead on the floor. She finally ran upstairs, packed her things, and stormed out the door." Mike pauses. "You know what? She never cried, not even a sniffle. Actually, I'm damn glad to be rid of her, that's for sure!"

"Do you think she's gone for good, or will she get over it?" Lilly asks.

Mike reaches into his pocket. "Here's the wedding ring I bought for her. She threw it at me. It's over, Lil. Maybe tonight I can sleep with both eyes closed."

Mike sits down on the rocker near a tall cobblestone fireplace. Lilly moves close to the fire and kneels in front of him.

"How much do you really know about this woman?" Lilly asks delicately, not wanting to incite Mike's defensive tendencies.

"I take it you and Grimaldi checked her out?" says Mike. "I figured you would."

"What did you expect?" Lilly chides. "Good Lord, Mikey, you know a woman for a week and you marry her?"

"Okay, so what did you find out?" Mike asks.

"You're her second husband," Lilly answers. "Her first husband *was* Captain Al Adelman. But she was never divorced. She was still married to him when she married you."

Mike is uncharacteristically calm, as if he has already conceded his mistake. "My entire relationship with that woman was a sham," he says.

Tommy listens to the conversation and wonders when he should tell Mike his father was also dating Jaclyn. Then he concludes there *is* no right time.

"Bender," Tommy interjects, "there's something else. I really hate to tell you this." Tommy looks around the room unconsciously stalling, not wanting to deliver such a catastrophic message.

"C'mon, Grimaldi, my clothes are going out of style waiting," Mike complains.

"Bender, I hate to say it, but they were out of style when you bought them," Tommy retorts.

Everyone laughs, and for the time being, the tension begins to dissipate.

"Listen to me, Bender," Tommy continues. "Jaclyn was your father's girlfriend. She was the mystery woman with him on the Lake Placid trip."

Mike arches his head back, closes his eyes, and says nothing. Lilly moves closer to him and softly places her hand over his.

"How did you find that out?" Mike asks.

"Tommy found a picture of the two of them at Lake Placid. It was buried in a stack of papers in your garage," Lilly replies. "We were surprised you hadn't seen it."

"I *did* see it," says Mike.

"What do you mean, Bender?" Tommy asks with astonishment. "You knew she'd been dating your father and you still pursued a relationship with her?"

"That was the *only* reason I pursued it," Mike says, "and I mean the only reason!"

"Mike, what the hell are you talking about?" Tommy says, showing his indignation.

"Well, you know I've been obsessed over my father's plane accident for a long time," Mike begins.

"We both knew that," Lilly says.

"I found the picture of the two of them in my garage after we returned from Toronto," Mike explains. "I was really pissed at first. Later, I decided not to confront her and play along, just to see what she was up to. Also, I wanted to find out if she had anything to do with my father's accident."

"Why didn't you let me know what was going on?" Tommy asks. "We could have at least discussed what to do about it."

"I'm not sure I can explain it," says Mike. "It was something I had to do on my own. I had to find out if she really killed my dad. I thought of nothing else. I was intoxicated by the idea of learning everything I could about her. I would do anything to find out the truth."

"Even marry her?" Lilly asks. "That's carrying it to an extreme, don't you think?"

"No, not at the time I didn't."

"Even without a prenup, I presume?"

"What's a 'prenup'?" Mike asks with a blank look.

"It's when you get rid of the playpen and keep the toys!" Eaton declares.

"Eaton!" Lilly scolds.

"Sorry, I couldn't keep my mouth shut any longer."

"Mike, this is our friend, Eaton Stone," Rebecca explains. "He's been helping us research some things about Tommy's ancestry. He's saying that unless you have a written prenuptial agreement forbidding it, your wife has the qualified right to inherit all your property if you die."

"Really? But that's only if she's my wife, right?" says Mike.

"What do you mean?" Lilly asks with a stunned voice.

"I'm sorry to put you all through this. No. She isn't my wife. A fraternity friend who lives in Toronto posed as the justice of the peace."

"What about the fifteen million you transferred to her bank in Bridgehampton?" Tommy asks.

"I showed her the paperwork. Then I rescinded the transaction within the allowable cancellation window. Once we were on the boat, I knew she'd never check it again."

Suddenly, Mike seems like the smartest guy in the universe to Tommy. "Okay, Bender, touché," he says. "In fact triple touché.

Despite the fact that you put us all through so much grief, I have to hand it to you."

"But, Mike, how could you risk your life diving the North Atlantic with someone who, at any second, could turn on you and try to kill you?" Rebecca asks.

"That was the coup de grâce," says Mike. "I found out the truth and everything I did was worth it. I may never know how or why, but I do know who. She definitely is behind the death of my dad. I overheard their conversation in the pilothouse when they thought I was sick on the deck below. Captain Al wanted to end their fraudulent business scheme. I never expected that she'd kill him, though. She wanted me dead, too. That's why she disappeared on me when we were inside the wreck. Thank God for Craig and Sean Holloway!"

"Excuse me," Eaton says. "We don't know for sure she killed Captain Al, do we?"

"Listen, I know for sure," Mike says with his typical brazenness. "I have all the evidence I want or need!"

"We'll know for sure when the autopsy report comes in," Tommy says. "Captain Holloway is supposed to call me."

"Or you can ask Meggie," Rebecca says. "You know what, Tommy. I definitely buy her story."

"I agree with you, Rebecca," Tommy replies. "I wonder if any others will."

"So you're the famous Eaton Stone, the guy that writes all those articles in the *Prancing Horse*?" Mike asks.

"Yes, I'm that genius, thank you," says Eaton.

"My father said you know more about the history of Ferraris than anyone," says Mike. "It's a pleasure to meet such a well-known Ferrari advocate. I read your article about Antonio Grimaldi and the GTO. In fact, that's what got me so stirred up about the car."

"That article received a great deal of attention," Eaton acknowledges, "much more than I intended."

"By the way, Grimaldi, did you ever uncover a connection between you and that Antonio character?" Mike asks.

"With Rebecca and Eaton's help, we learned that Antonio is my grandfather," Tommy replies.

"Oh my God, really? So what about the rumor that he was a member of the royal family of Monaco?"

"It's true," Tommy confirms.

"How about that!" says Mike. "Now I'm really glad you are my best friend."

"It's a lot more complicated than that," says Tommy.

"Well, you've always been one big walking complication. But I still love you," Mike grins, standing to embrace Tommy.

"We were ready to write your obituary. Thank God you're alive!"

"Listen, buddy, I hated to set you up like that with Jaclyn. I had to find out. I knew you would have been angry with me and would try to talk me out it."

"You're right about that, Bender," Tommy confirms. "I would have gone ape shit had I known what you were up to!"

"But now I know!" says Mike.

"What about that gazillion dollar Ferrari you ordered from Jaclyn in Toronto?"

"I picked out the interior trim before we left for Montauk."

"You really *are* unbelievable, Bender!"

"I can guarantee you one thing," Mike asserts, "the GTO is still intact inside the *Andrea Doria*. Your grandfather did one helluva job!"

"I sure hope that doesn't mean you're still interested in salvaging that thing," Tommy says with a stern voice.

Mike beams. "Only with you, good buddy, only with you. First, I have to get my job back over at Fairchester Academy. I'm really not built for the world of intrigue on the high seas. I miss the kids a lot."

Tommy smiles. "I'm glad you want your job back, Bender. You have a lot to offer the young people of this community."

"Well, all I can say is that it's been a long, exhausting day," Lilly says.

"I'm ready for bed," Eaton agrees. "You know sleep comes so naturally to me, I can even do it with my eyes closed!"

## November 8, 2008, Saturday

A few days pass after the surprising revelations at Mike's place. Tommy and Rebecca's emotions are still unsettled by their harrowing adventure in Montauk. As they sip wine and nibble on snacks on the sofa at Tommy's apartment, Rebecca is eager to tell Tommy about a special invitation she received by mail.

"When I opened my mail this afternoon, there was an invitation for my father and me to attend a special Ferrari event in New York City. I told you about NART, didn't I?" she asks.

"Yeah. But could you explain the details to me?"

"Sure. NART is an acronym for North American Racing Team, and was started in 1958 by Luigi Chinetti. He was a race car driver who came to America and opened Chinetti Motors, the first Ferrari dealership in the country. Since he was a very good friend of Enzo's, he received financial support from Ferrari. During the seventies, Chinetti Motors employed my father. He worked there during the day and prepared race cars on evenings and weekends."

"Whatever happened to NART?" Tommy asks. "They don't race anymore, do they?"

"No. They ran out of money in the early eighties. Chinetti sold the dealership not long after NART folded."

Rebecca takes the invitation card out of her purse and shows it to Tommy.

"Hmm, it sounds interesting," he says. "NART: A Fifty-Year Salute. Miller Motorcars is sponsoring it. Didn't that used to be Chinetti Motors?"

"Yes, it was," Rebecca replies. "It's a shame my dad's Alzheimer's is so bad. He would have loved to be there."

"I'm sorry, Rebecca. That would have been a great experience for you and him."

"Tommy, my invitation is for two people. Would you care to join me as my guest?"

"Of course!" he says. "Where are the festivities?"

"At the Radio City Music Hall. Dinner before the event is in the Roxy Suite."

"Sounds pretty swank to me," Tommy says. "Wonder if Eaton received an invitation."

"Good question. He's become quite a well-known figure in Ferrari circles," Rebecca notes. "I understand his article in the *Prancing Horse* about Antonio and the GTO has some Ferrari aficionados doing more research, especially that guy Eaton mentioned, Miles Cantor. I would really love to know what they find out."

"We will," Tommy says, "one way or the other. We haven't heard much from Lilly lately, have we."

"Haven't heard anything from her in several days. That's unusual. I think she's spending a lot of time with Eaton," Rebecca exhibits a devious smile.

"You really think they have something going on?" Tommy asks, raising his eyebrows.

"I'm sure of it," she replies. "They spent a lot of time alone together in Montauk. Come to think of it, Tommy, how much do we really know about Eaton? Where did he grow up? Was he ever married? Does he have children? How was he disabled? But most importantly—why did he ever get so heavily involved in all that Grimaldi family research? I realize he did an exhaustive study on the royal houses of Europe. Still, why so much about one European family? I just wonder about his motivations, that's all."

"Fair question. We've been so preoccupied with Mike, we never did any fact-finding on Eaton. Now that he and Lilly are together, I'd like to know more about him. Speaking of Mike," Tommy continues, "I still can't get over his brilliant ruse. I never thought he had it in him. He threw us one of his epic curve balls. I totally underestimated him, and I've known him my entire life. One good thing, though; during the last few days all the knots in my stomach have gone away. I honestly thought I'd never see him alive again. What an incredible outcome."

"Well, you were almost right. He came very close to being one more *Andrea Doria* statistic," Rebecca points out.

"Oh, by the way," says Tommy, "I checked his investment statements. The fifteen million *is* back in his account where it belongs."

"Wouldn't you like to see Jaclyn's face when she discovers the money is no longer in her bank account?"

"I'm sure she'll blame me too," Tommy laughs. "I hope she does!"

Just then, Tommy's cell phone rings. When he answers he hears Captain Holloway's voice at the other end of the line.

"Hello. Captain Holloway here. Just wanted you to know that the autopsy results couldn't confirm there was any foul play. According to the coroner, it was a case of drowning from divers' sickness. They found nitrogen in his blood, just like the other divers who have drowned inside the *Doria*."

"No bruises on his foot?" Tommy asks. "Remember Jaclyn saying that Al got his foot wedged between two pieces of sharp metal girders and there was blood? I would think there would be some evidence of a leg or foot wound."

"I asked about that," the captain answers. "There was no blood on his suit and no sign of any wounds on his body. The coroner believes some sort of underwater trauma caused the narcosis. I tend to agree. Al was an experienced diver on the wreck. It seems odd that he would allow himself to get trapped like that."

"So she deliberately lied," Tommy concludes. "Have they brought her in for questioning?"

"Al's death was ruled an accident by the coroner," Holloway reiterates. "The Suffolk County District Attorney told me there is simply not enough evidence to open a case."

"Tell him to speak with Meggie. She'll give him an earful. I'm serious, Captain Holloway. I'm surprised no one has spoken with her. She has everything all figured out."

"I'll convey that information to the DA, but Meggie has a reputation for being somewhat of a peculiarity down here."

"Somewhat? We were lucky to escape that place with our lives!" Tommy exclaims.

"Yeah, I heard she fired at you. You can have her arrested, you know."

"I've been fired at before," Tommy says. "Anyway, I don't want her coming after me in the future."

"I hear you," says Holloway. "Oh, another thing. Craig and Sean are taking the *Ocean Diver* to the Nantucket Boat Basin tomorrow. The weather is supposed to be unseasonably good. They're getting paid quite well."

"That's interesting. Do you know who's paying them?" Tommy asks.

"Yes, of course. Jaclyn called them. I don't know from where. She already sent them a check. At first I was concerned, but then

I thought it'll be just the two of them and they have a lot of experience on the water. After all, they learned from me! I'll have the Coast Guard keep an eye on them, too. They'll be fine."

"Next of kin inherits the boat, huh?"

"No. The boat has always been registered to her, Al just operated it," Holloway explains. "The boys have been deckhands on the boat for a few years."

"I'd still be concerned if I were you, but that's your business," says Tommy.

"Thanks for sharing your thoughts but they can pick up a fast couple grand. Believe me, they can use it."

"Well, okay, Captain Holloway. Thanks very much for calling. Please let me know if anything changes regarding the DA. I want to underscore my earlier suggestion. He should interview Meggie, and he should do it ASAP, before Jaclyn finds another Ferrari paramour with a blind obsession to own the GTO."

"I hear you loud and clear!" says the captain.

"Have a good day."

"You too. I'll call if anything changes. Goodbye."

"Tommy, what was that about?" Rebecca asks when he hangs up the phone.

"He said the DA couldn't press charges against Jaclyn," Tommy repeats.

"I hope he understood you were serious when you said they should speak with Meggie."

"We'll see," Tommy replies. "He also said Jaclyn called Sean and Craig to arrange the transportation of the *Ocean Diver* to Nantucket."

"Sure, Meggie and the gang would have pulled her fingernails out one by one and then hung her from the highest fish hoist in Montauk. Too bad. The scam lives on!"

# 23

# NART:
# A Fifty-Year Salute

### Radio City Music Hall, New York City
#### *November 15, 2008, Saturday*

Few venues in Manhattan match the opulence and grandeur of the VIP Roxy Suite on the fifth floor of Radio City Music Hall. Years ago, it was the living quarters of Samuel Lionel "Roxy" Rothafel, storied theater entrepreneur and the creator of the Roxyettes, later renamed the Rockettes.

Bright red curtains hang from the twenty-foot-high, gold-flaked ceiling all the way down to the luxurious brown and gold carpeting. Black and silver art deco tables with shaded table lamps line the cherrywood walls. Elegant buffets are offered in an intimate setting right next to the suite.

Two hours before the main event, a concierge escorts Tommy and Rebecca from a private entrance at Radio City Music Hall to the iconic Roxy Suite. While they admire the ambience, they feel some apprehension regarding the weightiness of the event. With a glass of white wine each, they sample the passing hors d'oeuvres, including blinis with caviar and oysters on the half shell, then roam the suite, appreciating its history and the many celebrities that are in attendance.

"Look, Tommy!" exclaims Rebecca. "There's Piero Ferrari leaning on the bar talking to someone. He's Enzo's son and the current vice chairman of Ferrari S.p.A." Rebecca pauses a few seconds. "Wait a minute, he's talking to Coco Chinetti, Luigi's son! I met him a few times at the dealership. He's the nicest man. What a sight, seeing the sons of two automobile legends having a drink together!"

"Rebecca, we're supposed to blend in and not act like a couple of starstruck teenagers," Tommy scolds her while smiling broadly.

"I can't help it! Oh my God," Rebecca sighs. "Look over there near the window. Ralph Lauren and 'Gentleman' Jack Sears are having a drink together. They each own a Ferrari GTO! Isn't it amazing being here with them? Let's go get their autographs."

"No, Rebecca!" Tommy laughs. "We'll get thrown out. Just act like one of the celebrities. After all, you happen to be with a Grimaldi, one of the most celebrated names in the world."

"That's right, I almost forgot. Should I make an announcement?" she teases.

"Rebecca!"

"Can you imagine the chaos that would create? Do you think Prince Albert will show up?" Rebecca asks with a half-smile.

"You mean Cousin Al? I understand he's quite a car buff."

"Not enough security here. He never ventures very far from Monaco."

"Let's check out the guest book over there on the podium," Tommy suggests. They stop at the bar and order two more glasses of white wine. Tommy says, "The book is filled with signatures of famous people that have been feted in this place like Elton John, Bette Midler, Frank Sinatra, and Paul McCartney."

"Hey, Tommy Grimaldi should sign it! You're a famous person," Rebecca says, hugging him gently and looking into his eyes.

"Sure, Rebecca, but speak softly. I want to protect my anonymity. Besides, bodyguards are expensive, especially in New York City," Tommy jokes. "C'mon, let's get something to eat."

The reception room flows into a more intimate dining area where other VIP guests are helping themselves to the sumptuous buffet. Tommy and Rebecca feast on succulent roasted chicken over Mediterranean-style mashed chickpeas with sides of green beans, smashed potatoes, and a mesclun salad.

After dinner, they discover the dessert table near the far wall. It is full of luscious delights such as Amaretto cheesecake, dense chocolate brandy cake, and tiramisu.

"The passion fruit and raspberry tart looks amazing!" Tommy says excitedly.

"I like passion too!" comes a voice from across the table.

Tommy looks up. "Jaclyn!" he exclaims.

"Why are *you* here?" Rebecca asks tersely.

"I run this event," Jaclyn replies. "It's my gig! I'm the one who sent you an invitation."

Jaclyn is dressed in a bright red evening gown with a plunging v-neckline, thin crisscrossing straps, and an exposed back. Two muscle-bound bodyguards with full black beards wearing tight blue sport coats and polo shirts are standing behind Jaclyn. They are casing the area as if someone might pop out the woodwork with a pistol at any moment. A tall woman holding Jaclyn's hand is standing so close to her they seem welded together.

Tommy feels an intense hyperacidity rise up to his esophagus. He swallows hard.

"Why hello, Jaclyn," he says uncomfortably. Responding to the woman who killed Captain Al and attempted to murder his best friend feels perverse. Tommy stands rigid, unable to say anything more, desperately wanting to walk away from her.

"Too bad your father couldn't make the event, Rebecca," Jaclyn says. "At least you and Tommy are here."

"Thanks for the invitation," Rebecca says with obvious insincerity.

"Say hello to my new girlfriend, Ambrosia. Isn't she beautiful?" Ambrosia nestles even closer to Jaclyn, placing her arm around her waist.

"Ahh . . . yes she is," Rebecca replies uncomfortably.

Ambrosia is a tall, lanky, boney woman with rounded shoulders, a shapeless figure, a pale complexion, and straight black hair. Her black evening gown, also with a plunging v-neckline, is ill-suited to her frame. Tommy tries to stop a slight smile from blossoming into a larger one. All he can think of is Morticia Addams.

"Her father is Sergio Stavropoulos," says Jaclyn. "I'm sure you have heard of him."

"The Greek shipping magnate?" Rebecca asks.

"Yes, that's right," Ambrosia says with a giddy laugh.

"Ambrosia, it's a pleasure," Tommy finally acknowledges. "Do you live in New York?"

"I live in Greenwich, Connecticut," she replies. "I'm helping my family with the business at Port Newark. I met Jaclyn at the Ferrari dealership."

"Millers?" Rebecca asks with a look of astonishment.

"You look surprised, Rebecca," Jaclyn says curtly.

"No . . . I just . . ."

Jaclyn interrupts her. "Ambrosia is one of my best clients."

Tommy starts to fume. *If she asks me about Mike, I'll lose it.* He needs to remove himself from this situation before he explodes.

"We're going to sit down now," he says. "Nice meeting you, Ambrosia." Tommy nods as he and Rebecca walk back to their table.

Jaclyn, Ambrosia, and the two bodyguards sit at a table across from them.

"OH . . . MY . . . GOD! Jaclyn is selling Ferraris at Millers!" Rebecca scowls. "I shouldn't say I don't believe it, it makes perfect sense! That dealership really has a wonderful reputation around here."

"Well, it won't be wonderful for long once Jaclyn cranks up her machine," says Tommy.

"I grew up down here, Tommy. The median income in Greenwich is the highest in the country."

"Fertile territory for Jaclyn. Plenty of capital to raise the GTO."

"Or the Titanic!" Rebecca quips.

"What do you think about her entourage?" Tommy asks. "Those blackbeards tell the whole story, don't they?"

"They sure do! It's only a matter of time before she'll need them."

"That poor Ambrosia!" Tommy laments. "We both know what's in store for her. Suddenly, I'm not in a very good mood."

Tommy stares over at where Jaclyn and Ambrosia are seated. Jaclyn returns the stare as if to say, *Catch me if you can.*

Amid the large crowd, walking through the grand foyer to the theater in the Radio City Music Hall, Tommy and Rebecca pass eight elaborate lounges, several sitting rooms, and beautiful art deco furnishings. Sparkling chandeliers suspended from the sixty-foot ceiling illuminate the gold and brown carpeting and wallpaper flecked with real gold.

They marvel at the main staircase. Its rich reds, lush greens, and golden tones complement all the other colors in the foyer.

"I love this mural," Rebecca says.

"The Fountain of Youth?" Tommy asks.

"Yes. It portrays an old man nearing the end of his life, confronted by the choices he made during his lifetime. It's a sobering thought, isn't it?"

"It reminds me of my grandfather and the choices he made during his lifetime."

Rebecca looks at Tommy empathically. "According to Eaton, he didn't have too many choices. Eaton believes he's one of Monaco's greatest heroes."

"I don't disagree," Tommy replies, "but I still think he's more of a tragic figure than a heroic one. Antonio's biggest mistake was getting involved with Charone. Otherwise, he was a victim. Life dealt him a pretty lousy hand. Anyway, let's sit down," Tommy says, wanting to change the subject.

An usher in a red tuxedo hands them each a program and escorts them to front row seats near the exit on the first mezzanine.

Tommy and Rebecca are in awe of the refined golds and browns that saturate the theater. Bright orange and yellow lights shine on the semicircular ceiling. They resemble the setting sun as they slant down to the stage. The dazzling gold curtain is enough to take their breath away.

"They say that curtain is the biggest in the world," Rebecca notes as she bends her head backward to capture the moment.

"This place is absolutely magnificent!" Tommy exclaims. "You're right, Rebecca. What a thrill to be here. Thanks for inviting me." He places his arm around her and hugs her tenderly.

Then he says, "Rebecca, do you see Jaclyn anywhere?"

"Tommy, I told you to forget about her!"

"There she is in the front row to our right, sitting in the middle of her two bookends!" says Tommy, spotting her.

"The program is starting," Rebecca says as she nudges him with her elbow.

A single podium in the middle of the 10,000 square foot stage seems like a lonely flagpole on an empty football field. The crowd is silent. From behind the curtain, a tall and distinguished man appears. Lights are dimmed. A spotlight shines directly on the podium. As the man assumes a position behind it, he seems like the only person in the theater.

"Ladies and gentlemen," he says. "Welcome to NART: A Fifty-Year Salute, sponsored by Miller Motorcars. My name is Blake Stevens, President of the Ferrari Club of North America, and I am honored to be your master of ceremonies this evening. Before we start our program, I ask that we have a moment of silence for the American driver, Phil Hill, who passed away last August. He was the only American to win a Formula One Drivers' Championship and the 24 Hours of Le Mans, which he won exactly fifty years ago this evening."

"I met Mr. Hill, too," Rebecca whispers. "My dad was part of his pit crew."

"Thank you," Stevens continues. "This event has a wonderful cause, one that was near and dear to Mr. Hill's heart. All the proceeds from this evening's event will be donated to the Pennsylvania College of Technology to support their brand-new degree program in automotive restoration. As many of you may recall, Mr. Hill had his own restoration shop and won awards at the Amelia Island Concours d'Elegance several times. I'm sure he would be delighted with Miller Motorcars and their decision to support students in the field he loved so much.

"And now we have a special treat for you. Wait until you see the special tribute car we have on display!"

Stevens turns off the reading light on the podium and walks off of the stage. Three stagehands quickly remove the podium. The curtain's rise is laborious, almost tormenting. The loud hum coming from the audience sounds like honeybees fanning their hive. Hearts are palpitating. Then an austere silence comes over the crowd.

When the curtain is finally up, to everyone's amazement, the stage is empty. Gradually the crowd noise increases, becoming vociferous, and on the verge of anger. From their front row seats, Tommy and Rebecca can hear the hydraulics from stage elevators go on and off again as if they are stopping at floors in a tall building.

Then a very sexy female voice comes through the loud speakers. "You know, ladies and gentlemen, it is impossible to salute NART without paying tribute to its founder, Luigi Chinetti."

"That's Jaclyn," Rebecca whispers so quickly it takes Tommy a couple of seconds to assimilate her words.

"See, I told you!" he says. "You have to watch her every second. You never know where the hell she's going to show up!"

All eyes are on the stage. They see two Brookland half-moon windscreens rise from the stage floor. The red bolted-on fenders appear next, covering the gray painted 48-spoke wheels. Soon they see a long front hood with bug-eye headlights with the number 54 on its rounded nose. The car keeps rising until it is several feet above the stage, then it rotates in a clockwise direction on its pedestal.

Jaclyn continues speaking through the sound system. "Ladies and gentlemen, I present to you the 1948 Ferrari 166 Spyder Corsa, also known as the Tipo 166—the first Ferrari to reach American soil!" The audience breaks out in spontaneous applause.

"Rebecca, isn't that the car my grandfather was accused of stealing?" Tommy asks.

"Yes, I'm sure that's the car Eaton mentioned!" she confirms.

Jaclyn continues, "Before Luigi Chinetti imported this car and sold it to Briggs Cunningham, it was stolen from Enzo Ferrari by Antonio Grimaldi, heir to the throne of the famous Grimaldi dynasty in Monaco. In fact, Antonio's grandson, Thomas Grimaldi, is sitting right here in the front row. Stand up and let them see you, Tommy!" The crowd buzzes but the applause is tepid, almost nonexistent.

Tommy is mortified. "That bitch! Tell them he was exonerated!" he says under his breath.

"C'mon now, Tommy. Stand up!" she says again.

Tommy slowly stands with his back stooped and his face beet red, then quickly sits down.

"We are grateful to the Collier Museum in Naples, Florida, for loaning us the car specifically for this event," Jaclyn says as she walks out from behind the stage and stands next to the Tipo, as if *she* is the main attraction instead of the car. Photographers rush to the foot of the stage to take pictures as Jaclyn assumes a variety of fashionable poses. Her bodyguards stand by just in case the frenzy she has created gets out of control. Then the curtain slowly descends. Jaclyn, the bodyguards, and the photographers head toward their seats. As Jaclyn walks in front of Tommy and Rebecca, she leans over, grabs his face with her two hands, and blatantly kisses Tommy on the lips.

"Consider yourself lucky, Tommy boy," she croons. "That was for screwing me out of my fifteen million!" Then she walks to her seat, waves to the crowd one last time, and sits down next to Ambrosia, who appears eminently impressed by Jaclyn's performance.

Tommy fidgets nervously in his seat and loosens his collar.

"Stop squirming," Rebecca says quietly. "The whole theater is looking at you."

"How does *she* know that about my grandfather?"

"We'll ask her later," Rebecca replies, attempting to calm him down.

"If I ever had an urge to punch a woman in the face, I have it right now!"

The evening's festivities run their course with introductions, speeches, and tributes to people who were involved with NART. Not until Blake Stevens begins his discussion about the GTO do things change dramatically.

"As many of you know, as President of FCNA, I am as concerned as you are about the story written by Eaton Stone in the *Prancing Horse* newsletter." He pauses and takes a sip of water. "It has stirred a great deal of speculation regarding the Ferarri Prototype GTO Berlinetta, as well as the impact Antonio Grimaldi has had on our beloved hobby."

"Tommy—look!" Rebecca says in a barely audible voice. "Over there near the exit door on the far side of the stage. See those two men in black suits?"

"Yes, I see them," he nods. "They look familiar."

"They're the two men who were in Eaton's hospital room the first time we met him."

"That's right, they are! I wonder what they're doing here."

Stevens continues, "Miles Cantor, one of our event organizers, has volunteered to share his most recent research on the subject. When he's finished, we will have a special slide presentation by Jaclyn Le Harve."

"Tommy, that's Eaton's writer friend, the guy who owns the Leisurama place we stayed at in Montauk," says Rebecca.

"Yes, it is," Tommy smiles, "the scruffy guy who only showers on odd days."

"And wears plaids with stripes," Rebecca adds.

They both quietly laugh as Miles Cantor walks to the podium wearing jeans, a blue and red striped blazer, and an open collared green plaid shirt. A full orange beard complements his full head of orange hair. A slim, diminutive figure, he struggles to raise the microphone before he speaks.

"Tommy, look at his thick orange eyebrows!" Rebecca says.

"He looks like a pintsize Fat Bastard from that *Austin Powers* movie."

"*The Spy Who Shagged Me*!" Rebecca covers her mouth and laughs.

Miles looks up at the audience and begins. "Hmm . . . Antonio Grimaldi. For the record . . . he was exonerated from the crime of stealing the 1948 Ferrari 166 Spyder Corsa. I don't know from where Ms. Le Harve gets her information, but it is clearly erroneous. It's too bad. The man spent five years in prison for a crime he didn't commit. Later, he saved the Monaco dynasty from being taken over by a ruthless and powerful rogue organization known as the Charbonneries. Antonio Grimaldi is a hero."

Miles adjusts his heavily framed horned rim glasses that seem far too large for his small face. Then he starts unconsciously pulling at his orange beard.

"Now, while I'm at it," he continues, "let me tell you something else about Antonio Grimaldi. After being removed from the dynastic order of the House of Grimaldi in Monaco for supposedly committing this crime, he went on to become one of Enzo Ferrari's best Formula One technicians. Thanks to Eaton Stone's article, we know for a fact that Antonio transported the Prototype GTO Berlinetta to the *Andrea Doria* for delivery to Chinetti Motors in New York City. Of course, we all know what happened to the *Andrea Doria*, don't we?

"Now I don't know if it was a premonition, or exactly what it was, but not only did Antonio Grimaldi save Monaco, he also saved the greatest Ferrari ever made. You see, after delivering the GTO to the Genoa pier, he must have had some sort of forewarning that the *Andrea Doria* was going to sink. He immediately drove to Naples and when the *Andrea Doria* docked there, he had the GTO removed from the ship and delivered it back to Enzo Ferrari. He saved it from being forever lost and ending up at the bottom of the ocean. Mr. Grimaldi . . ." Miles looks down at Tommy. "I would like to ask you to stand again, sir. Only this time I am asking the crowd to give you a standing ovation!"

Tommy blushes as he stands up straight and tall. He is proud his grandfather's name has finally been cleared. So is the audience. They're on their feet cheering him.

"Ladies and gentlemen," Miles says, "I'll bet Miss Le Harve can tell us all about her experiences diving down to the *Andrea Doria* in search of the GTO. Unfortunately, she won't be giving her presentation this evening." Miles looks over at Jaclyn. She has a terrified look on her face.

"Listen, Rebecca, he's going to nail her right here and now!" says Tommy.

Jaclyn and Ambrosia get up to leave. Her bodyguards wisely remain seated. The two men in black suits that were standing under the exit sign follow her up the center aisle.

The audience rumbles and turns their heads to the back of the theater. The two men in black suits have already handcuffed Jaclyn and are removing her from the theater.

"FBI!" Tommy says. "They must have spoken with Meggie."

"Or Mike!" Rebecca adds.

"Goodbye Jaclyn, hello Leavenworth!"

"I'm sorry for that brief distraction, ladies and gentlemen," says Miles. "I just wanted to clear the air. She made me a little nervous sitting right in front of me." He laughs awkwardly. "Now on the lighter side, a little bit more about my good friend, Eaton Stone. I would call him by his nickname, Sandro, but he gets nervous when I call him that in public." Miles laughs, as if he has just shared a private joke.

As Miles is speaking, the groan from the stage elevator nearly obliterates his words. Then Eaton Stone arrives on stage and positions his wheelchair next to the elevator shaft. The audience cheers, anticipating the biggest surprise of the evening.

"Look, it's Eaton!" Rebecca says. "Or should I say 'Sandro'?"

Tommy's face is contorted with shock. He starts to tremble, unable to speak.

A bright red cover ascends from the stage floor. Now the audience is completely entranced. The groan from the elevator finally stops.

"Now what could be under that cover?" Miles asks, teasing the audience.

Tommy lowers his head. "I can't watch," he says.

"History is littered with significant Ferraris," Miles remarks. "But I submit to you that the car Eaton is about to unveil is arguably the most significant Ferrari ever made. Calling it a car is like calling the Mona Lisa a sketch. It truly is a unique expression of fine art."

The audience rises to its feet. Red balloons drop from the stage ceiling. Twenty-five trumpeters from the Garibaldi Bersaglieri Fanfara line up across the stage. They are impressive in their black and red ceremonial uniforms with crimson-red flame patches, black berets, and black gloves. Never before has such fanfare been displayed for an automobile. Never before has a more important automobile been showcased.

As the fanfara plays "Il Canto degli Italiani," the Italian national anthem, Eaton clutches the front end of the cover, places his wheelchair in reverse, and as he moves backwards the cover is slowly removed.

"Fantastic! Spectacular!" Miles yells. "On loan from the Ferrari family's private collection, until recently kept hidden from the public, and the first time this car has been publicly displayed, the most famous Ferrari of all time. Ladies and gentleman, I give you the exquisite Ferrari Prototype GTO Berlinetta, the first GTO made, and certainly the most beautiful!" Several armed security guards surround the car as if they were protecting the crown jewels.

"Thank you everyone! This concludes our evening festivities," says Miles, attempting to speak above the roar of the audience.

"Look, Tommy, there's Lilly standing next to Eaton," Rebecca notes.

Tommy feels severely nauseous. His hands are shaking from a panic-induced adrenalin rush. He's fighting against the urge to vomit.

"Tommy, what's going on with you?" Rebecca is alarmed.

"I have no words, Rebecca. Like the poet says, 'my mind is a big hunk of irrevocable nothing.' I feel numb all over and sick to my stomach. I'm not sure I can even walk."

"Tell me, what's the matter?" she says.

"Eaton! Eaton is my father, Rebecca. He's my father. I don't know whether to be happy or sad. I feel no emotion. All I feel is shock."

"Why do you suddenly believe he's your father?"

"It all adds up!" Tommy exclaims.

"What adds up?" Rebecca asks.

"Remember his answer when we asked him how he became paralyzed?" says Tommy. "He said it was a bad boating accident when he was seven years old. He was seven years old in 1956 when the *Andrea Doria* sank."

"How do you know that?" she asks.

"He said he's fifty-nine years old now. Do the math!"

"Okay, yes . . . so he would have been seven years old in 1956. You're right," Rebecca agrees.

"He also said his wife died," Tommy adds. "He said 'it wasn't pretty,' remember?"

"Yes, I do."

"My aunt and uncle always told me my mother died of the AIDS virus in the eighties. And what about all that research he's been doing on the Grimaldis? I think he's trying to figure out his ancestry, too."

"How do you know all this isn't just a series of coincidences, Tommy?" Rebecca asks.

"Because Sandro is one of the most common Italian nickname for Alessandro!"

# 24

# Proud and Honored

**Cacio e Pepe Restaurant, East 77th Street, Manhattan, New York**

*November 15, 2008, 9:00 p.m. Saturday Evening*

"I am ashamed and embarrassed," Eaton laments. "I never wanted you to know what a loser your father was. And I never wanted you to know what really happened to your mother. I apologize, Tommy, from the bottom of my heart."

Tommy's near meltdown at Radio City Music Hall has him insisting on some kind of explanation. After almost thirty years, he realizes the truth has been purposely concealed from him. *It's time for me to discover what happened to my father and mother and why.*

Eaton makes late reservations for drinks and snacks for all four of them at his friend Salvatore Corea's Manhattan restaurant. Once they order beverages, Eaton struggles to recall his unpleasant past.

"How about if you start right from the beginning, Eaton," Rebecca encourages.

"I'll start about the time I became Eaton Stone. How's that?"

"Go ahead," Tommy nods. He's not smiling.

"Okay." Eaton takes a large gulp of water, leans back in his wheelchair, and reaches for Lilly's hand. "Even though I was only seven

259

years old, the sinking of the *Andrea Doria* left an indelible scar on my mind. It was 1956, fifty-two years ago. My mother and I were on our way to a new life in America. We were in a two-bed forward cabin. It was late in the evening when we kissed each other goodnight."

Eaton grimaces as he wrestles with his thoughts. Separating his feelings from the tragic details of his life has always been a painstaking, almost futile exercise. Alcohol dependency insulated his reality for many years until he was able to plunge his life into eighty-hour workweeks. He trembles as he forces himself to resurrect his heart-wrenching memories.

"I'm sorry," he says. "Chronicling my life experiences is unpleasant for me. Tell me Lilly—where was I?"

"You have just kissed your mother goodnight," recounts Lilly.

"Okay. That was just minutes before the riveting impact of the *Stockholm* on the starboard side of the *Andrea Doria*. As long as I live, I'll never forget the sound of the two massive ships colliding with a combined weight of more than fifty thousand tons and a combined speed of forty knots. I was petrified! The crunching sound of the initial impact was like a thousand sledgehammers hitting the ship at once. Then the inside of the ship was imploding around us, with tons of debris flying in every direction. My mother and I were thrown to the floor, and seconds later an enormous metal beam fell on top of us. We were buried under a collapsed elevator shaft. We were both conscious. I was numb all over. My mother was in great pain. I found out later her spine and both legs were shattered.

"Once the *Stockholm* pulled away, water rushed in through the thirty-five-foot gaping hole created by the impact. A crewmember used every ounce of his strength and courage to fill the hole with wood planks, preventing my mother and me from being washed out to sea. Three other men desperately fought to free us. They struggled to find tranquilizing painkillers for my mother. For hours one of the men searched for wire cutters and a jack. We were relieved when they finally arrived by lifeboat from the *Ile de France*, the French liner that rescued so many passengers. But the jack wasn't powerful enough to dislodge the heavy elevator shaft. Remember—all this was going on as the *Doria* was listing and in danger of sinking at any moment.

"The men struggled for nearly an hour trying to move a 150-pound hydraulic jack from the promenade deck to the lower level deck where we were. Once they had it in position, one of the men pumped the jack lever frantically and screamed to us to hang on. But my mother drifted quietly to sleep. Her last words were, 'My dear Alessandro, I think I'm slipping away.' I had been crying throughout the experience, but when my mother said that, I became hysterical. It took them a long time to settle me down."

No one says a word.

"Eventually the jack worked and I was carefully pulled out from under the shaft. It was too late for my mother, though. I was strapped to a stretcher and placed on the last lifeboat departing the *Andrea Doria* before it sank. Later in the morning, I was airlifted to Bellevue Hospital in New York City. That's when the full extent of my injuries became known. None of the five operations I had did much good. Rehab was ineffective. The doctors told me I would never walk again. It's pretty tough to hear that when you're a seven-year-old without family support. That's when I learned to joke around a lot. It keeps my spirits up!"

Lilly moves closer to Eaton and places her arms around him. "I can't imagine how devastating that news must have been," she says.

"I cried myself to sleep for months. Yet my year in Bellevue included the best possible treatment. To this day, I believe someone had to have intervened."

"Was it Prince Rainier?" Tommy asks.

"I don't know," says Eaton. "Based on the care I received, I wouldn't doubt it."

"Tell them what happened next," Lilly advises. She has heard parts of the story earlier.

"I grew up in St. Joseph's Children's Home, went to NYU, graduated with honors, and began my career. For a while I tried my hand at writing novels. On July 1, 1978, I married a massage therapist I met at a Manhattan rehab center. I was in my late twenties, Margaret was only nineteen, but I fell hard. Our first few years of marriage were wonderful. Tommy . . . you were born in 1980 and to this day, I have to admit, it was the happiest day of my life. But this is where my life began to spiral down into the abyss.

"Margaret felt trapped. My being incapacitated greatly hampered her life. She had to do almost everything around the house and still continue her work as a therapist. I stayed home, took care of you, and tried to get America's next great novel published. After fifty or so rejections, I gave up. Soon our expenses exceeded our income. As a new novelist, I was broke. We struggled financially. That's when we started to argue. One day she packed her bags and left. You were just two years old. That, Tommy, was the saddest day of my life.

"The situation only deteriorated from there. Unsuccessful as a writer, I became a serious alcoholic. One day, a police officer knocked on the door. He had you in his arms. You were wandering around the neighborhood. That happened a few more times before social services became involved. That's when I realized I was unfit to be a father, emotionally, physically, and financially. I became desperate. I asked Margaret's sister and her husband if you could stay with them until I got my life together. I'm *still* working on that. The good news is I haven't had a drink in three years."

Eaton clears his throat and drinks some water. "They moved to Fairchester, taking you with them. I moved to Syracuse when I found a job as a sports journalist for the local newspaper."

"Whatever happened to my mother?" Tommy asks.

"The answer to your question is one of the reasons I've been putting off telling you this story."

"But I need to know," Tommy tells Eaton. "Based on what you had to endure growing up, you must know that."

"Sure, I do," Eaton replies. "It was cowardly of me not to tell you before. I could say I was trying to protect you, but you probably wouldn't buy that excuse."

"No I wouldn't. So what happened to her?" Tommy persists.

"She made some poor choices and got mixed up with the wrong crowd. She died of an HIV infection in 1984."

Tommy bows his head, attempting to digest the weight of the information he is receiving. Feelings of despair and alienation penetrate his mind. He needs to learn more about his mother.

"You said you were with her when she died?" Tommy asks.

"Listen, Tommy," Eaton responds. "I don't blame you for being upset, and I'm not making excuses but . . ."

"What did she say, Eaton?" Tommy presses him.

"She said she wished she had never met me and that you had never been born. She died right after she made that comment. There were no apologies."

"Can you imagine how distraught she must have been?" Rebecca asks. "I feel so sorry for her."

Tommy's eyes fill with tears as he removes a handkerchief from his coat pocket.

"I was so deeply moved by that experience, I wanted to die too," Eaton continues. "In fact, a few weeks later, I almost did. I discovered alcohol and heroin didn't mix very well. I was taken by ambulance back to Bellevue. For the next several years I went from job to job. Then I got my life in order. I started a major genealogical research project. I was also trying to figure out who the hell I was. The result was a nonfiction bestseller entitled *The Imposition of the Inquisition: A Study of European Demagoguery.* That's when I learned all about the Grimaldi family. After that my life changed. The work poured in, and so did the money. Unfortunately, Tommy, that didn't matter much to your aunt and uncle. I tried many, many times to see you. I called. I went over to their house."

Tommy reaches for the onyx and gold rosary he has carried in his coat pocket ever since he learned the centerpiece is the House the Grimaldi coat of arms. He places it on the table with the crucifix facing Eaton.

"Have you ever seen this before?" he asks.

Eaton closes his eyes and nods. "They were my mother's. She gave them to me before we left for America," he declares somberly. "On one of my attempts to visit you, I gave it to your aunt."

Tommy leans back in his chair. "Okay. That explains how I got it."

"I guess they thought I was some kind of dangerous alcoholic," Eaton continues. "They somehow obtained a restraining order preventing me from seeing you. They were very stubborn people. I'm sure they held me responsible for your mother's death."

Tommy looks directly at Eaton. His lips are quivering. He tightens them. "It's the choices we make, right Eaton?"

"I don't expect you to forgive me, Tommy. As you grew older, and I learned about our ancestry, I thought telling you about it would cause a major upheaval in your life. Now in retrospect, I wish I had tried harder. I am sorry I didn't have the courage. Then after my accident at Daytona, I thought your life might be in danger. I kept coming up with excuses not to tell you the truth. I realize saying 'I'm sorry' doesn't resolve anything."

Eaton looks into Tommy's eyes almost dreading his next remark as Tommy gazes in the other direction. The message he wants to deliver to Eaton is clear, however he needs to carefully select his choice of words.

Tommy turns his head and looks directly at Eaton. "Do you feel some relief now?" he asks.

"I just feel guilt, Tommy. What do you feel?"

"I'm over the shock. Now I feel selfish."

"Why?" Eaton asks.

"Everyone is so concerned with me—my feelings, my reactions. What about you? Words are totally inadequate to describe *your* suffering. I can't imagine how painful your life has been."

Eaton raises his eyebrows. A look of total astonishment blankets his face. Lilly closes her eyes in relief as she squeezes Eaton's hand, as if her team has just won the championship.

"You're also a big liar!" Tommy exclaims.

Eaton is speechless, wondering if the other shoe is about to drop.

"You said you didn't have courage. That's a lie! Let me tell you something. You just happen to be the most courageous person I have ever known, and I am so very proud and honored to be your son!"

# 25

# Murder in the Grotto

### Gorgona Island, Italy
#### *June 15, 1958, Early Sunday Morning*

Sitting in his blue prison uniform, Antonio is about to panic. Of all the times he has been shackled, this time has been the most physically painful. Handcuffs are tightly secured to a chain wrapped around his waist, immobilizing his arms completely. Manacles bite into his ankles causing him pain when he shuffles to walk. His wrists and ankles are swollen and cut from the Polizia Napoli motor launch bouncing on the waves of the Ligurian Sea. When he attempts to remain still, his forearm and shoulder muscles begin to cramp. He is physically exhausted from this experience and mentally drained from his ordeal with the Italian judicial system.

One week! That's how long it took the *tribunale* to convict him. Murder in the first degree for Giancarlo. Manslaughter for refusing to bring drivers Rene Pelletier and Edmond LaRoche in for a tire change at the 1957 Mille Miglia race. Life in prison—all as the result of Paul Charone's false accusations, trumped-up charges, and fabricated evidence. *The bastard finally got his revenge,* Antonio thinks to himself.

"Hope you like olives," a police officer says. "You'll be rakin' 'em for a long time!"

Antonio bows his head in despair. *It would have been better if I were never born.* Antonio's thoughts drift to his childhood when he was growing up in the lap of royalty and privilege, never suffering from the lack of anything. Had he not messed up his life, he would be Prince of Monaco now. Catherine and Alessandro would be living a wonderful life in the royal palace. *How shameful and useless my life has become.*

Soon, Antonio sees the ancient fishing village of Cala dello Scalo in the distance. The ride to Gorgona Island from Livorno on the mainland, is nearly over. *Thank God!* After a year of wasting away in Regina Coeli, Prince Rainier pulled some strings and arranged his transfer.

The harsh resonance of the boat's engine becomes a quiet hum as it slows down. Tuscan style farmhouses stacked on the steep slopes and terraces are now plainly visible. One of the farmhouses will be his home for the rest of his life. Antonio's thoughts turn to Father Nick. Despite being unsure of how much time he will be able to spend with him, he hopes his agony will dissipate to some degree when he sees him.

Four police officers from the penal farm wait on the pier ready to escort Antonio to his new home. One of them, a friend from his last stay at Gorgona, says, "Give me the keys!" to the police officer in back of the boat. He then immediately frees Antonio from his steel bondage and they walk to a light blue Fiat Campagnola police jeep parked on an unpaved side road.

"I'm taking you to see Father Nick," his friend says. "He wants to see you right away."

"Is he okay?" Antonio asks.

"He's dying."

When Antonio arrives at Father Nick's country house, he finds him slumped in a recliner with a cane by his side. His normally stout frame is gaunt and withered. While his face is weary, his eyes are serene and peaceful.

"Antonio! *Oh mio Dio!*" he says with his eyes full of tears. He reaches for Antonio's hand and squeezes it tightly. "Sit down, my son. We have much to discuss."

Antonio is overwhelmed. He leans down, embraces Father Nick, and weeps audibly. Marching inside of him is a parade of every emotion he has felt during the last year.

"Doctors call it lymphoma. I don't have much longer," Father Nick says sadly.

"I'm sorry, Padre."

"Please, Antonio, sit down. Do not be sorry. I've had more blessings than I deserve. Being here with the prisoners has been the great joy of my life. The Lord has given me great moral strength, and I have done my best to pass that strength on to them."

"And they are all better people because of you, Father Nick. Is there anything I can do for you?"

"You are here."

"Yes, I'm here."

"I see you made your decision, Antonio. It was a very courageous one, indeed."

"I told Il Commendatore that I had a premonition about the ship sinking, and that's why I had the GTO removed from the ship at the Port of Naples."

"A 'premonition,' Antonio? And he accepted that?" Father Nick asks.

"I was surprised. Maybe the prince interceded," Antonio smiles.

Father Nick laughs. "It's called divine intervention, my son. But I wouldn't be surprised if the prince used his influence, too!"

"He gave me a promotion," Antonio adds. "I became the chief technician for the Formula One team."

"Ah, Mr. Ferrari—he must be a very wise man."

"My life was going very well until Charone called me out with his trumped-up story about the Mille Miglia tragedy," Antonio continues. "He made it all up! I flagged them in, Padre, really, I did. They simply refused to come. I'm sorry all those people were killed, but I tried to get them off the track before the tire blew. And Giancarlo? Why would I want to kill my best friend?"

Father Nick slowly shakes his head. "I don't understand it either. But I can tell you this, my son, the Lord sure works in strange ways."

"I'm a loser. I've failed at everything I've ever done," Antonio laments. "I've shamed my family, myself, and anyone who has ever cared for me, especially Catherine. Oh, Padre, she was the love of my life. I'm not doing very well with the guilt."

"Catherine was a good woman who never stopped loving you. I am sure of that, my son."

Antonio's eyes fill with tears. "I tracked down information on every one of the fifty-one passengers killed on the *Andrea Doria*. It was a horrible day when I learned Catherine was one of them. She would never have been on that ship if it weren't for me."

"Don't despair. She is with the Lord, and I am sure she is happy," Father Nick reassures him.

"How I wish I could embrace that concept, Padre."

"In time, you will, Antonio. In time, you will. Do you know anything about Alessandro?"

"Yes. They were in a forward cabin on the starboard side," Antonio explains. "That's right where the impact took place. Thankfully, Alessandro survived the impact. He'll be paralyzed for life." Antonio bows his head and begins to weep. "But at least he's alive."

"I'm so sorry, my son."

"I found out his name is Eaton Stone, and he is in a children's home in New York City. How I wish I could see him again. The first thing I would do is apologize for ruining his life."

"I'm sure someday you will see him, my son," Father Nick says gently. "I just know you will."

Antonio breathes deeply, closes his eyes, and slowly looks out the back window facing the grotto.

"How are the finches doing, Padre?" he asks.

"Oh, they're still there."

"They're still escaping the sparrow hawks, huh?"

"Some of them, yes. Come with me, Antonio. I have something to show you." Father Nicholas reaches for his cane. "Help this old monk up, will you please, my son?"

"Of course, Padre," Antonio says.

"Not long after the prisoners finished the small cemetery next to the grotto, the two friars that have been here with me for nearly forty years passed away. My plot is all ready for me. Then there will be no one else here to care for the prisoners."

"I don't need to see your plot, Padre."

"It's okay, Antonio. Come."

They pass the grotto with flowerbeds filled with radiant red roses, gentle yellow daffodils, and peaceful blue hydrangeas. The sun is bright and robust. A slight breeze bends the small trees behind the grotto. From a distance, Antonio sees four vertical granite tombstones in a neat horizontal line in front of the cemetery, and begins walking in that direction.

"Wait! I want you to see something else first." Father Nick points to a clearing in the grotto behind the cemetery. They walk another fifty feet until they come to a small flat rectangular tombstone imbedded in the dirt and covered by a pile of olive branches.

"Every day I place another olive branch over the stone," Father Nick says sadly.

"Why is that?" Antonio asks

"Olive branches represent forgiveness and peace," he responds. "I come here to pray to our Lord and ask his forgiveness."

"I don't understand," says Antonio. "You've done nothing but sacrifice your life for others. Why would you need forgiveness?"

Father Nick strains to bend over. He removes a cluster of olive branches covering the top of the stone. "Look closely, my son. I always ask the Lord to forgive him."

Antonio falls to his knees and reads the inscription on the flat tombstone. *Here Lies Paul Charone. God Rest His Soul.* For a few moments, Antonio is anaesthetized. He is unable to speak and doesn't believe what he has just read. He reads it again. Stunned, he looks up at Father Nick with a blank stare.

Father Nick explains, "One day, just after I received the bad news about my health, I was planting flowers in the grotto. When I looked up, I saw a tall, thin man was standing over me. He said, 'My name is Paul Charone and I am here to pick up the Ferrari. Please take me to it now.' Apparently other than the Naples dockworkers, he was the only one who knew you had possession of the car after the *Andrea Doria* had sunk. When you never appeared in Lucca to give it to him, and after you went to prison, he somehow concluded the car was here. Believe me, Antonio, even after all my years of preaching compassion and understanding, it took all I had to restrain myself.

"I said to him, 'Antonio is gone; so is the car. You can leave now too!' I'm afraid I wasn't very hospitable. He replied, 'We can do this the easy way or the hard way. That's up to you!' I demanded that he leave. The last thing I remembered was the two prisoners who were working on the tombstones in the cemetery walking towards us with their shovels. Then Charone hit me so hard in the abdomen, I keeled over in pain. I was unable to breathe. For a minute, I thought I was going to die. As soon as I looked up, I felt a jarring blow glance off my jaw. I was out cold for a long time. When I came to, Charone was gone. The two prisoners helped me back to my house and tended my wounds."

"The prisoners. They killed Charone?"

"Yes. And buried him too," Father Nick says slowly with his head bowed.

Antonio remains hard-pressed for words as he rises and brushes the dirt from his blue prison uniform. An empty stare is the only communication he can offer.

Father Nick slowly nods. "I say prayers for the repose of his soul every day."

"Yes, Padre," Antonio agrees. "God rest his miserable soul."

"Come, Antonio. I have something else to show you."

They leave the clearing and walk to the four vertical tombstones in front of the cemetery. Father Nick reads the markers on each one.

"Reverend Richard Lopez, Reverend James Burns, Reverend Nicholas . . ." When he comes to the last one, he pauses. "Antonio Grimaldi."

"What? Why me?" Antonio asks.

"This island, my son, is now your permanent home. A long time ago, once I realized I would eventually die on this island, I decided to make my time here worthwhile. Antonio, my son, I believe with all my heart the Lord has something special in mind for you."

Father Nick's words are difficult for Antonio to comprehend, as is a tombstone already bearing his name.

They walk back into the house. Antonio helps Father Nick assume his former position on the recliner. His breathing is heavy—he is exhausted from their short walk to the cemetery.

"My son, this is my final message to you," says Father Nick. "Guilt will always remind you of your mistakes but please, never feel shame. Shame seduces you into believing that *you* are the mistake. See yourself as God sees you. He doesn't want you to feel ashamed. He wants to forgive you and help you with the courage to move on with your life."

"Antonio!" comes a loud voice from the front doorway. "It's time to leave."

"Thank you, Father Nick, and God bless you," Antonio sighs, trying hard not to break down and cry.

"Goodbye, my son. Always keep me in your prayers."

# Winning the Crown

**Fairchester, New York**
**Seven Years Later**
*October 23, 2015, Late Saturday Afternoon*

Bedlam erupts as the Fairchester Eagles handily defeat their cross-town archrivals, the Northport Raiders, to win their tenth county championship. Drenched in Gatorade, the coach is hoisted onto the shoulders of his two largest linemen and paraded in front of the wildly cheering fans, many of whom refuse to leave the football stadium until the coach gives his traditional postgame speech. Finally, the linemen deposit the coach on the 50-yard line where the microphone is waiting so he can deliver his victory message to the team and the fans.

"Winning isn't everything, it's the only thing!" comes the coach's voice over the speaker. "Well, far be it from me, a mere small-town high school football coach, to challenge the words of the great Lombardi. But I have to ask the question. What does it really mean to win?"

The crowd noise diminishes to whispers.

"That's probably a very strange question coming from the coach, isn't it? Especially one who just won the county championship!"

The crowd laughs.

"So what does it mean to win? Coming out on top? Taking out our opponents? Destroying the competition? Is this what we want to teach our kids? No, I don't think it is! The last few years I've tried to teach integrity. If winning requires us to sell our souls, compromise our values, or do harm to others, it can hardly qualify as a win. That's when something much more has been lost in the process, and everybody ends up losing.

"A very special lady by the name of Lilly Brandt created my new definition of winning: Winning means going as far as you can with all that you've got! Even if we don't win one game next year, if our kids have gone as far as they can with all that they've got, they are winners . . . big winners! As your new Director of Athletics, I hope you can support that philosophy with all our sports teams at Fairchester Academy. On behalf of all our kids who participate in all the school athletic programs, thank you for all your support! Okay, now let's celebrate!"

A thunderous standing ovation from the four thousand fans in the bleachers nearly deafens Mike Bender, the head coach and new athletic director. Those cheering the loudest are Katie and Tony Grimaldi, Tommy and Rebecca's six-year-old twins.

"Can we come to Uncle Billy's with you? Please, can we come?" Katie asks.

"Of course, you can!" Rebecca answers enthusiastically. "There will be lots of kids your age there."

The high school van drives up to the 50-yard line. Mike jumps in and is whisked away as if he is a dignitary and has an urgent engagement to attend. Lilly and Eaton and Mike's new wife Jessica, are already over at Billy Amato's place helping prepare the greatest celebration party ever.

"I thought that was the best speech I ever heard Mike deliver!" Tommy says to Rebecca.

"Sure is a far cry from the way things were a few years ago," Rebecca notes.

"That's for sure!"

When Tommy, Rebecca, Katie, and Tony arrive at Billy's place, they find it totally empty.

"Some victory celebration, huh?" Tommy asks despondently.

"There's probably tons of traffic after the game," Rebecca reassures him. "Let's sit at the bar and wait for everybody."

"I'm going to run into the kitchen and see what they're doing," Tommy says.

An elderly member of the Roman Catholic clergy walks into the restaurant after Tommy disappears into the kitchen. He is wearing a black suit and a tab collar shirt with a small white square at the base of his throat. He is tall with broad shoulders that have rounded with age. His full head of silvery hair has been combed back with a wide-tooth comb. Despite his advanced age, he appears confident, distinguished, and strong. Katie and Tony leap off of the stools and run to greet him. He embraces each one as tears fill his eyes. Then he greets Rebecca with a hug and kiss.

"Thank you for picking me up at the airport yesterday," he says graciously. "I also appreciate the wonderful dinner you prepared for me last night in your lovely new home. It was delightful."

"I was glad Tommy had a late appointment," she says.

"I know you want to surprise them, but are you sure Tommy and Eaton won't have heart attacks when they see me?" the man asks.

"After our conversation last night, I think I'm more concerned about your heart than theirs!" Rebecca replies.

They hear the hum of an electric wheelchair coming closer. Rebecca has never had so many butterflies. The hinge on the kitchen door makes a familiar clack as it opens. Lilly and Mike are walking behind Tommy and Eaton.

"I didn't know this was a masquerade party," Eaton says to Lilly when he sees the old man standing next to Rebecca.

Tommy's reaction is quite different. He seems to know instinctively. He walks slowly up to the man. Eaton looks up at Tommy. Now he is speechless.

Rebecca senses their bewilderment. "I'd like to introduce you to Father Antonio Grimaldi." She says his name slowly, almost imperceptibly, as if she is afraid of revealing a secret that has been hidden for four generations.

"Alessandro, my son, how I have prayed for this moment." Father Antonio falls to his knees in front of Eaton's wheelchair and collapses into his son's arms. Tears stream down both their faces as Father Antonio repeats, "Grazie a Dio! Grazie a Dio!" over and over again.

Tommy moves closer to Rebecca, almost afraid to interrupt their tearful reunion. Eaton was two years old the last time he saw his father, more than sixty-six years ago. In Tommy's mind, it is impossible to underestimate the significance of the moment.

"I guess you never know what kind of riffraff might walk into this place," Eaton says, sniffling. His characteristic good humor cracks everyone up, relieving the intensity of the moment. "Tommy, did you say hello to your grandfather yet?" Eaton asks.

Tommy is frozen solid, searching for the right words.

Father Antonio gazes in admiration at his grandson. "I am sorry for all the pain I have caused in your life," he says with deep compassion. "If I could go back and make different choices, I would do so in an instant. But I can't . . . and here we are."

Father Antonio is thinking about how much he wants to share with his grandson, about the false accusations and the choices, good and bad, he has made, but mostly he wants to tell him all about Father Nick and the great lessons of life he learned from him: how he learned to be strong in the face of devastating injustice, how he learned to do the right thing, no matter what the cost, how he learned to forgive, and finally, how he learned to turn adversity into a meaningful and productive life.

Father Antonio's outstretched arms are impossible for Tommy to resist any longer. He capitulates and they hug each other tightly.

"There will be plenty of time for all of us to get acquainted, Tommy," Father Antonio says. "I've taken up residence at a nearby clergy house. I'll tell you all about it later."

Mike walks over to them with an outstretched arm.

"Nice to meet you, Father Antonio," he says. Father Antonio extends his arm and they shake hands. "If you don't mind, Father, could you answer just one quick question for me right now?" he asks.

"I'll try," Father Antonio smiles.

"Tell me . . . how'd you enjoy the game?"

# About the Author

**Roger Corea** writes about things, people, and places he is passionate about. His first novel, *Scarback: There Is So Much More to Fishing Than Catching Fish*, was published in 2014. This award-winning novel tells the story of the critical time in the life of a mentally challenged man from the Italian neighborhood where Corea grew up.

His second novel, *The Duesenberg Caper*, was published in 2015. This classic car thriller follows two young teachers as they are drawn into a dangerous world of high-stakes intrigue when commissioned to solve one the oldest mysteries in the car world—the whereabouts of the priceless 1935 Duesenberg SJ Emmanuel owned by King Victor Emmanuel of Italy that remained hidden for decades.

Not only is writing a natural outgrowth of Roger's formal education, it is also a product of his life experience. While a bachelor's degree in English from St. Bonaventure University and graduate courses at the University of Rochester provided a solid foundation, Roger's most meaningful education comes from teaching English literature and a thirty-year field leadership position with American Express Financial Advisors (now Ameriprise Financial). He calls these experiences his "writer's apprenticeship," citing that the best preparation for writing novels is learning about people. Mark Twain's quote, "Never let your book learnin' interfere with your education," describes his philosophy.

Roger and his wife, Mary Ann, reside in Penfield, New York. They have three children and three grandchildren.

# About the Contributors to GTO

**Bill Warner** has been around automobiles his whole life. As a teenager he worked at the local Volkswagen and imported car dealership in the parts department and driving the delivery truck. Upon earning his degree in electrical engineering, he entered the family filter business.

Bill's photographs and articles have appeared in *Road & Track, Car and Driver, Autoweek, The Atlantic Monthly*, and *Automobile*. His photography has won awards from The Los Angeles Art Directors, the Creative Arts Yearbook, and the Sports Car Club of America (Photographer of the Year 1970). His photos have been featured in the Petersen Museum in Los Angeles as part of the 50th Anniversary of Ferrari and at the Meadow Brook Concours d'Elegance in Auburn Hills, Michigan.

In 1996 he founded The Amelia Island Concours d'Elegance near his home in Jacksonville, Florida. In the twenty-year history of the show, it has raised over $2.25 million for Community Hospice of Northeast Florida. Recently, the hospice named their new care facility The Jane and Bill Warner Center for Caring. In November 2013 and again in 2014, the Amelia Island Concours d'Elegance was awarded "Motoring Event of the Year" by *Octane Magazine*. This award represented worldwide recognition of The Amelia Island Concours d'Elegance as the best of the best.

In 2002 automotive journalists awarded Bill the prestigious Meguiar's Automobile Hobby Person of the Year. The ceremony was held at the Beverly Hills Hotel in California and was nationally televised. Other recipients of the Meguiar's Award have been Jay Leno, the late Chip Miller of Carlisle Productions, and Steve Earle of the Monterey Historic Races.

His wife of fifty years, Jane, has patiently put up with his automotive mania with an understanding beyond reasonable expectations, as have his three children: his son, Clay, and twin daughters, Demery Webber and Dana Shewmaker, as well as his granddaughters, Lindsey Jane Webber, Mildred Huxley Warner, and Ruby Meeks Warner.

**Marc Corea** began MotorCarTrader.com, LLC, a classic car business and website during his junior year in college in 1998 as Internet marketing was coming into its own. Since then, Marc has built MotorCarTrader.com, LLC into a successful enterprise known for its integrity, trustworthiness, and high standards of quality.

Specializing in Jaguar E-Types, Jaguar XKs, Mercedes 280SLs, Austin Healeys, and Porsche 911s, Marc has acquired a loyal clientele that appreciates his accurate and objective representation of his cars. Marc has also restored and sold several national award winners that have competed at the Hershey, Pebble Beach, and Amelia Island concours shows.

Marc operates his classic car business near Charlotte, NC. His love of classic cars is shared by his wife, Sarah. They live near Lake Norman in Cornelius, NC.